"A celebration of the joyful mysteries of language. . . .
Lemann's style is pure, sweet exaggeration, the exaggeration of a crazed lunatic batsman leaning unwisely, impossibly into a wild pitch and connecting."

—Ralph Adamo, *New Orleans Times-Picayune*

"An original in style and spirit, Nancy Lemann's is a talent rich in oddities and, in my view, a pleasing challenge in the benign and forgiving wit of her special vision of North and South, young and old, drunks and fools."

—Elizabeth Hardwick

"To read Lemann is to know how Dom Perignon must have felt when he discovered champagne. Each page is a delicious, dizzy-making, potentially dangerous surprise."

—Tom Robbins

VOICES OF THE SOUTH

SPORTSMAN'S PARADISE

SPORTSMAN'S PARADISE

Nancy Lemann

LOUISIANA STATE UNIVERSITY PRESS
BATON ROUGE

Copyright © 1992 by Nancy Lemann

Originally published by Alfred A. Knopf

LSU Press edition published 1999 by arrangement with the author

All rights reserved

Manufactured in the United States of America

08 07 06 05 04 03 02 01 00 99

5 4 3 2 1

Library of Congress Cataloging-in-Publication Data

Lemann, Nancy.

    Sportsman's paradise / Nancy Lemann.

        p.   cm. — (Voices of the South)

    ISBN 0-8071-2417-6 (alk. paper)

    1. Long Island (N.Y.) — Fiction.   I. Title. II. Series.

  [PS3562.E4659S66   1999]

  813'.54—dc21

                                   99-15678

                                      CIP

The paper in this book meets the guidelines for permanence and durability of
the Committee on Production Guidelines for Book Longevity of the Council
on Library Resources. ♾

To MC

My theme is memory, that winged host . . .

—EVELYN WAUGH

SPORTSMAN'S PARADISE

1. ORIENT POINT, Long Island.

It is very pleasant here. There is an enclave of houses done in what is, strangely enough, a sort of Mississippi mode, with imitation antebellum stone columns. There is a bay with green marshes at the front, which turns into a canal on the side, which turns into a green lagoon with lily pads and swans, oddly enough, in the back.

There was once a hotel across the canal, and this enclave was the staff quarters, giving it its humble air perhaps.

The setting is very beautiful but seems strangely tame. It is not as wild as my memories of the sea. The ducks and their little children file across the garden, escorted by swans when they reach the lagoon. The sight brought tears to my eyes for its tender domesticity. I have grown so tenderhearted that I shed tears at the slightest provocation. Then I found out that the ducks sometimes get eaten by otters. "It's the law of the jungle," said Grace.

It goes without saying I was horrified.

Grace Fox (the owner of the enclave) comes walking down the garden path. She is married to Constant Fox, the heart throb. He is currently absent, conducting travels in the world.

His pending arrival is actually a source of endless controversy and speculation. At least on my part it is.

The others are leaving from Manhattan at three-thirty to get to Long Island by six—such plots, you think, such long afternoons in the jazz age. In this raging green—everything is green outside of my marvelous imitation antebellum stone portico—there will be a storm tonight.

Much tender domesticity among the members of the Mississippi enclave, due at the moment to the family of six next door and the young couples. The others have not yet arrived.

This afternoon a man who could stand to lose about sixty pounds or more, with a handlebar mustache, bald, about forty-five, was in a rubber boat on the bay, weighing it down, with a tiny three-year-old boy. The latter asked me if he could sit on my lap, when he came over that evening. Naturally, I assented.

"Guess what?" said Al, the three-year-old boy. "Harry Locke drools. He drools on everything."

Then he lapsed into a pensive silence.

"And guess what else?" He looked at me intently. "I know how to play checkers."

"Time for your Geography lesson," I said, and got out my atlas of the world. If there is one thing that interests Al, it is Africa. He is interested in the famine. Also, he has girlie pictures all over his room, even though he is only three years old. And Harry Locke drools all over them.

"Where am I from, Al?" I said, using the Socratic method.

"Louisiana."

(Pronounced "Looziana"—where did he get that? I don't pronounce it that way—suddenly he's a drawling Southerner.)

"Very good. And where are the starving people, Al?"

"Florida?"

"No . . . Come on, you remember."

"Africa?" in his high-pitched child's query.

"Good, Al."

"I can jump like a rabbit," he confided offhandedly.

"Now, what did we study yesterday?"

"Maps."

"So what did we learn about?"

"The map."

"But what is the study of maps? Of different parts of the world?"

He and his sister, who had drawn near, started jumping up and down at this (for it is known to them how to jump like rabbits). "GEOGRAPHY," they chanted, in rhythm with their jumps, ecstatic. "GEOGRAPHY," they chanted in a litany, with shining eyes.

Mrs. Langguth came out with the baby. I gave the baby four silver doubloons from Mardi Gras. The baby analyzed each one individually, inside her mouth, and then studiously threw them away.

The children ran unsteadily across the lawn. Tonight we are going to play checkers.

Cedric, the unwanted guest, is lounging in a deck chair on the lawn. He is the frequent though unwelcome visitor from the house on the bay. No one likes the people in the house on the bay because they won't let you walk on their lawn. None of them associates with our party except for Cedric, who comes over every afternoon promptly at the cocktail hour and stays for what seems like an endless time. He is considered a discordant element.

Grace rides up and down the road in her white Cadillac.

Mrs. Langguth, the mother of six, next door, is sitting on the front porch smoking cigarettes, adding the dark glamour of vice to her otherwise upstanding household.

The red-and-white-striped lawn chairs sit in the moonlight on the raging bay.

The guests are arriving across the lawn. The young men are coming to us from Friday evening after work in Manhattan—wearing suits and ties and sunglasses, carrying their briefcases, uproarious yet exhausted, drunk yet sober, etc. They came in on the train in the parlor car and are somewhat the worse for wear, owing to the drinks.

The ducks, not to mention the otters, have already filled my heart with tender sorrow. I think I have had one too many cocktails. The Langguths insisted on concocting Sazerac cocktails, in my honor—"All the way up from Looziana," etc. I sit on my imitation antebellum stone portico, transfixed by the ducks and swans.

"So you came all the way up from Looziana on the Cotton Blossom, eh?" says the overweight fellow with the handlebar mustache, winking lasciviously, as though there is something ribald about Louisiana.

"Southern Crescent," I politely corrected him. "The train."

"Yes, I took that train once. The Orange Blossom, heh, heh. My heart belongs in Dixie."

I took a queazy excursion to town for a drink with the young couples. There is a very nice bar called Claudio's with ceiling fans and an old tile floor and green tablecloths, in a section of Orient that is known, oddly enough, as Port of Egypt.

John said he wanted to name his first child Tom and his second Elektra. Why Elektra, I wonder. It is not like him. He is what you would call a normal, regular guy, and all of the couples are normal and regular, with double standards, the men in banking jobs, the women with artistic interests. The men are jocks, but with certain eccentricities, like Sam leaning over at dinner, pedantic in his black-rimmed glasses, to say, "When Jane and I have sex, it's incredible, it's unbelievable, it's like—" making some ecstatic, lurid description, readjusting his glasses, and simply continuing dinner.

They are the love couple. She is a good, strong, sweethearted, fine girl. She does not have much personality. She is stupefied—in a constant state of even slightly ashamed stupefaction—by the amount of sex she has with her husband. He is a fellow who is endowed with everything—wit, brains, personality—and to top it off he is at the same time strong and tall and filled with sex ardor.

The amount of his sex ardor keeps his wife in a constant state of stunned love embarrassment. In a way, she is cowed. Although she is a very big-boned, very big, very tall girl, in his arms she is cowed.

Men when they get together find interesting the dullest subjects. How to get the ladder to the pier. Whether the water should boil longer. How much grease to use in a screw. How to repair the boat. Who should keep score in the bridge game.

Water-skiing, tennis, and the like, the occupations here— that people should concoct forms of amusement which they ply with such seriousness always strikes me as lovably absurd —the couples playing bridge at the card table on the lawn, the men wearing silly sports caps.

The bay is like a pleasure kingdom. The red-and-white-striped lawn chairs, the children in rubber boats far out in the bay, and people taking drinks on their front porches.

Everyone seems to be slowly getting plastered all afternoon.

The weeping-willow trees, some white wood deck chairs in the Langguths' garden. The rustling of the leaves, the waning light on the bay, and the green canal. The swans on the green lagoon. The drama of the twilight.

The love couple are having sex in the laundry room, where they retired after having embarrassed everyone in the kitchen, where the torrid scene began.

"Are they married?" said Al, eyeballing the love couple.

"Yes. They are newlyweds," I said.

"What are newlyweds?" said Al.

"It's someone who just got married."

"Is Grace married?" he asked.

"Yes, she is married to Constant," I said.

"Who is not married?" said the boy.

"You're looking at her, Al."

He pondered this.

"Storey, will you marry me?" said Al.

"I'm too old for you, sweetheart. But it's one of the most flattering proposals I've ever received."

He looked wistful.

"Do you have a boyfriend?" he inquired.

"A few."

Actually, my old flame is here. But he and I are estranged. When I came to this "slender riotous island that lies east of New York," I found that my old flame was here—a Southerner, like myself, from New Orleans—and I had not really seen him for five years when we were thrown together here.

"Stunning, kiddo," said Grace Fox, coming up, remarking on my dress. Then she warned me that there was a flu going around. "They're dropping like flies, kiddo," she said. There was something comforting about her jazzy attitude to disaster, serving drinks, issuing flat commands in an unimpressed drawl. A Mississippi matriarch of sixty, she had a talent for the small, concrete details of life. The real meat of life to her was how to hang the curtains or fix the oyster stew. That may be the key, strictly off in your own Mississippi world, coping so knowingly with the crises of life.

I brought the baby a small red wallet with a little chain that she could use as a purse. She promptly hung it on her nose, and dissolved into a fit of mirth.

Al, looking on, has a sweetness in his brow. He looks at the baby with a tenderness beyond his years. It is the consideration for others that is his chief attribute, even though he is only three years old.

Al takes a great interest in my boyfriends, although his conception of them is confined to whether or not they have a mustache, and his conception of a mustache seems to take in a wide variety of attributes.

"Time for your Geography lesson," I said to Al. "Where is Paris?"

Making an expression of polite interest, he studied the world atlas and put his little hand upon the page.

"California?"

"Now come on, Al, you remember. There are seven continents in the world, remember?"

"Guess what?" he said shyly. "There's a continent called Nuttin and they make nuts there."

"Oh really? Well, there's a certain continent I know of called Europe, with a certain country called France, and a certain person that I know of forgot the whole entire thing."

"Do you like cole slaw?" Al said urgently. "I don't."

Conversation with a three-year-old involves wide leaps among a disparate variety of subjects.

I spent a good deal of time with Al. We made a secret hiding place in a pole by the canal and put a marble in it. I put in three small tiles with the initials of the children. Al put a secret present in the secret hiding place but it floated out to sea, as he dropped it in the bay.

We observed the swans. The swans were acting extremely peculiar. They seemed to be in amorous stupors, taking their cue, perhaps, from the love couple. The swans flipped their wings heatedly and raced toward one another in the bay.

We built a sand castle and tried to dig a hole to China.

That night there were stars in abundance, including shooting stars.

I bought presents for the children. I would gladly buy them everything in sight.

At night I am consumed by worry for the children. Waves of worry consume me, on their behalf.

I couldn't sleep—is it the tender domesticity and the country, the bay, the gardens, the green marshes, and the slant of light? One's like a stranger in his rooms, his own rooms. But there is the black glamour of the night, the rustling of the leaves in the black night.

"Do you want to play the marvelous marble game?" said Al.

"No, thank you," said the moody bachelor.

"What's your philosophy?" said Al. (After temporarily despairing of Geography, I have moved to Philosophy.)

"PHILOSOPHY, PHILOSOPHY," the children scream in tragic attitudes, although ecstatic at their newest realm of knowledge.

"Okay, okay, okay, I get the picture. But I don't have a philosophy."

"Do you like cole slaw?" asked Al. Whether or not a person likes cole slaw, also if he has a mustache, is Al's real gauge of character, and much more important to him, quite frankly, than either Geography or Philosophy.

As it happens, the moody bachelor does have a mustache,

therefore automatically inciting Al's love. Al asked him why he had a mustache but the moody bachelor made his standard reply, "I haven't the foggiest," which I might add is an answer that Al tends to find hilarious, if enigmatic.

"Let's play the Silent Game," said the moody bachelor. "Sometimes Big People need peace and quiet. Okay, buddy? Do you know how to play the Silent Game?"

"I haven't the foggiest," said Al, disintegrating into a small pile of mirth. He lay collapsing on the ground. The moody bachelor, Hobby Fox, looked over at him skeptically, smoking his cigar.

There was a din among the houses of the enclave and in the gardens. Screaming children, low voices at cocktail parties, 1920s flapper foxtrot violins, low laughter of women and men, a din of families.

Dark fell suddenly tonight at about nine o'clock. I have never seen dark fall so suddenly as that. It was as if a stagehand had been given stage directions to cut the lights and shift the scene from day to night.

The guests were circulating in the gardens of the houses of the enclave, mixing drinks, amid the clink of glasses and martini shakers, the cries of the children in the night.

Someone is listening to a baseball game on the radio. New York is winning. Against Pittsburgh.

Crashes emanate from the next house over. Crockery is being thrown. Also loud Al Jolson music is being played. The occupant is Margaret. Margaret is in crisis. That is nothing new. Margaret is a Southerner, from Memphis, Tennessee. That itself explains a lot. Memphis is definitely a town with a dark side. Margaret gets into a lot of scrapes. She is what you would call a live wire. If she's not out getting in fistfights in nightclubs ending up in jail, then she is fixing bourbon old-fashioneds on her boat at midnight or getting in gigantic boating accidents and the Coast Guard has to come and rescue her. Margaret is no stranger to the Coast Guard. Or to the local police force. The Chief of Police, the Sheriff, the Town Supervisor, you name it, she's in trouble with it. And yet Margaret is a glamour girl and old-style Southern belle.

"She's over the edge," said Hobby, smoking his cigar.

"She's from the South," said Al, as if by way of explanation —a profit from his lessons in Geography?

"You're driving me crazy, boys," said Hobby to some little boys who frolicked loudly on the lawn.

"Why does he have a mustache?" Al asked, referring to his idol, Hobby.

"Mustaches seem to hold a great interest for you," I said.

"Does he like cole slaw?" Al inquired.

It's the cole slaw theory of human analysis.

"Buddy, that's all you care about—cole slaw. Cole slaw and mustaches."

"But *does* he like cole slaw?" said the little boy.

"Everyone in their right mind likes cole slaw," I said supportively.

The children grew somewhat riotous.

"Simmer down, children," I said. "Hobby will get mad."

This had no effect on their boisterous cries. But their mother called from the bay.

However, they showed no signs of removing. They dawdled on the lawn. "Flake off, dandruff," said Hobby, with his gruff demeanor, causing fresh hilarity, using apparently the single most hilarious phrase in the English language. It took the boys at least ten minutes to recover.

Then the boys rowed out to sea in their pint-sized boat and

showed no signs of returning. Hobby had to swim out and rescue them.

Now the boys are being yelled at by their mother.

"You're driving me insane, boys," Hobby said again as they ran back to him in rapture, for they find him to be fascinating. Perhaps because they know beneath his gruff exterior lies a certain tenderness to them. Also he taught them how to tie flies. The boys are all obsessed with fishing, though have never caught a thing. Often Al is seen heading for the dock, a poignant figure, his fishing pole against his shoulder, ever undeterred.

The little boy stood on the dock with his fishing pole, and then trudged home across the lawn—a poignant figure, as I say. I have reason to be concerned about the boy.

"I want to be with my Dad," said Al, a melancholy admission since his father is currently absent. He looked manfully off into the distance, noting a fact, a melancholy one. "I'm very proud of Dad," he said.

"He's very proud of you too, Al," I said.

"Where is he?"

"He's in New Orleans. But coming for you soon."

Al and his brother and sister are technically being looked after by a nurse; also they play with the Langguth children, into whose family they have been somewhat absorbed in the absence of their parents. It worries me. My cousin, Claude Collier, their father, is as usual in trouble.

"I'm falling apart," said Al, sounding like the soul of his father.

"Well then, let's paste you back together, son," I said.

The sky tonight is covered with stars, including shooting stars. The ferry steamed in on the blue sea at dusk, lit up with gay lights.

I saw the dark radiant green lawns and old rambling houses down the path, and people drinking outside under canopies.

In a mansion on the sea there was angelic music, in the garden on the sweet Northern sea in the night, the swans on the green lagoon.

An unknown pathos. Befitting, for it was a startling beauty, to sit in the old gardens looking at the old Southern-seeming houses on the bay, which remind me of the green place of my heart.

A month ago I saw Al's father.

"I've known that man for thirty years and I've only seen him pass out from liquor once," I said to the doctor, looking at the subject of discussion in a hospital in New Orleans. It was a weak argument. I don't know why I even advanced it.

"That may be. But I want a complete detoxification from alcohol and drugs," said the doctor.

"Am I going to be a vegetable?" said Claude, the patient.

"No, you are not going to be a *vegetable,*" said the nurse, scolding her ward. The patient was known to make a lot of jokes. He was the darling of the psychiatric ward.

"Maybe it would be better if I were," said Claude.

"Were what?"

"A vegetable," said the patient gloomily. He sat in a wheelchair in an old plaid bathrobe, an item he had had for too many years, but which he insisted on using as the chief element of his wardrobe, contributing, perhaps, to his look of ill health. He was thirty-eight. Outside it was pouring rain, as could be seen from the window in his room, which looked onto the Mississippi River, with tugboats and barges, against a rainy cobalt twilight, moving slowly as if in a tropic lassitude, in the glamour of the twilight.

A conversation ensued concerning the condition of the patient. The patient's face began to bear a look of anguish. The details of his situation were discussed. His three small children would be taken by a nurse to a summer house in the North, effecting a total removal from the scene for the duration of the crisis.

His children were brought in to say good-bye. He held his daughter awkwardly in his arms. When he set her down, the little girl lost her footing and fell down, and he bent to pick her up and brush her off, with his cigarette hanging out of his mouth, like an awkward and a slightly seedy father.

It was a scene that severely touched my heart, to see him so reduced, though I had seen him so reduced before. Into every love affair there comes a moment of dishonor. If you resolve it then you may reach a deeper and more permanent agreement, but if not, then on the ardors of your youth, on that the door may close. It had been so with Claude Collier and his wife.

"Look after Anne and my boys," he said to me when his children had gone, before I left the hospital. He stood formally. "They're very fond of you, Storey," he said. "They know a glamour girl when they see one," he added kindly; and then he looked away, into the glamour of the rainy cobalt twilight.

So I would go to the country on the weekends from work in New York, thinking of my memories and those held dear, and keep an eye on the children, for they would be my responsibility, in a sense.

The enclave consists of eight houses. It is quite secluded. You take a turn off Route 25 and drive down a winding road lined by fields of wheat. The houses in the enclave are humble and dilapidated. It looks like an army base in Mississippi, with white clapboard houses among overgrown green gardens. As I say, the architecture, strangely enough, is done in a sort of Southern mode, with stone porticoes, verandas, and white columns. But in the sterling Northern twilight, that sterner Northern air. One could sit transfixed for many hours straight, on the raging bay, in the black night, on the green canal. The ferry steaming in on the blue sea at dusk with gay lights. An occasional other pleasure boat.

The men come out on Friday nights drinking highballs in the parlor car of the train and discussing business, banking, bonds; or steam in on the ferry from Connecticut.

Their wives and children sometimes stay in Orient throughout the week.

The members of the different houses in the enclave form a complex and in many ways incongruent group, ranging from the humble to the great.

But above all the enclave has a humble air, situated as it is on the north and unfashionable shore of Long Island—unpretentious, humble, frequented by relatively few.

Music emanates into the night. At times it reminds me of my hometown in the South, some broken-down old place that has jazz music.

By a strange string of circumstance, the enclave is owned by a Southerner, Grace Fox, a Mississippi matriarch of sixty, with a talent for the small concrete details of life, issuing flat commands in an unimpressed drawl, serving drinks, coping with disaster.

Owing to the Fox connection, a number of Southerners are meant to arrive, many of them my cousins. The South is made up of vast networks of cousins, who are ceaselessly concerned about each other. I also have a number of younger cousins now floating around New York, in spectacular bands, in particular a band of two brothers in their twenties. If you want to find them, just look in a nightclub at four in the morning. Or if you happen to be in a nightclub at four in the morning, my cousins will be there.

One house in the enclave has been taken for the Collier family, of whom Al is the youngest. Their father, Claude Collier, my cousin, is in a sanitarium for alcohol rehabilitation in New Orleans. Orient is considered to be a more healthy atmosphere for the children in the present crisis. I am keeping an eye on them of course. As their father asked me to do. Then they can play with the Langguth boys. One house in the enclave is occupied by Mrs. Langguth, the serenely calm mother of six, and her husband, the morose overweight fellow with the handlebar mustache, and their six children. Their children are rather demonic, I have to admit. The boys seem to spend most of their time lighting explosives. I don't know how or where they procure these implements of ignition. Mrs. Langguth seems serenely calm throughout the turmoil. "Could you do that in another room, dear?" she says airily while the boys light diametrical explosives on the ceiling. She is elegant, dry, distracted, smoking cigarettes on the lawn at night when her day of toil and supervision of the boys is finally over. Her husband reads *The Wall Street Journal* on the lawn morosely.

Al is considered to be too young to be included in the wild adventures of the boys. He makes piteous entreaties to be included in their manly adventures. They light explosives, they smoke cigars, they follow all forms of pyromania. Nevertheless, it is an innocent atmosphere, among the gardens, on the bay and the green canal, among the swans. The young couples pursue their pleasures, boating, dinner parties, bridge. The baseball games emanate from the radio on Hobby's porch.

Some of the stray guests, such as Margaret or Cedric, seem to be plunged into crisis. Cedric is prone to weird outbursts, causing many moments of strain.

Music emanates into the night. Old jazz. Crazy old-time Mississippi jazz. Old saxophones and crooners. "Inseparable" and "Reconsider Me." The clink of glasses, the young couples having drinks, the piercing cries of the children punctuate the night.

The proximity of the houses in the enclave, their humble air, the fomenting scandals among the different guests—afford many opportunities for spying on the neighbors.

My old flame, Hobby Fox, is sitting on a deck chair in the night alone. He is the nephew of Constant Fox, the heart throb. Possibly Hobby is too gruff and crusty to be an exact heart throb. But he is one anyway. "His eyes are so blue it just makes you want to go jump in the river," as Margaret commented.

Usually he sits obliviously on the porch reading the stock pages or the sports pages, listening to the baseball games on the radio in a low masculine drone, and smoking a cigar, with his slightly burnt-out air. He has a certain burnt-out air. Distracted by his memories, perhaps.

"Don't go out tonight, Hobby," said Al, sitting on the porch.

"Why, sweetheart?" said Hobby.

"Because you'll turn blue."

Hobby contemplated this possibility.

"Don't go out dancing," said Al.

"Why, Al?"

"Because then we would miss you too much. I want to be with you," said Al with his blunt emotion. "I'm very proud of you," he said.

I do think the little fellow is falling apart.

"And I'm very proud of you, too," said Hobby. "Now come over here and sit on my lap in the rocking chair and we'll have some time together, son."

Hobby is the idol of the little boys. He wears sweatpants emblazoned with the legend DUCK HUNTING CLUB OF NEW ORLEANS, an old-fashioned sleeveless ribbed undershirt, and tennis shoes. He has a sort of crusty gruff demeanor, which for some reason has inspired the children with idolatry in his behalf. Although he is a misanthrope he often finds himself with the responsibility of the children, who follow him around and with whom he is quite gruff, but tender if the truth be told.

It is his peculiar blend of tenderness and disinterest, I think, that has inspired their confidence.

Then they are awed by his ex-athlete status, for he once was a professional baseball player.

Currently World Editor of the New York *Examiner,* he was an athlete, a man's man, an old pro, who had been around the block a million times, at age thirty-six. Among the young couples he is an outsider, but then so am I. The young couples ceaselessly pursue their innocent amusements—boating, dinner parties, bridge, etc. Their innocence bemuses me. I have more in common with the misanthrope.

He even seems a little seedy. Because he is burnt out. Nevertheless he is a source of fascination to the children, who have been inspired with idolatry in his behalf, and for the fading slightly seedy glamour that, in Al's case, must remind him of his father.

Thinking of my memories and those held dear, it's like watching other people than yourself and trying to paste them back together, these other people you once were, in such a different time and place. Like actually watching the different people you once were for those you have held dear—shocked at how it slips away, what was held dear, what one was to love it, and how to hold to those things here in this differing environment. It is a certain exile, even of my heart. My story starts in Orient, tame Orient, but pursues ever to the South— to the plantation of the Foxes in Louisiana, or to the stony grandeur of the Collier family in New Orleans.

But the Collier family was definitely in crisis.

The grandparents of the children are meant, at least, to arrive, but Mrs. Collier, grandmother to Al, was in the hospital recovering from surgery. She was now quite aged. The years had wrought on her a study of infirmities.

Her husband, who had now seen the last of seventy, made two brisk visits to the hospital per day, enigmatic, witty, kind. Lying in her hospital bed, denounced of her imperious mode, she looked at him with unceasing fascination. With what did he look back? It would be hard to say. His was an undemonstrative and understated love, but she was what he adored.

They were glamorous and quaint and droll, even in their aged condition, like the Southern city that they occupied. Where every street corner has its long associations. Mr. Collier's devotion to his wife was like his devotion to this Southern city which he occupied and in which his whole life had been spent. His life in New Orleans represented innocence and simplicity, as did his rigid routine.

Mr. Collier's reaction to the sorrows of life, and in his life there had been many, was to become rather more eccentric. But he was steadfast. He viewed the troubles of his son in the alcoholic ward with equanimity, and as he trod the halls in his well-worn but dapper attire, he had a certain unassailable dignity. But his grandchildren were the delight and consolation of his life. Once he had lost a son.

He brought the children to the hospital to visit his wife before they were sent up North to Orient. It was his wife's

birthday. "Congratulations, my dear, on being sixty," said
Mr. Collier. "You have accomplished a great deal."

"Everything I have accomplished is here in this room," she
said, looking at the children, and she wept.

The members of the enclave here form a complex mixture.
But the idea is that here there are a number of people who can
look out for these children, and provide for them forms of
amusement.

Al said he had a present for me and ran inside to get it. It
was a plastic bracelet, which carried the word FOREVER. When
presenting it to me his brow was furrowed in perplexity and
concentration for several moments in silence looking up at me
before he then announced, "I have something to tell you, Storey, if it would make you happy." He paused, concentrating.
"I love you so much that I would like you to stay here forever
with me if you want to."

"Al, thank you, sweetheart."

His crooked brow was still furrowed in perplexity, looking
at me, thinking. He sometimes makes dramatic pronounce-
ments such as these, uttering them in a sort of stiff, rehearsed
way, as if to make them even more dramatic.

"Storey is my girl," said one of the Langguth boys who
dawdled near, age four.

"No, she is my girl," said Al.

They glared at each other. I thought that they might come
to fisticuffs. Unaccustomed to being the object of such idolatry, I had to pry the little boys apart.

"Al asked me first," I said. I am the darling of the four-
year-olds.

We then had to vacate the premises, for the love couple
came near, and started looking at each other in a way they

have that just makes you want to get out of the place and let them at it. This can happen of course at any time and in any place. The other members of the enclave have their differing reactions, each his own. But even Al takes notice of it, calmly eyeballing them with his brow furrowed in perplexity. But Al is a ladies' man himself. I mean his first word was "train" and his second word was "tunnel," if you catch my drift.

"If you don't eat oatmeal, you'll dry up," Al informed me. "Never throw away cardboard," he added.

Maxims of a three-year-old.

Actually, cardboard is very dear to him, for some reason. He collects it. Like many little boys he is obsessed with war, guns, soldiers, etc. His room is a virtual arsenal. A box of his beloved cardboard contains his weapons. "If you throw away cardboard, my heart will break into a million pieces," he says inexplicably. It is hard to fathom where he gets these quaint ideas. Hobby commented that he gets them from me. It is true we have been hanging around together a lot, Al and I, because I find his situation to be bad. He suffers from the absence of his father. It is why I have grown so tenderhearted, watching over these children. There is only one solution and that is their father but I do not know when he is meant to arrive. Hobby saw him in New Orleans recently and said that he looked terrible.

"You'd look terrible too if you'd been through what he's been through,"

"I know. It's a miracle he got out alive."

His problems derived from one source, at least on the surface, alcohol.

Cedric has been tying flies all day like some sort of zombie at a card table on the lawn, taking his cue, perhaps, from

Hobby and the boys. One of the young couples mildly asked him, passing by, if he wanted to come with them to the grocery store.

"I can't take the pressure!" said Cedric, and put his head in his hands.

"What pressure?" I said, as he had just been sitting there all day, watching everyone perform their innocent amusements, boating, playing bridge, etc.

Someone is always going to pieces, among the different guests.

"Are we being gracious enough?" I said to Hobby, sitting on the porch, as in a situation like this, an enclave of summer houses, with the guests circulating on the lawns and among the gardens to the beach, it is of paramount importance, in my opinion, to be gracious. Especially as the place is riddled with smoldering faux pas and gaffes, especially on the weekends when the various extra guests arrive, and drive each other crazy.

Crashes emanate from Margaret's house, as usual. Then she ran onto the lawn, seemingly in crisis, wearing a leopard-skin bathing suit and a huge bow in her hair.

"She's so glamorous," I said.

"You're glamorous too, Storey," said Al.

The children are swimming in the bay with rubber boats. "Lower your voice, F.R.," their mother calls from the shore. F.R. always picks fights. The man with the handlebar mustache who could stand to lose about seventy pounds sits alone under a beach umbrella, pensive and a tad on the morose side.

The swans are on the green lagoon.

F.R. (son of the overweight fellow with the handlebar mustache and not so trim himself) comes trudging across the lawn, wrapped in a towel, carrying a toy pail. The forlornness of children is always enough to break your heart.

There is a floating bar in the bay—and a dinner party, with long tables in the twilight.

The drama of the twilight.

2. NEVER HAS one group of people conducted such a ceaseless series of activities. Boating parties, boating accidents, tennis, bridge, loud music on the lawn, dancing late at night, golf, sailing, water-skiing, dinner parties, etc. This afternoon, for instance, the men went to the golf course and Margaret sailed over to the links in her boat and picked them up and sailed them over to Southampton to look at the mansions on the bay. Or she will drive down the boat basin and sail over to the tennis courts and pick them up and sail them to Paradise Point. Then there will be cocktails on the beach. The young men rigged up an elaborate floating bar on a raft with attachments they got at the hardware store. They also have special rafts with attachments for cocktail glasses and martini shakers. Every weekend Margaret gets in a gigantic boating accident and has to be rescued by the Coast Guard. The waters are so Yankeefied that, unlike in the South, if you get in a boating accident no one helps you because they are so Yankeefied, and someone at your house has to call the Coast Guard instead to come and rescue you. Margaret takes the boat out at midnight, on wild escapades. I think she has had one too many martinis. This frenzied zenith of activity shows no signs of abating. Today I saw a pamphlet for sky-diving lessons next to the telephone.

On the beach the women sit talking darkly of Mr. Underwood. His fits of temper, his stern demands, etc.

However, I myself adore Mr. Underwood. My favorite, aside from Mr. Underwood and Al, is Speed Weed, a snaggle-

toothed egghead eight-year-old with gigantic glasses and an
awkward mien. Al loves him too, and makes piteous entreaties
to be near him. "I want to sit by Speed." "Speed, will you
help me?" Once Al said, "Speed Weed frightens me." "Why,
darling?" I asked. "Because I . . . I love him," said Al, with a
very blunt grasp of human emotions.

Mr. Underwood frightens me. Because I love him?

Everyone sits talking darkly of Mr. Underwood, cowering
in fear, trying to placate his stern demands, being on pins and
needles. Everyone is relaxed until he comes, then they are
anxiety-ridden and filled with grievances but meekly submissive toward him.

Everyone is obsessed with grievances against Mr. Underwood, but everyone acts meekly submissive when he actually
appears.

Mr. Underwood is the editor-in-chief of a major New York
newspaper. He does not play this part down, but up. Everyone is obsessed by his position of importance in the world.

Thursday night we ate at the club with Mr. Underwood.
He chewed his cigar in a frightening manner and conversed
with his guest, the Governor, while we cowered in fear. Mr.
Underwood's small troubled son was also there. Mr. Underwood's small son is "troubled," but not through any fault of
his father's character, in my own opinion. Many may malign
Mr. Underwood, but although he frightens me, I think he is
an angel.

It is true that Mr. Underwood has many important guests.
The Governor has visited twice, a millionaire racetrack owner,
politicians, magnates, and thinkers. As a result the enclave
is constantly inflamed with gossip and spy mania. Two
champagne-soaked authors came once and they still haven't
left (they were invited for dinner two weeks ago) and are
causing a scandal of major proportions. At least, I think so.

Mr. Underwood sometimes invites me to dinner at the club or cocktails but my Crippling Shyness prevents me from engaging in actual conversation in a gracious manner. After dinner Mr. Underwood told me to go out and have some fun. So I went to the bar at Port of Egypt and I think I had some fun. But I'm not sure.

Actually, Mr. Underwood is worried about me. You might wonder why I even know Mr. Underwood. It is because he is my boss. He has been my boss for five years and of course I have talked to him personally a number of times, even though he is the big cheese. The New York lunatic big cheese. I'm not really sure why he has taken a sort of special interest in me, I only know it fills me with anxiety, because it is a little hair-raising having to hang around with the big cheese. A lot of times he invites me to have cocktails at the club with other aged parties and big cheeses, but then, when we get there, a lot of times they all just sink into a daze, brooding, like the other night he asked me to have cocktails at the club, and then he sank into one of these dazes, distracted by his memories, smoking his cigar, just staring off into space, brooding. Then, if I try to leave, he says, "Stay here, kid. We're having fun. This is fun for me. I like you, kid." Then he'll sink into silence for a while. Then suddenly he'll say, "How old are you again, kid? Jesus Christ!" he'll say, out of the blue, in his reverie. Then we just have to keep sitting there, brooding.

But I am not the only person whom Mr. Underwood has attempted to take under his wing. He favors the young people, the underdogs, the peons. He always tries to take them under his wing. The only problem is, he ends up terrorizing them.

For example he will call you into his office. Which is hair-raising enough in itself since he is the big cheese. Then when you get there he just sits there in dead silence staring at you. I mean you'd think he meant to tell you some huge philosophi-

cal thing or give some type of guidance, maybe. But instead
he gets this dazed expression, just staring off into space, smoking his cigar. Then after about five minutes of dead silence
scaring you out of your wits, he'll finally say something like
"What makes you tick, kid?" or possibly he will brood about
his memories, and start telling you some of his reminiscences.

I find him to be poignant. But then again, I find a lot of
things to be poignant. I also find him to be crazy.

And the reason why a big cheese like Mr. Underwood is to
be found in our humble Orient enclave can also only be explained by a series of somewhat coincident and circuitous circumstances. But to make a long story short, it is because Grace
Fox, the owner of the enclave, is an old friend of Mr. Underwood's family, and Constant Fox, the heart throb, is Mr.
Underwood's idol.

Of course, Constant Fox is my idol too. He is everyone's idol.

3.   I REMEMBER the first time I met Mr. Underwood. It was, oddly enough, at an old hotel on an island off
the coast of Alabama. It was the type of place populated
strictly by Southerners, so it was strange that a Yankee like
Mr. Underwood would be there. But I had noticed at cocktails
a foursome who kept to themselves. One was a dark man with
horn-rim glasses. It was two gents with vivacious wives. The
wives talked convivially and seemed to be driving their husbands crazy, sort of. The husbands knocked back their cocktails. The man drank methodically and seemed very morose.
He was crashingly handsome.

There was a lengthy cocktail hour, as is the custom at
Southern hotels, and a convivial dinner, after which we main-

tained our position in the Magnolia Room—a position of strategic importance.

The Southerners socialized ceaselessly, the two wives joining in, and the morose man played backgammon with his friend misanthropically in a far corner of the room.

It was hurricane season. There was the ceaseless news of hurricanes coming up from the Gulf Coast. Born-again Christians raved on the radio. There was a hint of disaster. The palm trees were slightly awry in the storm, leaning dangerously toward the old hotel, in the black night.

But the news of the hurricanes only made it more exciting, adding a certain dark gaiety, while the storm lashed against the palms.

You had to fly into an old town on the coast to get there, to a small tropical airport in an old unpainted town, and then take a ferry up the coast to the old hotel. Old boats, tugboats, old-time fishing boats, and the levity of a green old frivolous place with no pretensions to anything else.

The man I had noticed had also been on the plane and the ferry with me. He was striking, somehow. He chewed on his cigar in silence while his party socialized. He must have been at least sixty. He had an elegance. But he was morose. He was a misanthrope. But so am I.

In the Magnolia Room the Southerners socialized ceaselessly. Some shuffled toward the dance floor. Others maintained vivacious, drawling conversations. Black men in starched white uniforms served drinks with a sort of ancient abiding hospitality. The massive oaks and palms swayed outside.

And so the evening passed until most people had retired, save for a few who socialized endlessly in the Magnolia Room, while the morose man smoked his cigar in the corner with a crusty expression and lapsed into long crusty silences.

Suddenly the morose man addressed me.

"Where are *you* from?" he growled from across the room, with his odd air of antagonism—or mixture of sarcasm and moroseness. He seemed to be engulfed in depression.

"I'm from New Orleans."

"I know some people from New Orleans."

"Who do you know?"

"I know the Colliers."

"Well, you're looking at one of them!"

He registered little surprise at this alarming coincidence. Nor did it do anything to dispel his depression, I might add.

He lapsed into a brooding silence.

"Storey Collier. Pleased to meet you, sir," I said.

"Stokes Underwood."

Then he sank into a wordless daze.

I remark again that the striking thing about the man, aside from his engulfing depression, was that he was a tall stalwart Yankee who was crashingly handsome.

The man was drinking heavily and as the night wore on seemed rather pixilated. The rest of us were chatting about our travel experiences, and a general discussion arose on the subject of Charleston. The man would make gruff comments in a morose manner, or otherwise lapse into gruff, morose silences. Sometimes his wife would ask him a question and pure silence would be his answer.

"Where was that hotel in Charleston, Stokes?"

Dead silence.

Desperate gaiety would then ensue, on her part, and on ours, trying to make up for it.

"Charleston should be bombed off the face of the map," the man suddenly contributed. He was not fond of Charleston. He had relatives there. In fact, his wife's relatives were from there.

Someone gaily remarked on a hotel in Savannah, trying to shift the conversation from the menacing subject of Charleston.

"It should be bombed," said the man.

The man started asking me questions and after I answered he would say, "And?"

Then I would elaborate.

"And?"

I would continue.

"You always have a lot of Ands," he said. But this was only because he asked a lot of questions.

"There's more to you than meets the eye," he said enigmatically, puffing on his cigar.

A silence ensued.

"There's a lot more to you than meets the eye, I think," he repeated.

As there's really not a lot more to me than meets the eye, I said nothing.

He regarded me silently.

"Am I right, kid?" he suddenly bellowed, scaring me out of my wits. He seemed to be having some sort of mood swings. Not to say delusions. "Come and see me at my office when you're in New York, and we'll see about giving you a job. You and me, kid, we're going straight to the top."

"Huh?"

"Hah!"

He stared at me happily for a while. Then again he spoke. What's your name again, kid?"

"Storey Collier. Pleased to meet you."

"Jesus Christ!" he bellowed happily, inexplicably, out of the blue, as in conclusion. Then he sank into another daze.

He began to chew on his cigar in a frightening manner and ordered more brandy and soda. He sat in his silent trance. His face was like a death mask. I began to worry that maybe he had some sort of gigantic mental problem that everyone knew about or knew how to handle ordinarily. The others had long since retired.

Quite to my relief a strangely normal conversation then arose on whether I was qualified for the job, which I happened to be, though he certainly wouldn't have known it or didn't know it before he made his inexplicable offer, unless he was a mind reader. Furthermore, when I mentioned the name of my boss, Constant Fox, the long-revered editor of the *Southern Democrat,* who turned out to be the man's idol, I saw that the man shed a tear. He mentioned Constant Fox had done a favor for him once, and he shed a tear.

Then with his customary resilience he bellowed, "And you're not working for him now?"

"No. I left to travel and—"

"And you're trying to find yourself? You're trying to find yourself!" he screamed. "Well, go out and have some fun, kid! Congratulate yourself! You've got the best job in New York! Go out and pour some liquor down your throat! How old are you, kid? Well, it's you and me now. We're going straight to the top."

It was his wacko big-cheese mode. The thing about Mr. Underwood is, he's a lunatic. It's like having a lunatic for a boss.

So that was how I first came to know Mr. Underwood, later the Senator from New York, or as we called him at the paper, and as he was known at the enclave, The Terror.

Okay, so my boss was a nut. But that was New York to me. Only New York could breed the particular kind of nut that he was. It could not have happened in New Orleans, for his behavior was a result of being in the big time, New York.

Or maybe it was that he played the part so well, of a lunatic New York big cheese, you hardly felt he was dealing with you personally, but more like in a script from the 1940s of how he thought it should be, as if Central Casting had just sent him over.

But it was Mr. Underwood who brought me to New York. He stretched out his hand to me.

In a way he did have a soft spot for the South. He loved the underdog. He would never root for the favorite. It's the broken-wing theory. He liked people who had broken wings and then he could pick them up and paste them back together. The same was true of Constant Fox. This is the way to the heart of the old, of the wise, of the great, odd as it may seem. But then again it is not so odd at all.

I read an article in *Time* magazine about eccentrics that said that what we need is an oddball in the White House. If so, and seeing as Mr. Underwood later won his race for Senator, they ought to elect him President and they can see what it's like to have a nut in the White House.

He always talked like an impresario in Las Vegas. He and I were going straight to the top, all the time. On our way to the top, the road was studded with anxiety. Actually, it was so traumatic working for Mr. Underwood that many people who worked for him at the paper ended up moving to Bombay to work with Mother Teresa or going back to graduate school to take degrees in religious philosophy. I never knew the meaning of the word "anxiety" until I met Mr. Underwood. I never knew the meaning of the word "stress" until I met him. Do you see what I'm getting at?

On leaving the Southern hotel the next day, I went on to another resort on the Alabama coast. It had a garish decor of green and yellow, the green opulence of the country-club mode. There I unexpectedly ran into Mr. Underwood again, and his wife, and the other couple. It was as if I were pursued by the man—the crusty Northerner out of place in these Southern haunts. I couldn't figure out why he was there and kept popping up. It seemed unexplained. He was perhaps not enjoying himself—if the trip had been meant for enjoyment. But I would never expect a Northerner to enjoy himself in certain places of the South—it always seems too foreign to him, too hot, too humid, too desolate. Familiarity alone explains that passion for an untoward place, as for the South. The twisted oaks, the grey humid air, the black maids drawling in the kitchen—familiarity alone explains.

The same scenes of socializing persisted, the wives with their desperate gaiety, in the heat, drinking martinis, glamorous in their black sunglasses, and the man's dark comments. If this trip had been meant for him to repair exhaustion or overwork or malaise, it was perhaps not working, although there were certain moments of hilarity—pitchers of martinis, opulent dinner dances in sweltering gardens.

It was the kind of place where you eat in the Magnolia Room, dance at Julep Point, and golf on the Azalea Course. There were girls in antebellum costumes in the lobby. These are not the type of places where you find many Yankees. Torture and Lust on Plantations comes to mind. But these were the ancient oaks and velvet lawns and wrought iron of my youth. What was familiar to me, though, was not to them.

Still, I thought that if I had to spend another night in the Magnolia Room I would die. But my hopes were dashed of not spending another night in the Magnolia Room, for I could not get a reservation in the Country Club, the sole alternative. But that night in the Magnolia Room I ran into Mr. Underwood and his party, a party into which I had already been integrated and seemed to perform an integral diplomatic function. Their nerves were starting to go. First I saw his wife. She was a cornball. But she was extremely kind. She stopped and stared at me in a dramatic posture of silent amazement. Then she screamed, *Storey Collier!''* She took my hand and stood in her dramatic pose. *"Aren't you darling!"* She stepped back, frozen.

"Isn't she precious!" said her friend.

"Where did you find *her?"* said a black man in a starched white uniform, chiming in.

"Hah!" said Mr. Underwood. "Jesus Christ!"

A small crowd began to gather. We were creating a scene. Unaccustomed to being the object of such idolatry, I alternately cowered in embarrassment and basked in my glory.

Finally everyone began to calm down. There was a convention of Southern Baptist senior citizens in the hotel. Many aged Southerners were shuffling toward the dance floor.

Mr. Underwood seemed a little down in the mouth. Other times he would cause you to cower in fear. But one thing was constant: he was crazy. He talked like an impresario on Hollywood Boulevard. (You and me, kid, we're going straight to the top.) But I later found that a lot of big cheeses in New York talk that way, plus they're all crazy.

His hair was kind of slicked back by this stuff his wife gave him, and he was wearing an ascot. He did look tired and quite old. He looked uncharacteristically seedy, in short. He certainly did not look like a Southern Baptist senior citizen. He looked like a falling New York big cheese with one foot firmly planted in the lunatic fringe.

Mr. Underwood had also integrated others than myself into his party. There was an aged Southern Senator whom he knew, and several others. Cotton-tops, I call them. White-haired gents.

Mr. Underwood and his original party, too, had seen the

last of sixty, I would judge. I was the only person in the hotel under sixty. But that was all right with me. The older the better, closer to God.

The wives and I fell into a pattern of secret congeniality common to women who regard their husbands and fathers and brothers as men whom they tend to admire from afar, while cowering in fear at their dark moods and positions of power, being on pins and needles, just attempting to be gracious. In short, it is how you act if you are married to a nut. Or if your father was a nut. Something I am very familiar with. In my family the men were nutty misanthropes who puttered around making little incomprehensible comments and the women were gracious and normal. Why is such a man and such a situation bred so often? I have come across it very often.

So the wives and I would engage in normal interesting conversations, and then if Mr. Underwood walked up, we would quickly fall silent and start being on pins and needles.

The theme of our conversation throughout the entire trip was, as it had been before, Travel Experiences in the South.

I was telling a sad tale of Asheville one night. "North Carolina always seems so sad."

"It's sad, doll," said Mr. Underwood. "It's very sad."

"I had some problems there," I said.

"I had some problems there, too," said Mr. Underwood.

"It was a sad situation."

"It's sad, doll. It's a sad situation."

A lot of times he would just go on like that, agreeing with you. It was rather kind. But then he would have a mood swing.

"It's fabulous," he said suddenly. "It's a fabulous, fabulous feature story in the Travel Section."

"It is?"

"You had some problems, you say?" said Mr. Underwood.

"I guess I had some problems."

"'Baby, everyone has problems!" he suddenly screamed. Everyone cowered in fear. A silence fell. "So what's the problem?" he screamed.

The wives tried to change the subject.

"Isn't she darling?"

"Aren't you darling to sit with us?"

"Isn't she precious!"

I think her vehemence startled us. It snapped Mr. Underwood out of his mood. Then he lapsed back into his enthusiastic or even beatific mode. We were discussing ideas for stories in the Travel Section. I would give an idea for a story.

"Fabulous. Fabulous," he said. "It's a series."

"No, it's a story."

"Right, right, it's a story. Fabulous. I love it."

I think that if I had said I wanted to write a column called "Torture and Lust on Plantations" he would have said, Fabulous, it's a fabulous column, I love it.

What with traipsing from the Magnolia Room to Julep Point to the Azalea Course, the atmosphere was enough to make your entire personality disintegrate. But you could not take the grandeur from the setting. Aside from the cornball Southernisms, there were the ancient grounds and gardens, among the green, with velvet lawns and long tables with white tablecloths set up on the lawn for a dance in the black night.

For a while the Southern setting seemed to affect Mr. Underwood's personality. This happened more and more the longer I knew him, back in the North in Orient and in New York, where he was surrounded by a good many Southerners, a number of whom he had hired, like me. He had a habit of slipping into a Southern mode from time to time, when he would speak in a sort of drawl and suddenly start saying things

like "The Delta is prettiest when the cotton is high." I mean
not even Southerners say things like that. He slapped people
on the back and called them Chief or Coach or Colonel. Meanwhile our party assumed its strategic position in the Magnolia
Room.

"Would you like to freshen up, dear?" his wife asked him.

"If I get any fresher, I'll die!" he drawled.

Some people began to retire. "Stay here, kid," he said to
me, when I tried to depart. Then he sank into a moody silence,
staring menacingly at the Southern Baptist senior citizens shuffling toward the dance floor. Then we just had to keep sitting
there, brooding. I mean there the old gent sat, silent as a tomb,
brooding. To me it didn't seem proper to try to make gay
remarks or instigate gay conversations. So I sat there and tried
to look gracious.

The aged Southern Senator was also there. He was a bachelor. As Mr. Underwood had informed me at dinner. "We have
a bachelor," he whispered. "You're next to him."

"Very kind," I said.

Then this eighty-year-old Southern Senator sat down next
to me. He made some mischievous comments. Then he fell
asleep.

Mr. Underwood sat staring moodily into space.

The aged Southern Senator woke up abruptly and said,
"How's that?"

"What's that? Come again?"

"What's that you said? Eh?"

"I didn't say a single word!"

"Ha ha. That's grand," said the Senator. "Just grand. I've
been listening to your conversation, my dear. I heard every
word. Quite the wit you are, dear one."

Dear one? He dropped off again and Mr. Underwood continued to sit staring in a dazed manner into space.

"I guess I'll call it a night!" I said gaily.

"No, no, we're having fun, kid," said Mr. Underwood. "This is fun for me. It's a lot of fun being with you, kid," he said.

Naturally I could not make my departure after that. We sat in silence. He was crashingly handsome, at sixty. He chewed on his cigar in silence. I performed my customary task of sitting in a group of white-haired gents brooding. Why that is my fate I do not know. It was sort of like a Latin American dictator surrounded by yes men, who laugh when he laughs, and frown when he frowns, etc. I mean that's what I was like with Mr. Underwood.

The storm rained into the gardens with a downpour, among the leaning palms. The sea had a light green color. There were white markers in symmetrical paths against the green in the garden, marking out tropical walks.

There was an air of disaster. People played solitaire in the bar. Mr. Underwood drank numerous cocktails throughout the day, which however seemed to have no effect on him until quite late at night, in a sudden finality.

As it was hurricane season, a storm would come along and then as suddenly there would be moments of calm. The air looked green. The Azalea Course looked like a green ballroom stretching out into the night.

Mr. Underwood regained his misanthropic corner, while I looked for further signs of personality problems in him. He puttered around the Magnolia Room with his cigar, making little incomprehensible comments, the crusty Northerner.

None of us had meant to stay so long. But the hurricane came, and you couldn't leave. You could only have left if you were incredibly hardy and felt like driving your car out into the Alabama night on the Gulf Coast in the middle of a hurricane.

"The Lord just makes the cross as heavy as we can bear," said Mr. Underwood's wife one night—and I couldn't tell if she was looking at her husband when she said it, referring to his—shall we say—peccadilloes personality-wise, or if she meant the storm.

As we were cooped up in the Magnolia Room due to the hurricane they brought in a TV and we watched an old movie. Claudette Colbert and Don Ameche in divorce court in Paris and the judge asks what are the grounds for divorce. "Mental Cruelty," recites her lawyer with dramatic indignation. "Oh, that again," says the judge with a John Barrymore sidelong glance. It reminded me of Mr. Underwood.

Mental Insanity? Oh, that again.

Either that or they would play the radio—born-again Christians. "The devil offered Elvis Presley a cup of custard and a gold lamé suit. That's all he had to offer. That's all he had!" screamed the preacher.

Three things are a constant of the South: palm trees, born-again Christians, and hurricanes. Those were the themes.

The usual discussion ensued on our travel experiences in the South.

"North Carolina is a vale of humility between two humps of pride," drawled Mr. Underwood, in his Southern mode, quoting the Civil War Governor of North Carolina, Zeb Vance. I contributed that the two humps of pride, Virginia and South Carolina, certainly did seem different from North Carolina, for their society aspect. It does seem odd that two such close neighbors as the Carolinas could be so different, South Carolina having a genteel, ladylike aspect and North Carolina being manly and rugged. South Carolina having many social niceties or pretensions or hotly differentiated strata of society, much more so than North Carolina. Mr. Underwood contributed some drawling quotes and comments to this conversation, as if he had been born and bred in Alabama. He kept slipping in and out of his new Southern mode.

But actually you couldn't get more Yankeefied than Mr. Underwood, who was from Troy, New York.

As with many a Northerner, baseball was his great love. He was following the progress of his New York team while we were at the old hotel.

"My head is in Chicago but my heart is in New York, if I may be candid with you," he would say, regarding the fact that his New York team was playing that night in Chicago and he thought that New York might lose. He loved New York, but he knew Chicago had a better team. His heart was with New York, but his brains could calculate in favor of Chicago. Head, heart. See? Head in Chicago, heart in New York. It took me awhile to figure out what he was talking about, see, because they don't have baseball in New Orleans.

"He's a very disturbed individual," he would say, regarding the Chicago coach, "if I may be very candid with you."

He would always make these utterances in his deep New York accent, sounding like a gangster.

Even though he knew Chicago would win, he went off on a rampage about how disturbed and terrible they were. "Losers are losers," he screamed. "They're losers! Schmucks!" Heads began to turn in the Magnolia Room.

"There's a man on the phone for you in the lobby and he says to tell you to come to the phone," said Mr. Underwood's wife, coming in, with an ecstatic expression, looking at me.

"Who is it?"

"I don't know. He just said to tell you to come to the

phone." The caller had charmed her, it appeared. He had had
a strong effect on her, plainly. A heart throb? Calling for me?
By the same strange string of circumstance, Hobby Fox was
also at the old hotel. He later came to work for Mr. Underwood as well. He was the World Editor. He did, in fact, go
straight to the top. But when among the leading newsmen,
journalists, and politicians that comprised Mr.
Underwood's surroundings in New York, Hobby seemed remote, as if in
his seersucker suit and white bucks, the odd innocence or
gaiety of the South and his old attire and North Carolina
drawl, he just wasn't a regular guy like the Harvard types of
East Coast journalists pontificating. What added to his glamour, and amounted in Mr. Underwood's eyes to greatness,
was that he had once been a professional baseball player.

He wasn't hard to look at, either. I just remember then his
old blue eyes, khaki pants, and that he'd put a camellia at my
place. And he looked at me the way a man looks at a woman.

I presented Mr. Underwood and his wife to Hobby in the
Azalea Room. "Jesus Christ!" said Mr. Underwood, by way
of introduction, apparently his mode of greeting.

"Likewise, I'm sure," said Hobby.

At dinner with the new addition, Hobby, in the Magnolia
Room, the mood was general hilarity. We made a hilarious
party. First he was doted on by the wives. Hobby and Mr.
Underwood's wife became closeted in private conversation
throughout the night, strangely enough. I had to pry them
apart with a crowbar. And what did it turn out they were
talking about for the entire night? Boxing. And then they went
into the den to watch the prizefight and laid bets on it. This
genteel old girl, Mr. Underwood's wife, and her brittle high-
society gaiety from Charleston, and it turns out her main interest in life is boxing. Or at least it was when she was with

Hobby. A lot of things were sports metaphors to him, it is true. Everyone tried to get him to talk about baseball but it didn't work. When you take a man like that, who has to go into a regular walk of life, you will find he doesn't tend to really talk about those days. Which in his case gave him his dignity. They were heroes and their season was short. It's poignant. At least I thought so. He did talk about baseball to me. In fact although he and I had a motley past, we didn't talk about feelings, we just talked about baseball. Later on in New York, that is, where it is a Northerner's great love. He was thirty-six and you could see an athlete's grace in him, and a sweetness, however much he tried to hide his sweetness, with his gruff exterior. Or however much he may have been distracted by his old haunts, the ball parks.

There is a fine old boulevard that runs along the Gulf Coast, lined by old oaks, with gay white houses on the Gulf. The Gulf is not a ravishing sea as in the North. It is strictly the tropic zone. It is less stern than the North. It is not melancholy in its beauty as the North can often be. It is a frivolous, green old place with no pretensions. How could it have pretensions? It is remote and stifling. The Gulf is brown and swelters in the heat.

But I left my heart there. And like all people who have left their hearts behind, I yearn for someone who is gone, or for a place that I have parted from.

There were ancient unpainted houses crumbling on the Gulf beside huge palms, and plaques on the houses designating their old age with French heraldry—it being a French town, near to Mobile. Mardi Gras was begun there one midnight by some drunk young men who later brought it to New Orleans.

Everything was green, immensely green, and everything was sweltering in a tropic heat. At the hotel there was one tiny beach with green deck chairs and jaunty green umbrellas. No one was ever there. But the place had a sort of grandeur. Frequented by no one. On the Gulf. No one was there, in general. No one would go there. It's the South, the Gulf Coast, the "redneck riviera," stifling and remote. No one would ever go there from the North, only a few Southerners would ever go there, which is why it was so striking that a type like Mr. Underwood was there.

It was shortly before the World Series. It was early October. "It's a winter wonderland," I said to Hobby, in the garden, on the Gulf.

"It is many things, but one thing it is not is a winter wonderland," he said—as the weather was eighty degrees, with hot rains and hurricanes, which is the Southern fall. Old oaks, ancient gardens, and black nightclubs with exotic names and martini glasses in the town. Don't go anywhere near the equator if you prefer an ordinary autumn.

Our party had become so enamored of each other's company, aided no doubt by the Early Times and pitchers of martinis, that the entire party elected to go to Charleston the next day. This was where Mr. Underwood's in-laws resided. The sky was black from stormy weather, adding a certain philosophical thrill, the palm trees adding to the tropic aspect. The car broke down and we were stopped at a seedy dive, a dark gaiety in this broken-down old place, a seedy dive with saxophones and Ray Charles and the real thing. Born-again Christians raved on the radio, in an atmosphere of Torture and Lust, soul legends wandered around South Carolina getting in fistfights in nightclubs, yet with the crusty Northerner out of place in these Southern haunts, and hurricane season in Charleston, causing tumult in my heart.

. . .

I went on a series of job interviews with Mr. Underwood in New York before he hired me, coming out of the subway at Forty-second Street with the old ruined architecture, as ever, sleazeland, which is what I like best, for some strange reason. Maybe it reminds me of the South, the dark side, etc. Bourbon Street, Times Square, sleazeland, for I only know that I love the dark side, with everyone falling apart walking around just wondering how to control their desire.

He would be sitting typically in darkness, for he never would put on the light when it grew late. He was wearing horn-rim glasses, which made him look erudite. Uncharacteristically erudite. Especially when he would be screaming out his Las Vegas sayings.

First he would get a phone call and say to me, "Close the door." So I would close the door and he would say into the phone, "I adore you." He said that to a lot of people who called. It was an advanced form of You and me, kid, we're going straight to the top.

He looked at my résumé. Then he crumpled it up into a little ball and stared at it. Then he put it through his paper shredder. It was hair-raising, needless to say. That is the only way I can describe it. Hair-raising.

"Some people call me a fanatic," he screamed. Then he laughed maniacally. "Now go out and pour some liquor down your throat. Go to a couple of nightclubs or something. Have some fun! It's okay to have fun around here, kid. You and me, we're going straight to the top!"

Strictly wacko.

4. OUR OFFICE in New York, formerly the Majestic, with its glamorous Art Nouveau entrance, which had a darkened court and Beaux Arts wrought-iron overhang

painted dark green, was very incongruous to the swirling madhouse of chaos surrounding it, though bits of architecture of its kind could still be seen in Times Square at that time. The Majestic, the Barrymore, the Century Paramount.

The newspaper office had originally been built as a hotel called the Majestic in Times Square in New York. Owing perhaps to the overwhelming grandeur in which it had been built, at the turn of the century, it shortly failed, and the newspaper publisher had been able to buy it, as they say, on the cheap. Although it had been cut up into offices, some remnants of its former grandeur still remained, as in the lobby, with an old white marble floor, cracked armchairs, and potted palms. The exterior of the building was an old limestone beauty with a verdigris roof in turrets and domes.

Walking past the office with its name lit up dashingly in bare bulbs above the old arcade, the old architecture of the Majestic described a beguiling history of which there were few other representatives. The office had its crumbling aspect—it was not gleaming new or refurbished but had grown quite decayed, the cracked armchairs in the lobby, the missing floor tiles, an engraving of the name of the former hotel, Majestic, in the stone above the entrance, whose encrusted remains could no longer be deciphered in the stone. Columns, capitals, and a long gallery behind the lobby, elegant, faded, and defunct. Forty-five-foot ceilings, long corridors, bare bulbs in rows above the window transoms, arcades, and the iron Beaux Arts overhang of the entrance, among the potted palms.

As I have said, Mr. Underwood seemed to take a sort of special interest in me. He would often call me into his office, while I cowered in fear.

"You're looking for meaning, kid," he would say. He found it amusing, for he chuckled. He puffed on his cigar. "You're always looking for meaning. Sometimes there *is* no meaning." This seemed to make him very happy. "You're a kid! You're just a kid!" he screamed. "But you're hitting with the bases loaded, kid," he said. Often he spoke in baseball metaphors. "Show them your curveball, kid!"

He was full of stories. He had met Babe Ruth, Barrymore, Bessie Smith—or so he said. At times it seemed as if anyone you happened to mention Mr. Underwood had met. Prize-fighters, Presidents, washed-up Southern bandleaders—you name it, Mr. Underwood had met him, usually when the person was all washed up, and then Mr. Underwood had picked him up off the floor, dusted him off, and pasted him back together. Roosevelt, Al Jolson, and the entire Beat Generation, to hear him tell it, Mr. Underwood had met, and pasted them back together when they fell apart.

I did not get much chance to talk to Hobby at the office, because he was a big cheese, the World Editor. He often had to work until two in the morning. It was in Orient that I would see more of him.

Ordinarily I would ride into town on Sunday nights with one of the young couples. One of them lived in the same apartment building as me. It was called the Grunewald. Sudden bursts of salsa music after midnight, remorseless gaiety; careening sirens, huge disasters, sudden screams; sirens, chaos, madness.

It was definitely a contrast to the country. On Friday evenings I would descend into Penn Station and take the train out to Long Island among the sweltering summer crowds, to emerge, at the end of the line, into the sudden sweetness of the summer night in Orient.

5. Orient Point, Long Island.

The guests are arriving, across the lawn. It is Friday afternoon. The men are coming in on the late train in the parlor

car, and others have come on the ferryboat steaming in on the
blue sea at dusk with gay lights.

Friday evenings after work, the young men go to the baseball games, in their suits and ties and sunglasses, having plain
American fun. It touches my heart, because they don't have
plain American fun where I come from, it is too exotic and
remote for that, it is the dark side. They don't have baseball in
New Orleans. It's not normal enough to have baseball.

In New York I learned quite a bit about baseball as to many
a Northerner it is his great love. But what interested me about
it was not perhaps the same thing that interested them. I like
how all the ball players have marital problems and personality
problems and need sports psychiatrists, and especially in baseball where you don't have to be that athletic or it's not as
strenuous in a way the players are all dissipated wrecks with
drug problems, chain-smoking. That would maybe work in
New Orleans. Baseball would maybe work in New Orleans
because all the players are dissipated wrecks with troubled
relationships with their fathers, chain-smoking. But they are
tough guys. Except for when they retire, then they cry. The
whole thing is an emotional roller coaster, at least for me,
trying to keep up with their problems. That's what I like
about it.

I saw a baseball player hold a press conference to announce
his retirement. Big burly guy with a mustache. Six feet tall,
extremely manly, big rough tough guy. "I had a dream," he
said. "Ten years ago I was a kid with two bad knees who
wanted to be a baseball player." He stopped and looked down
at his speech. He bit his upper lip. Time passed. He was silent.
Finally you realized that he was stopping because he was
trying to compose himself. Still he remained silent. You got
the picture, he was struggling. But then finally he said, "And
I'm just glad that dream came true"—sobbing, screaming,
crying, literally falling completely to pieces. Then he just

walked away from the whole podium and cried. See what I mean?

I like how they have so many emotions even though they are crusty sports figures. Actually I know one ex-baseball player who is a crusty figure without having so many emotions—Hobby Fox. At Carolina, Chapel Hill, he was drafted by the Major Leagues and spent a season with the Atlanta Braves. He was a pitcher. Then he decided to go to Law School. It seems he had a motley career.

6. A NEW ARRIVAL was seen on the ferry to Orient. He was wearing an ancient seersucker suit with a bow tie and smoking a cigar. He had an upright posture and a spare diminutive build. You could have taken him for fifty, but he had seen the last of seventy. This was the dapper and courtly Mr. Collier, grandfather to Al.

He had a profound elegance. I think it was his rather madcap attitude that comprised this elegance.

His habits were undeniably eccentric. The oyster diaries persisted, as did the shoeshine diaries. Every day at lunch in New Orleans he would leave his office in the Louisiana Bank Building and go across the street to the Acme Oyster Bar. There he would have a dozen oysters, often grading them by quality in a small black book. Then he would descend to the basement of the Louisiana Bank Building and have his shoes shined, sometimes noting the results by the same procedure. It was his way of bringing order out of chaos, which was his ceaseless pursuit. In the same black book he noted interesting aspects of dendrology, in Latin, and other esoteric observations.

Mr. Collier had had a mental crisis in Italy thirty years before while looking at a cypress tree and was seized with his interest in dendrology. Since then he had hired a series of professors to tutor him in obscure subjects. He was up in the clouds. But his clients found him reliable and suave, and his opponents in the courtroom found him impossible to defeat. Often I felt truly sorry for his opponent, in a courtroom, simply because it wasn't a fair contest. Nor did he exhibit his work in a pretentious manner. He wasn't lofty. He had a great simplicity about him. "My heart is in the law, you know," he said.

Those of his oldest acquaintance still called him Saint for his full name, St. Louis Collier, which was also the name of his boy who had died. His other son, Claude, father to the three children in tow, was meant to arrive with his wife at an unspecified time in the summer. Delayed by various crises, they sent word on developments from the "central bureau" in New Orleans.

Mr. Collier was my father's brother. But never have two brothers been such diametric opposites. My father was what you might call a man's man. Duck hunting, fishing, sports, cigars, these were his loves, and politics. But they did have some points of similarity, and they were partners for thirty years. They saw each other every day, and loved each other just the same. Theirs was a gruff devotion, but devoted entirely. In their infinite simplicity, they wrote memos to each other throughout the day on small concrete subjects of daily life. "This morning I parked in the Whitney Building. As it was raining, I thought it might be more convenient. The parking lot was not yet full at 9:05." Some moments later, the answer, in a piteous scrawl, "Me too."

They could be seen every evening walking down Gravier Street together in their ancient seersucker suits; it was as if they were still boys together. Devotion was a trait of theirs. To their work and as well in their personal lives. Each cleaved to one woman, in a mixture of duty and love, for love alone could not have held them. That was their type. An old-fashioned and perhaps Southern, highly cultivated sense of duty characterized them.

7. "YOU HAVE to take what comes to your door," said Mr. Collier in his philosophical fashion. "And they came to my door," he concluded—referring to the two champagne-soaked authors, who reposed on his lawn. "Two degenerates," he said crisply, but fondly. "Pathetic," said Al, his new word, with relish. He had just learned a new word, *pathetic,* and was expressing it richly. "Oh yes, very pathetic," rejoined Mr. Collier crisply, puffing on his cigar. "No, they're not pathetic, Pop," said Al, with feeling. "But the grass is pathetic."

"How do you mean, heart?" I asked, interjecting.

"It's just pathetic. It needs to be watered."

"Oh yes, it needs to be watered," agreed Mr. Collier.

"Is Dad coming soon?" said Al.

"He's working things out, Al," I said.

"He suffers from human frailty, perhaps," said Mr. Collier.

Mr. Collier cut a rather quixotic figure. That fellow becomes more madcap the older he gets. But of course that is one of my major discoveries, the madcap demeanor of the elderly. The basic import of our conversation today, which centered on Mr. Underwood, was that at the end he said, "Don't worry about anything! Don't worry. Don't worry about anything!" sounding very like Constant and his customary advice on most subjects, "Don't worry about it, doll!"

But if the old, thus the wise, give me that advice, you understand it must be quite true. There is a deeper meaning in their words.

I mean these people are definitely brainy, so if that is the advice they give, it is brainy advice. Mr. Collier with his arms so resolutely folded, in the family photograph—they were happy as in Socrates, happiness of the temperate and the just.

He told me not to worry.

"Jeez," I said.

"Very well put," said Mr. Collier.

"Yuk," commented Al.

"I'll go along with that," said Mr. Collier.

I went to Prudence Island to a party for the Governor in Mr. Underwood's behalf. The scene had such a beauty to it that I went to the sea and cried. Hetty Green's mansion on the lawn by the stern blue Northern sea, white tents, white deck chairs, the men in white tie and tails. Of course one loves what is familiar—familiarity breeds passion—when drawing back toward Orient I felt the love of the familiar. It is strictly humble here in Orient, where Prudence Island is more grand, the gay rambling mansions situated on green meadows by the harbor and the blue sea at dusk. That is a dark gaiety which stops my heart—reminding me again—for only certain places have a pure gaiety, and New Orleans is such a one.

The dapper and courtly Mr. Collier sat on the green lagoon listening to *La Traviata* and I noticed that toward the end he got choked up. I love when dignified people get choked up.

The boys rowed out to sea in a rowboat and showed no signs of returning. Hobby had to swim out and rescue them.

8. MARGARET GOT into another boating accident. Then she fell in love with a shipwrecked sailor. She sailed across the bay to Prudence Island and moored the boat and walked up to town. Then she turned around and saw that the boat was floating out to sea, plus had turned over. People were

standing on their front lawns having cocktails, but they were
so Yankeefied that none of them would help her, plus no one
would even let her use their phone to call the Coast Guard.
Finally some hood in a sailboat picked her up at the shore but
he wouldn't even take her all the way to her boat and made
her dive out in the middle of the bay.

Finally the Coast Guard came by because they had just rescued someone else—Edward, the shipwrecked sailor.

Margaret is a Southerner, as you recall, from Memphis,
Tennessee. By an incredible coincidence, it turns out that Edward, the shipwrecked sailor, is from Memphis too.

Margaret took the boat out last night at 10 p.m., heralding
of course another disaster. It sank.

"Come on, we'll just drift. We won't sail far," she said. She
came equipped with silver-plated mint-julep glasses from
Montgomery, bourbon, and etc. It was a starry night, but the
wind seemed low. Then when we were halfway out into the
bay I noticed that the pinions of the rudder were submerged.
Suddenly I realized, we were sinking. Then the Coast Guard
came and rescued us.

Margaret got into a barroom brawl at the Arrow Inn. The
Shore Patrol brought her home. It is amazing to me that Margaret is not behind bars or restrained by police directives. I do
not know what will happen to her next. Life runs high in
Margaret, that much is very true.

The enclave is alive with gossip. Mr. Underwood's small
troubled son "ran away from home" and was found by Margaret (who had been picked up by the Shore Police) pedaling a
tricycle on the road to Port of Egypt. A forlorn and poignant
figure, he was picked up by the squad car and taken down,
along with Margaret, to prison.

Mr. Underwood got drunk and was not able to pick up his small troubled son. Mrs. Langguth retrieved the boy and kept him at her house that night. Mr. Underwood went on a sort of diabolical bacchanalian binge. No one has ever seen Mr. Underwood drunk before, apparently, except myself, and the whole thing has been a shock. In the morning he behaved as though nothing had happened, and everyone cowered in fear at his stern demands. He also made a number of startling complaints about the weather, the music, the food, and the company.

Margaret was abducted by a yacht captain at a wedding party who cut his arm on her boat and the Coast Guard had to come and take him to the hospital. Margaret was held at Police Headquarters for questioning and her boat is in dry dock. Never has one person's life been such a ceaseless series of nautical misadventures.

Several houses in the enclave are occupied by the young couples, some with small children, others still newlyweds, such as the love couple. But some strays are not ensconced in love, such as Cedric, Margaret, me. Margaret is plunged into crisis. So is Cedric. Their behavior tends to be more eccentric, or disturbed, than that of the settled married couples. Margaret's behavior tends to be somewhat Satanic. From her quarters crashes emanate, strange swami music plays, or forms of jazz, sometimes strange hammerings are heard. She was recently fired from her job and is trying to find herself before she gets another one but her father is coming to take her away.

Cedric also is trying to find himself, equally without success I might add. He is a little disturbed. But I like people who are a little disturbed. He has a job, but is on vacation. As a result he comes over to my house in the enclave all the time, sometimes discussing his problems and having weird outbursts. "I am an individual!" he screams, apropos of nothing. No one understands him, so he says.

He is extremely garrulous, in my opinion at times refreshingly so, as when among the distinguished white-haired gents like Mr. Underwood. Even among his elders he talks incessantly about his struggles. It would be easier to ride a hog to Memphis than it would be to get him to stop talking.

Today he came over to my house as usual talking incessantly. I commented that he looked bright-eyed. This was a mistake, causing one of his weird outbursts.

"Well, what do I usually look like, a reeling alcoholic heroin addict?" he said.

Margaret was also there.

"How are you?" I said to her.

She burst into tears.

"What's wrong?" I said.

"Don't say, How are you. It's an insult," she said.

"How are you is an insult? What? Why?"

"Because it implies that I have some huge problem," she said.

"No, it doesn't! It's just a pleasantry. How are you. It's normal. How are you."

"Don't say that!"

Etc. I have to admit also that all of the people who are plunged into crisis are Southern. But I can't really blame them. The Yankees make you feel like a crackpot. I mean the upright victorious plain Yankees, and plain American fun like at the baseball games. They don't have that type of stuff in New Orleans. They don't have plain American fun there. They don't have baseball there. Instead they have decaying hedonists and jazz-crazed nightclubs and smoldering dives, etc. So among the Yankees I always feel like a crackpot. It makes you want to go get succotashed or at least put on the Bessie Smith

or Ray Charles or Al Jolson right away and get cheap bourbon. Maybe this is one reason why Margaret is always getting
into trouble. Because being around the Yankees makes you
want to go get into trouble, or drink bourbon, or dance your
heart out in a dive. Or end up in a jail cell. In my mind's eye,
it's Torture and Lust on Plantations, while the Yankees are out
having plain American fun.

But that is the charm of Orient—that people should concoct
forms of innocent amusement, and ply their summer pleasures
—the guests arriving across the lawn or steaming in on the
ferry with blue lights at dusk.

9. AT THE ENTRANCE to the enclave this eve-
ning I saw a somewhat piteous spectacle. It was a small boy of
ten at the side of the road, flanked by a little girl on one side
and by Al on the other, whose wrists he was sternly clasping,
holding them back while he looked both ways down the road
for cars. Such gallantry in the little fellow severely touched my
heart. These were Al's older brother George, and his sister,
Anne. They are to me a somewhat piteous spectacle. It is
perhaps their gallantry or their seriousness or their forlornness
that strikes me so. A certain quaint gravity of the Colliers.
Aside from their father, Claude, the Colliers tended to be
somewhat erudite or bookish or severe.

I had to get Al dressed after arising from his nap. I'm not
that good at it, I tried to do it all correctly and not make his
buttons or his laces on his shoes too tight. "How does that
feel?" I said finally, when he was dressed.

"It feels yukky."

"Okay, sweetheart, then let's do it over."

"Yuk," he commented, an expansive remark covering a
wide range of his personal observations.

Finally it was all done, and he stood before me, freshly laundered.

"Am I cool?" he asked suddenly.

"Whaddya mean, Al?"

"Hobby is cool. Baseball players are cool. Hobby is like them."

He and I have baseball mania.

Al and I retired to the sandbox.

The sandbox had a crack in it that bothered him and he washed it with a hose.

"Why does it bother you, Al?" I asked.

"Because it's so pathetic."

He grew philosophical.

"What do you want to be when you grow up, Al?" I asked.

He thought it over.

"A person who owns a giraffe," he said pensively.

I certainly can confirm that Harry Locke does drool. And it's quite true he drools on everything. The poor fellow is like a pint-sized lunatic. He brings the mild and quiet Collier children to a level of boisterousness to which they are much unaccustomed.

We found a mole. It was studied with interest.

"I wish I had a mole," said Al.

"It would kill you," said Harry Locke. "It's all fluffy but it would kill you. Maybe. MAYBE MAYBE MAYBE—" His conversation tends to simply degenerate into a series of loud screams. Then he ran maniacally away. As for the baby, she fled.

I must say the children find him hilarious, although Al takes a protective attitude toward the baby when Harry Locke is in the vicinity and often tries to calm him. But every time Harry Locke becomes hysterical, which is every two minutes, the children fondly guffaw and shake their heads in admiration and amusement.

"Is he your best friend?" I said to Al.

"Oh yes," he said. "But everyone is my best friend," he added. "So are you."

The hand of God is in that little fellow.

"I'm trying to show him how to do the right thing," said Al, even though he is only three years old. I have not seen in any child what I saw in him.

The piercing cries of Harry Locke penetrate the night. Harry Locke has a large number of ailments, it turns out, many of which are self-inflicted—he hobbles around the garden like a ninety-year-old, because he has so many accidents, from when he is hysterical, which is all the time, and often he is covered with blood. The bloodcurdling shrieks of Harry Locke have become a regular oft-heard sound.

I thought Al might want to take the opportunity to bone up on his Geography, while Harry Locke's numerous wounds are being dressed by his mother.

"Al, my heart, what is Paris?"

He thought it over. "A river?"

"France, buddy, France. Remember? It's called the capital of France."

"Harry Locke cut his jaw," said Al.

"I know, I know. He also skinned his knee."

"I tried to help him but he's very wild." The thing about Al is, he takes personal responsibility for everyone, even though he is only three years old.

Vernon, the aging playboy, a madcap older gent, is paddling down the canal in his madcap boat—a canoe rigged up with a red-and-white-striped sail and odd-size paddles. If not gaily paddling his paramours across the bay in his madcap boat, he is seen walking along the beach wearing a blue beret at a rakish angle, with a cigarette hanging out of his mouth.

Also, he has a protégé, Nick, who is known as the rogue of the island. At least so he is known by me. Nick is a young man with piercing eyes for whom the telephone constantly rings.

Also, Vernon used to be a glamorous figure in New York, where he was the publisher of a magazine. Mr. Underwood well knows of Vernon's former position in the world and graciously entertains him often. But Vernon doesn't need Mr. Underwood in order to have a great time. Although Vernon is retired in a business sense, not in a worldly sense, if you see what I mean.

Perhaps taking his cue from Vernon, Al rendezvoused with Hilary, the baby, at the sandbox.

"Hi," said Al to the baby, Hilary.

"Hi," she said.

"I'm three," said Al.

She sat in fascinated silence.

She went over to play with him.

"You can have my apple juice," he said. He gave a rambling, incoherent discourse. Then, being rather manful for a little fellow, he pulled himself together and told her in plain language that when he was in high school he would hunt bad animals with a gun.

Hilary went over and sat next to him on the bench. He got that sweet smile of happiness, such as he gets with me at times, when he is flirting (three and already flirting!) and when we went inside he told her good-bye and said, "Wave, Hilary—" and he indicated how, showing an example of waving. She waved. Then he actually blew her a kiss, before departing. She fled.

10.

VERNON ACTUALLY has a number of like-minded companions, for the Southern contingent has arrived. The Southern contingent are all over the age of sixty, many over seventy, some over ninety. Mrs. Stewart, the elder, at ninety-six, and her cousin, a young man (as she calls him), of eighty, sit knocking back scotch and chain-smoking, in the garden.

How I loved her is untold.

She frequently reminisces about her honeymoon, taken seventy-eight years previous, but seems to lament that the sex revolution had not occurred in her time. Her cousin, at eighty, relates his own adventures. "That's an amusing story, young man," she replies. I am spending a lot of my time with those over eighty, but believe me, this is no geriatric ward, this is a group of raging hedonists sitting in gardens knocking back scotch, reminiscing about their sex lives.

The young man of eighty was describing how he recently had done himself injury.

"Alice, I broke my back last week."

"Batty, how?"

"I was in the shower, and I slipped."

"Did you call the ambulance immediately?"

"I most certainly did not," he drawled. "I said, Well, no, first I'm going to have some bourbon, and then I'm going to have some champagne, and then—"

On leaving them last night, for I could not withstand the late hours they do, I found, again, a heart-heaving beauty on the bay and the green canal, in the sweet black night, the rustling of the leaves, the glamour of the black night.

Among the elderly in Orient, Mr. and Mrs. Collier were not the least infirm. But Mrs. Collier still had the same blond hair and ruddy complexion as the Wellesley girl whom I so well envision meeting Mr. Collier's eye at the Harvard Library some forty years ago. I see her as a college girl, for some reason, in my mind's eye, with the same glamorous blond hair. She had an indomitable spirit and a malevolent wit, through her many sufferings in later years, having grown quite frail. Mr. Collier walked in the garden or to the park pursuing his eccentric hobbies, making me recite the Latin names of trees in his beloved dendrology. In their household in New Orleans, infirmity had become the keynote. The old butler, Chester, had endured several heart attacks, though he mended each time. Usually he had heart trouble while watching the boxing matches or the horse races. Sardinia, the maid, had become very garrulous, and continued talking long after people had left the room. Everyone in the household was at least sixty. On Sundays Mr. Collier attempted to visit his old friends, but one he called wasn't up to it, and another hadn't come downstairs, which meant he wasn't well, and so on. They all hovered near a twilight world, yet often with considerable gaiety and wit.

I am patiently awaiting the cocktail hour. I feel I don't know the Meaning of it all anymore. So now I am on a Search for Meaning.

I miss everyone. It's strange, since they're all here. It seems strange.

Among the young couples there is a fellow whom I call Mr. Joviality—for obvious reasons. His overriding trait is joviality. His jovial laughter is oft heard resounding through the grounds.

He made a startling contrast to Hobby Fox, sometimes known as the misanthrope, and yet the two were oddly fond of one another.

The misanthrope was comforted, startlingly, by the company in Orient—whose joviality however shallow comforted him—their comforting shallowness, their resounding guffaws, a certain robustness for life—always fixing hampers, playing bridge, etc. It comforted him, secretly.

I mean they can't go anywhere without fixing a hamper, joking with strangers, and yet—Hobby felt that chief among them, Mr. Joviality was at heart a very fragile, even hollow, construction, and that it could suddenly crumble at any moment.

In a rare outburst of sports activity, the misanthrope descended and went swimming. Hobby.

On the beach he wears a bathrobe and the headdress of an Arab sheik, and sunglasses. On this occasion he discarded them and swam out into the bay.

I was involved in a near catastrophe. I took the children rowing in their pint-sized boat. I rowed them out to Margaret's catamaran, as she was on it making repairs. The children did not have on life belts nor did I have their parents' permission to row them out into the bay. The children cannot swim. Margaret has tried to teach them, but they are unable to learn, being possessed of an overwhelming fear of water. When we had rowed to Margaret's boat, suddenly a current seemed to take us farther out, and despite my efforts we were floating out to sea. Margaret called directions from her boat, the children cowered in fear, and yet we floated farther out to sea. Then, in a dramatic rescue, the misanthrope swam up and pulled us back to shore.

A chorus of thanks emanated from the children, in a piteous high-pitched cacophony. Continued forms of gratitude ensued, from the children jumping up and down and offering expressions of affection to the misanthrope, who maintained his composure and relit his cigar. Then he started reading the newspaper. Margaret sauntered past and batted her eyelashes at him but he retained his hard-boiled demeanor, smoking his cigar. He certainly plays the misanthrope—while saving everybody's lives or pasting them back together when they fall apart, particularly the children, who fall apart the most. But nursemaid to the children is not a role I would have thought would fall to him.

A chorus of good-byes issued from the children as their mothers came to get them and dragged them off apologetically. Hobby made a quaint courtly gesture as if to tip his hat—reminds me of the baseball players when they get a home run.

As if spurred on by this, the mothers started in again on another round of profuse thanks, and apparent adoration.

He had an old-fashioned air, of the South, after all. And thus he had the air of someone who has led another life. Seeming rather wry—courtly and windblown and stoic—he proceeded to the sports page, tuning in the baseball game, looking with amusement at the children who still stood around observing him.

11. I KNEW Hobby in New Orleans. He was a prosecutor in the District Attorney's office. He seemed a little wild to be a prosecutor. He had long hair and baggy suits and black sunglasses, was seen at Galatoire's for lunch, or dancing his heart out in a dive at night. His idea of a date was to take you to a drug bust in the Quarter. Or if you called him up sometimes he would mistake you for one of his FBI or DEA agents. He was in the White Slavery department. You wouldn't think that there would be a lot of White Slavery floating around, but apparently there is.

Actually an ornate piece of language from an old French code, I believe it refers to a form of illegal immigration. But when his father died he left the law. His heart was never in the law. So he made the somewhat rare transition from the law to journalism—as had his uncle, Constant Fox, the long-revered editor of the *Southern Democrat*. Hobby covered politics. The old sinner was the Governor then. He was Constant's cross to bear. On the other hand, he was Hobby's idol. That was the difference between them.

But I can't say that the old sinner was actually Hobby's idol. It was just that he didn't blame the old sinner personally. He blamed his human frailty. Or maybe it was partly our environment, growing up in New Orleans, where you went to Bourbon Street and saw strippers in the afternoon, looking in the doorways, among the screaming saxophones and seedy dives. A childhood memory—Bourbon Street. They don't have that up North. Bourbon Street with screaming saxophones and strippers as your childhood memories. You always heard that type of music, old-time jazz, with its dark gaiety, the instruments in languid unison, and yet the inexorability or steadiness of the beat in this old jazz is what strikes the heart, and the dark wit or cynicism of the music, a gaiety in dark conditions. My town had the guts to be sleazy, starting right from the airport, driving into town on Airline Highway with cheap motels and palms.

You cannot leave one world and go into another without misgivings, regrets, confusion. But one night he blew out of town on a midnight flight wearing a seersucker suit—to New York, of course. I did not know then that I would later follow.

Now he was burnt out. Hobby, that is. He had a certain burnt-out air. Pursued by his memories, perhaps. There's a lot of human frailty floating around in politics. I think that politics is where the most human frailty is to be found. He had been around the block covering politics, then a foreign correspondent, currently World Editor of the New York *Examiner.*

There was a certain gulf between those old haunts in New Orleans, his White Slavery days, not to mention the old sinner, and tame Orient. It is hard to reconcile such innocence, as at tame Orient, with the dark side, such as he knew. To me the theme of Orient is innocence, despite the sometimes boisterous jollities, boating accidents, and dinner parties of the young couples. These are innocent amusements in the odd overtaking innocence of Orient. It's Yankeefied. It is plain American fun.

Whereas I can remember Hobby and Claude Collier, his crony as it happens, walking down the Avenue in the black night in New Orleans. The nights had grace, among the massive oaks, the weather sweltering. It is truthfully a more painful place than the North, a truthful place, a downtrodden place, with a certain constant adversity toward which the people are rather debonair. That is what strikes my heart, their elegance, in that adversity.

And so to see another representative of my past here, Hobby Fox—it is not often that I see here these ghosts from the past. He had a dark Southern wit and a dark Southern glamour to me.

Constant Fox, who was now seventy years old, had looked out for Hobby and his brothers since their father died. Constant's own family was numerous, Grace being devoutly Catholic. In fact they had ten children. Constant had always worried. He used to say that he would go to the Archbishop and get some sort of dispensation for her, but she always said, "I'd rather have them on my knees than on my conscience."

They were from a parish in Louisiana where some members

of the Foxes looked after the family interests, a sugar-cane plantation and refinery among them. There was an old store on what was once the main street. With high galleries and wrought-iron falling into disrepair and pigeons flying in from the cupola. It was wondered how to bring it into modern times. I thought it could be a beautiful hotel. But no one would go there, after all, being that the town was so out of the way.

"This could be a ballroom, though," I said, on the second floor, with the columns and the twenty-four-foot ceilings.

"I know. This could be a ballroom. But there's no balls," said Constant, cheerfully.

He was simplicity, from the heart. Constant knew far better than another man what life is—no balls, just malaise, simplicity, duty, ten children. Like many Southern men he had an almost quaint simplicity, a conception of honor, of the honorable estate.

"You'll wake up one fine morning," he said once, "and realize that there is someone you cannot get along without." He said that he himself woke up one fine morning at the age of thirty-one—he was a late bloomer, you might say—and said, I have to get a life. I'm going to (1) live in Louisiana (2) take up the gauntlet that my father left me, and (3) marry Grace.

Constant had known Grace since the age of two. She said that one day at the age of five he ripped a hole in her dress at school and she was mortified. "And I've been ripping it off ever since," said Constant. Seventy and in love, it is a fine thing to see. He was jocular and sweet like some sort of North Carolina boy though he was a white-haired gent of seventy. He wasn't grand—he was unpretentious. I was ever struck by his grace. A man in command of his depths, that was Constant. But he was a gent from another era.

All of these were gents from another era to me—Constant

Fox, St. Louis Collier, my father also—and when I heard their bass-voiced drawls, from across the years—they were a bit larger than life to me.

I have a photograph of Constant and my father in Greenville, Mississippi, when they were boys. Constant has an enigmatic smile, but a certain sweetness, his quality that recalled an angel or a saint, though as I say he was sarcastic and had the devil in him. My father was more stern and brooding.

He was a partner with his brother in the family law firm. But it was not my father's calling, the law. His older brother had returned to New Orleans after taking a law degree in 1936. He was admitted to the Louisiana bar in the following year. He became associated with the family law firm, Collier & Labouisse, whose decor featured old Oriental runners in the hall, old-fashioned arrows painted on the glazed glass doors describing which direction to pursue among the maze of corridors, and the senior partners ambling through the halls in their seersucker suits. They were old-fashioned lawyers who were privy to the secrets of powerful men at the bank and the cotton exchange. Then my father came into the firm, still but a boy, at twenty. Both of the boys had graduated early, and gone to work early, which is one reason why I think my father may not have had the chance to find his calling. Several years later the boys' father died of a heart attack suddenly. Then Mr. Labouisse, the senior partner, was similarly stricken, and the two brothers, then both in their twenties, having recently arrived and been confronted with the series of disasters, were left with the firm in their hands, realizing that it would be "a lot of work" to carry on, a mild understatement in a memo from the time that I have seen—the daily memos then began and never stopped—as the two boys wrote their ceaseless memos to each other on a variety of subjects. Others might have met in the hall, you understand, or in their offices, to discuss these problems, but that was not the mode. The brothers, though they were together in the firm for thirty years, saw each other every day, and were devoted, communicated on all subjects, from the frivolous to the grave, in the typewritten yellowed memos. No one could deny that the brothers were quaint. One had gone to Harvard, the other to Ole Miss, my father being the latter, where he met Constant Fox. "To my beloved friend" was written on the framed photograph that graced the hall, from Constant, among the other faded portraits of judges and great men.

As the law firm counted among its clients the railroad, the newspaper, the bank, and the cotton exchange, it was an absorbing practice. But at night my father strolled in the park, in his dream of his work, while Beethoven or Bessie Smith or the *St. Matthew Passion* emanated from his study. Whenever I hear the music he had loved, it calls forth all that I hold dear, as if retrieving something I had thought unrecoverably lost. Each man goes out to his own music.

The only piece of advice my father ever gave me was, "You are a Collier. You are bound by your word."

The Mississippi Delta is not a place that I know much about, but I have heard. Everyone sleeps with a pistol and a bottle of whiskey under their pillow, they wear white linen suits, and they fight a lot. If they go somewhere, to a strange place, they stand up on a table and yell out, "Where does the Southern cross the Yellow Dog?" and then if someone else yells out "Moorehead," then they know they have a friend there— someone from the Delta. It comes from the Bessie Smith song "Yellow Dog." This my father told me once, from his days at Ole Miss. My father and Constant, gents from another era, their haunts in Mississippi in the thirties.

It's like this. After my father was gone, one day I was at the Fox plantation in the country, and Constant was playing those Bessie Smith tapes that my father used to be so wild about, that would emanate from his study late at night. I was looking at Constant, who was one of those old-time Southern gents, and I was looking at him thinking that, and this thing came over me that said: Everything is going to be all right. As though if I went to that place where the Southern crosses the Yellow Dog, I would be all right. I lost my father years ago, but I am pursued by my memories.

I have a soft spot for the old. The older the better, closer to God. Their love is pure. It is the same with the very young, like Al. Constant and Al, the very old and the very young, beloved and closer to God.

When I said good-bye to Constant Fox that day, he took my hand in both of his, in the Southern fashion, and looked at me with his benevolence. I remember this, for as he smiled down at me with his blue eyes, he seemed to look into the years ahead, and a long time seemed to pass.

I see now that he knew then what he would be to me. I didn't know. I was just a kid. It's like when ten years later you look back and understand that someone whom you would not dare to hope would even like you or ever be your friend has loved you all along.

"I insist that you keep me posted on your beaux," he would say to me.

"Well, what about your nephew, Hobby?"

"Watch out for him. That boy is wild."

But in Hobby I saw more of Constant, more as the years went by. And I can never be other than I have been, for whenever I love anything, it is because it reminds me in some way or other of him.

It happens in life that sometimes two people will befriend

each other due to the familiarity with one dear to them both. It is this middle man, never present, who inspires you or gives you hope. Thus he travels at your side.

12. ORIENT POINT, Long Island.

From one house in the enclave music emanates. Old-time jazz and violins. That dark gaiety—how can something so dark have such gaiety—that old-time jazz is debonair, for the dark wit and cynicism of the screaming saxophones and inexorable beat. It reminds me of stormy weather in Biloxi or a night in Harlem, passing This Bitter Earth nightclub next to First Tabernacle of Prayer with a neon cross on the way to the midnight train populated by wino lunatics. The jazz-crazed house is occupied by Hobby.

He was lying on his bed wearing sweatpants emblazoned with the legend DUCK HUNTING CLUB OF NEW ORLEANS, an old-fashioned sleeveless ribbed undershirt, and socks with holes in them. Although the radio was playing screaming saxophones his eyes were closed, his hands folded on his chest, in an attitude of sleep. Several children sat on the other twin bed observing him closely. I went in and stepped over to the radio to turn it off, and as I bent over him to turn the switch he calmly opened his eyes and stared straight at me.

"Hello there," he said calmly.

The children were seized with mirth.

They jumped onto his bed.

"Okay, okay, you're driving me crazy," he said.

"Where have you been?" I asked him.

"I was at the Seven-Eleven, one of my glamorous haunts."

He kidded me because I thought he was glamorous.

I was asking Hobby his advice about Mr. Underwood. He

too worked for Mr. Underwood. He was the World Editor. Being crusty and burnt out and manly he could deal with Mr. Underwood better than I could. While I would be cowering in fear of Mr. Underwood. Currently Mr. Underwood wanted me to think about writing a column for which I had no desire. "I'm just trying to do the right thing," I said to Hobby.

"That's a mistake, baby doll," he said. It was his dark Southern wit. But he added, "You should do what makes you happy."

"I love Hilary and I love Sarah Rooney," said Al. "Man oh man."

Gee, I wonder where he got that. I can't tell what he is going to come up with next. Then he started jumping up and down in a hyperbolic manner on the bed.

"You're driving me crazy, son," said Hobby.

"I need to drive you crazy, Hobby," said Al.

"What are you boys doing inside anyway?" I said.

"We're waiting to see if Argentina is going to blow up," said Hobby. It was a story in the World Section. They were having some type of earthquakes.

He had recently returned from Costa Rica, where he had had to meet with the Central American Bureau Chief and brief the stringers.

"What did they have to be briefed about?" I asked.

"The deteriorating situation in El Salvador, the shaky situation in Honduras, the untenable situation in Nicaragua, the increasingly alarming situation in Guatemala, and the remarkably chaotic situation in Panama," he said while reading the sports page, smoking his cigar, and listening to the baseball game. I guess he could do four things at once. The children looked on, wide-eyed.

"Well, let me ask you this," I said. "Were all the reporters wearing rumpled white suits and drinking rum in seedy bars under ceiling fans?"

"You mean, were they romantics masquerading as cynics, as you would say?"

"Yes!"

"No." A silence ensued. "I don't think Mr. Underwood pays them well enough for that," he said, and looked at me sideways, askance, with those dazzling blue eyes.

"Mr. Underwood wants me to interview the Governor," I said. "I don't think I can. I'm too shy."

"You used to do it in Louisiana. The best reporters are shy."

"It's very sweet of you to say that."

"People who aren't shy are crumbs," he said.

"Crumbs," chimed in Al. "Sick," he added. This is his new word. Sick.

"But I'm not like you," I said, "going all around the world, 'ousted from Panama,' 'ousted from Havana,' all that type of stuff all over the entire world. How can you handle all that?"

"Because I'm so glamorous. Because I'm so brave."

A sarcastic silence ensued. But to me it was the truth, after all. The World Editor had to keep track of all the horrifying world events and constantly tell the bureau chiefs and reporters and stringers and everyone what to do, and they would always write him long tortured analyses of everything, asking for guidance.

"It's poignant," I said.

"It is many things, but one thing it is not is poignant," he said and looked at me sideways, askance, with those blue eyes.

"But it's poignant."

"You find a lot of things to be poignant."

"And another thing that's poignant—think of this—you and me and Al, for instance, Southerners, here in Yankeeland."

"Oh yes. That's big-league poignance." Another sarcastic silence ensued. "You had your picture on the society page," he said mildly.

"I know. It disgusts me."

"What does a glamour girl like you have to be worried about?" he said kindly. "Except for romanticizing, glamorizing, and idealizing everything? Actually, you worry me, Storey."

"I love it when I worry you."

"I'm worried about you."

"I love it when you're worried about me."

"You idealize these things. These people are crumbs. That's what I'm trying to tell you."

"What people?"

"Some people . . ." he trailed off. "I know how to handle you."

He would make a sweet remark and then just look at you masterfully, inquiringly, dry-eyed and blunt, with those sorrowful, dazzling blue eyes. To see what you think. After making some drawling remarks. Just like his uncle, the heart throb, with that crazy North Carolina drawl.

I have too many memories. I just remember his old blue eyes, tennis shoes, and baggy khaki pants, and that he'd put a camellia at my place, when we met in Alabama at the old hotel.

He looked at me sidewise, askance, with those dazzling blue eyes.

"I wish for one thing, peace," I said. "I just want peace," I said.

"You won't get it. None of us will." He wryly looked askance. "But you'll wake up one fine morning and realize that there is one thing you cannot do without. Be true to it." He encouraged me, but more than that, I knew it cost him dear.

He would not wear his heart on his sleeve. But he had vast reserves of sweetness, and an elegant old heart. He was the real thing, for brains, and sweetness—however much he tried to hide his sweetness, with his gruff exterior.

"Let's stick together tonight, kid," he said gruffly. "Are you scared to be alone with me?" he said.

"Should I be?"

"Maybe . . ."

But we already had a past, and a troublesome one. Into every love affair there comes a moment of dishonor.

As I left I heard Al talking to Hobby still. "Does Storey want a sad man, a happy man, an angry man, or a silly man?" said Al.

"I don't know, Al."

"I want to marry her," said Al.

"Don't you think you're a little young for her, champ?"

"She doesn't need to be alone," said Al, ever sagely. "We're going on our honeymoon," he added.

"Where are you going on your honeymoon?" said Hobby.

"Mars," said Al matter-of-factly.

13. HOBBY ALWAYS has the radio tuned in to the baseball games, in a low masculine drone, redolent of Yankeefied spring and summer afternoons. Mr. Underwood too has a love of baseball and also keeps the games on in the office at night if he works late. Due to these influences I find that I myself am developing a growing obsession with baseball and the need to chronicle the progress of the New York team that I follow. Hobby taught me a lot about it. He doesn't follow his old team, in Atlanta. He follows the New York team, while here. His father loved the St. Louis Cardinals, because in his day, they were the team of the South. They were an all-black team who were all extremely cultivated and they had the

most beloved manager in baseball. The manager of the New York team is completely listless. The personality of the New York team mystifies me. They have a certain elegance, I think because they are so stoic. If they get a home run or something good they try not to smile or act excited. If someone gets a home run, he comes out of the dugout and gives a curtain call —tipping his hat to the crowd—seeming rather quaint or courtly—and they only do this in New York, I'm told—but maintaining a gruff though courtly exterior. Equally if they lose or get slaughtered they betray no emotion other than seeming mildly dejected. It results in a certain elegance because the other teams are more volatile and make obnoxious displays at every sign of advancement.

Also the New York team is riddled with problems. If you like problems, you've come to the right place, with the New York team. Each player has a dazzling array of problems. Drug problems, drug rehabilitation, alcohol detox, injuries, marital problems, personality problems, nervous breakdowns, and psychological problems, also confidence problems.

Yet at the same time as they are afflicted with a ceaseless array of problems, it is the national pastime, plain American fun, heartwarming, wholesome, one thing that draws everyone together, the very young and the very old, and has an innocence, a certain basic innocence, good for the children, etc., a chance to go forth with the heroes, a good thing for the boys.

The other thing I like about the New York team is that they are underdogs. I love that. I would never root for the favorite. I like how they are always struggling, getting slaughtered twice in one night in double-headers, being exhausted in rain delays or playing extra innings until two in the morning, losing. Adversity becomes them, as adversity can be becoming if its object has character. There is a poignance in their struggle.

Plus, then if they suddenly win, it is all the more affecting. The New York team always loses and is stoic, elegant, dejected. But to the stars through adversity.

Then if they suddenly win I am suffused with a sense of well-being, and if they lose I feel doleful and listless. I have a ceaseless need to listen to every single game and keep up with everyone's problems. But my love for baseball is inexplicable —never before did I ever take the slightest interest in sports. Never was there one subject so boring to me as sports.

Now I even listen to the sports talk shows in the middle of the afternoon on the radio hosted by falling New York lunatics who remind me of Mr. Underwood, who sound off in deep Bronx and Queens accents about what burns them up. "I've had it," they passionately avow, referring to sports figures who irritate them or contracts negotiated that are too expensive. Often they slip into dreamy recollections of ball players from the thirties on the Yankees team or Brooklyn Dodgers, distracted by their memories, exhibiting a marked preference for the older teams of the American League, and if someone calls them up to ask a question about upstarts in the National League they say, "I've had it," etc. Sometimes they go berserk on the show and start insulting the callers and have complete breakdowns, ending up screaming out to the caller, "Shut up! Shut up! Shut up!" and then disconnect the phone line in a fury. "You're a schmuck. You're crazy. You're giving me a nervous breakdown. Shut up!" etc. Once I heard a nut call up who was equally as much of a lunatic as the announcer. The nut launched into a rambling unconnected story about a glamour girl who kissed him at a baseball game. Then he started swearing. "Do not take the name of the Lord in vain," said the announcer solemnly to the nut. "That is where I draw the line." It's a funny place to suddenly draw the line, considering that he spends the rest of the time raving like some kind of insane maniac. Then the nut started sounding off about what burned him up in sports and the announcer lost his cool again and started screaming. "You need a brain transplant. You're driving me crazy. Shut up!" etc. etc. And these nuts go at it forty-eight hours a day. They spend forty-eight hours a day analyzing these subjects on the radio. Sports, baseball, contracts, they analyze it for forty-eight hours a day. I turn on the radio at two in the morning and there they are, talking in strange voices like they're mentally unbalanced, analyzing everything. "New York did not play Philadelphia tonight," the announcer will be saying in a ghostly strangled voice, "Tidewater played Philadelphia tonight. A minor-league team played Philadelphia tonight. Schmucks!" he screams, in his New York parlance. This analysis had to do with one night when a lot of people on the New York team had injuries and they had to call up a lot of rookies from their farm team. I know about these things now. Suddenly I'm a sports fanatic, listening to sports talk shows twenty-four hours a day.

"Cincinnati is not going to make it. Cincinnati is through. Finished. It's over for Cincinnati!" Screaming. Long silences, Tortured strangled voices. Here they were referring to the pennant race, and who would be in the World Series.

In New York they had a romance with failure—uncharacteristic of the North. It began in the old days, at the Polo Grounds, with a series of eccentrics as managers, and a ball club that could never win.

Everyone was in tortures over it. That's what kills me about baseball, how everyone is in tortures over it as if it were the most serious thing that could ever be. Like the nuts who call up the sports channel on the radio all day to analyze everything. In the articles in the *Tribune* the Commissioner of Baseball would always have all these tortured quotes about integrity and self-delusions in long, tortured ponderings, when it is only about baseball. I mean you'd think they were talking about World War II. Like the most grave subject. The Baseball Commissioner agonizing over principles, integrity, abstractions as if he were Aristotle, not the Baseball Commissioner.

What I prefer is the team that had the romance with failure. They used to be "arrogant" and "cocky" and make obnoxious displays at every sign of advancement just like everyone else, and everyone hated them for it because they were so arrogant and cocky. Then the manager told them not to gloat or make such displays so now they all act like laconic Southern gentlemen. I personally like them better that way. But of course it's not a New York type of attitude and the New Yorkers hate them that way. They have articles in the newspapers interviewing the players about how they feel about this and their resultant tortured ponderings—like the Baseball Commissioner agonizing over sporting matters—as they ponder their broken dreams or fond hopes or failures, in sports.

Mr. Underwood had a box at the baseball games with other big cheeses, the Governor, millionaire racetrack owners, retired bandleaders, etc. Actually the retired bandleader in his entourage was a poignant figure, somehow out of place, being Southern. He could care less about baseball. He was used to seedy dives on Bourbon Street. Baseball just wasn't his thing. It was written on his face, in his countenance, everything about him did not say Baseball. Being from Bourbon Street, New Orleans, I can certainly understand why the Southern bandleader did not feel an affinity for baseball, as I never did before either until I realized how it has its dark side, or generally from spending five years in New York. But certainly on Bourbon Street the idea of baseball is but a remote image of a boy in the 1920s with a baseball cap in the sweet afternoon sun or sterling Northern twilight in some halcyon idea of America from which New Orleans is indescribably remote. But Mr. Underwood loved it all—retired sports figures, troubled prizefighters, washed-up Southern bandleaders—in his box of big cheeses at the game.

Hobby had a more ambivalent attitude, having played in the Major Leagues himself, and there were times when I got the feeling that he had left his heart there. Being thirty-six and out of practice I doubt he could go back. Though I hear of players who are forty-two and forty-three, such as relief pitchers. I guess he did not play long enough or make enough of an impression to come back in a career in baseball as a coach or manager. He listened to the games but did not often speak of his past in it. Also he had been a newspaperman now for too many years to think of much else. But once I saw in his room in Orient the Louisville Slugger that he used in Atlanta, for it was inscribed with the team and had his named burned onto it. He kept it with him, then. Some reminder of an innocence, which baseball surely represents, though it certainly has its dark side, so it seems to me at least. As every time I ask him about one of the players he always launches into a long story about how the fellow was a drug addict, or on trial, or just got out of alcohol detox or jail. I had no idea that baseball had such a dark side, or was so riddled with problems, but, of course, that's what I like about it.

He was telling me about a pitcher who thought it was his day off and took LSD. He happened to hear on the radio that his team was playing that night in Chicago—which he had forgotten. So he hopped on a plane to Chicago tripping on LSD and pitched a no-hitter.

Later he was on trial and told the judge that when you're on

LSD in a ball game, it makes the ball look like a grapefruit when it's coming at you so it's easier to hit.

Also Hobby told me that on his team in Atlanta it was one of the first years that they had a sports psychiatrist for the ball club. He went crazy at the end of the season. The TV announcers discuss these problems during their ceaseless banter at the game even though they are so All-American it seems they wouldn't want to admit it, and were all players themselves before they became announcers. The other night New York was playing Philadelphia and the announcers were discussing the pitcher for Philadelphia before the game. One of the announcers is a kindly old man who seems at times virtually senile and can't seem to keep track of what is going on. You'd think that maybe baseball in his day had less problems to it, at least in terms of psychiatry. But they were talking about the pitcher and he said, "Frank is back on the mound right now but it seems last year he had some psychological problems," looking out at ten trillion viewers on TV. Then he chuckled fondly, after saying the word "psychological problems," shaking his head in bemusement, but at the same time with concern, and then got a sort of rueful, whimsical smile, looking at the other announcer to elaborate.

"I was talking to him and he explained, 'I was giving myself a nervous breakdown.' Ha ha. He went to Harvard but he just got out of alcohol detox. He's a great pitcher, Bob. The only question is, can he keep out of the hootch."

Keep out of the hootch—I'm not sure whether that means stay out of the looney bin—or whether it means stay off the sauce.

Harvard, alcohol detox, baseball, and psychological problems—you have to admit that's a pretty weird mix-up.

There was a rain delay and they called in a sort of sports

weatherman. He was a cornball. The announcers are always sentimental and enthusiastic.

"What about the weather, Jim? Do you think we'll play?"

"I know we will, Bob. In about forty-five minutes, you'll see this storm clear up and they will start the ball game."

"How can you be so sure?"

"This is my life, Bob. I'm obsessed with the weather. I love it. It's my life."

Then the announcers chuckle and shake their heads fondly in bemusement.

On certain Fridays since this April Hobby had been taking me to the baseball games, when he could get away from the office.

Friday night we went to a double-header. The stadium announcer keeps droning on throughout the game on a loud-speaker in a cheerful voice, "Alcoholic beverages . . . Anti-social behavior . . . People drinking . . . Taking drugs . . ." admonishing potential abusers of these vices. There are a lot of police. Sometimes horrifying brawls break out in the stands. "Here comes trouble," said a fan when a weirdo with a menacing expression came up to take his seat and the weirdo heard him and got mad. "Shut up! Who are you calling trouble, schmuck, shut up. Shut up!" etc. As everyone knows, the attitude of the New York fans is "What have you done for me lately?" Meaning if the team is losing the fans are filled with loathing and disgust—this is why they call the radio talk shows at two in the morning to ceaselessly analyze all the problems and complain about how disgusted they are and go berserk etc. The New York stadium is like a latent catastrophe waiting to happen. But it never really does, in baseball. An innocence is inexorably attached to the game no matter how many people go crazy or how many drug problems or etc. arise.

Hobby and I had left the office late, to go out that night to the ball park, which had been named, oddly enough, for a pitcher from Louisiana, Sportsman's Paradise. It was a glamorous night in New York. The temperature was ninety degrees. I take a perverse satisfaction in the heat because the Northerners can't stand it, they're not used to it, whereas the Southerners are. Also it was humid and the sky was a thick cobalt blue as night fell.

We left the office at 7 p.m., in the midst of the usual gigantic summer traffic jam to Long Island. With everyone leaving all at once for the same place, Long Island, at exactly the same time. It does seem kind of ridiculous. That route out of New York, it's a dying-looking sort of place, but it's gutty, as they say in baseball. And that's why I find it glamorous, because it is gutty. The ball park is the most glamorous place in New York to me, because it is the most gutty. When I was young the East Coast was beauteous and promising; now it is gutty. There's one benefit of growing older, for I like it better gutty.

We were listening to the radio announcers call the game on the way out, as we were late due to the traffic. The radio droned on, describing as usual a demoralizing loss, but a certain rugged masculinity emanated from the sporting world, as the game droned on.

While passing that gutty landscape to Queens, Hobby was telling me about his father, one's parents' love. Though in his parents' case it was something less than love, which made him misanthropic, I think. Then we came into the ball park in a hot summer twilight. The stadium was a swirling vortex of chaos, as usual. It remained hot throughout the night.

It had been a fair day at the office for Hobby. The President of Burma quit, causing some flurries in the international section.

"Now it will be a swirling madhouse of unled people," I said. "Do you think you'll have to go there?" I asked him.

"No. But I am going to call Dolores." Dolores was his new secretary.

"How do you like Dolores?"

"She's a swirling vortex of human secretarial potential," he said, to kid me.

He was having some problems with his secretary. It was a measure of his character. He always answered his own phone, for instance, which I find that no one in a reasonably high position in New York would ever do. And he was a true big cheese. The reason why he always answered his own phone was because his former secretary, a woman of a certain age named Mary Louise, was such an antiquated person that as she perambulated slowly from office to lunch to the fulfillment of her personal errands, her official duties often fell behind . . . and Hobby was too courtly to ask for a different secretary. Finally Mary Louise retired. Then came Dolores.

I felt that Hobby seemed to seclude himself. "You go to work, you go to Long Island, but you seclude yourself," I said to him.

"I go to work, often I have to work in Orient, too. This doesn't leave much time for square dancing," he said. "But I am not totally secluded. I know you, don't I?" He looked at me sideways, askance, with those dazzling blue eyes.

It was a hot July night, and we lost very badly twice, a double-header. But there is something dashing and brave about the huge cavernous stadium with its excessive quality, I mean its excess, too many people, claustrophobic, as the stadium is a swirling madhouse of chaos. A vortex of true and complete chaos. I mean it's not exactly bucolic, being as it is in New York City. Though outside of Manhattan, in Queens, unpretentious, gutty. Of course I like it that way. Stan's Sports

World and Stan's Sports Bar populated the area. Pulsating with madness. What I like best is when the young men come straight from work, in their suits and ties and sunglasses, emanating a certain gentility or plain American history. They in pairs or threes. Brave of them to withstand the heat and the chaos, for the sake of their innocent sport, and dashing of them in their cavernous unlovely stadium, in the bad conditions, losing. The gallantry of their broken dreams and shining hopes in each situation, such as in the double-header Friday night.

There was one moment of hope. The New York team got a three-run homer. The one who got the home run is the most stoical person on the entire team, and that is saying a lot. He was trying his damnedest not to smile as he ran the bases, as you could see on the video screen, where they had a close-up of his face. They showed the dugout on the video screen and you could see his teammates pushing him back up out of the dugout to give a curtain call to the crowd. He didn't want to, because he is so stoical, but finally he came out and briefly tipped his hat.

"I wonder what his personality is," I said to Hobby.

"If he has one, you mean," said Hobby.

They definitely are the most stoical group of people I've ever seen in my entire life. "I can't believe how stoical they are," I said. "I can't believe that. I can't."

"Could you reiterate that please?" said Hobby and looked at me sideways, askance, with those dazzling blue eyes.

After all he was as stoical as they were. He was the type of man that if you wanted to talk about Feelings and Emotions he would either (1) fall asleep, (2) read the newspaper, or (3) watch a sporting event. But whatever happened he would not (4) fall apart.

He was an athlete, an ex-jock, etc. Meaning that if he were what is called "sensitive," he would probably try not to show it, and he may not even have been, since sports, stocks and bonds, politics, these were his interests, duck hunting, bourbon, cigars. Expressing Feelings and Emotions was just not his thing. Nor had it been his father's. Communication is very important, but I know a lot of people who don't think so, like Hobby, his brothers, and his father. They weren't that wild about communication. Of course it would be true to say that many men aren't. Maybe it would even be true to say that many Southern men aren't.

In their family, for some reason, as I remember it in New Orleans, everyone was always slipping each other hundred-dollar bills, in a sort of quiet magnanimity, as if that was how they expressed their emotions, indulgent, magnificent, suave. For some reason they carried around a lot of cold cash. The father would always slip one of the boys who was broke a couple of crisp hundred-dollar bills. And then, paragon of paragons, one of the boys who had gotten the hundreds, would then slip them to someone else, whom he thought needed it more.

In his baseball days Hobby, playing in the Carolina League, was the type of player who would come up to the plate when they were losing and "patiently smoke a fastball to left" as they say, ready when called, to help. His father might go up to Memphis or somewhere they were playing and watch in the stands. Then he would go into the clubhouse and slip Hobby a few hundred dollar bills. As I say, I think it was their way of expressing emotions.

His father met Babe Ruth once. It was at the Peabody Hotel in Memphis. It was in the twenties, and his father was a boy of twelve. His uncle knew that the Yankees were playing in Memphis, with the Class A teams, on exhibition games through the South as was done at that time. His uncle held the boy by the hand (his uncle always took the boy on many adventures—he would take him to Chicago on the Pullman train, with a sleeping car and a little compartment where you left your shoes at night to be shined—the boy's father was dead, his uncle took care of him). His uncle went straight to the front desk and jovially said to the clerk, "What room is the Babe staying in?" The clerk supplied the information. Those days were more innocent, as his uncle recalled when he told the story. The uncle and the boy went up to the room and the uncle knocked on the door. A man the color of mahogany opened the door. It was Lou Gehrig. "Is the Babe here?" said the uncle cheerfully. Then Babe Ruth came out of the sitting room and shook their hands and said that he hoped he would see them again and tousled the boy's hair. He had a drink and a cigarette in one hand.

The boy grew up to be, in his turn, the father of Hobby and five other boys, but he was a most unhappy man.

I knew Hobby's father just before he died. I felt sorry for him, for the condition of his wife. Their marriage was a long combat, to which they were dedicated. Parted from his family often, he had an air of unaccountable solitude. He had a wife and six boys, but his solitude remained, owing perhaps to his dangerous trade. He was in politics.

"A man of honor was hounded by men without honor— not unusual, perhaps—but the man was my father." That was Hobby's attitude to him. He was a suicide.

In his youth in Mississippi he watched rapt in the night as W. C. Handy and his orchestra played at dances at Ole Miss, the young men in white tie and tails. Then he was called to the spurious allure of the North. He fell in love with a girl in Boston. She was the local belle. But she married a man from New York. Five years later she returned to Boston with a divorce. Hobby's father was still waiting.

They returned to New Orleans. He used to quote the 137th Psalm—If I forget thee, Jerusalem. The South was his Jerusalem. They had sons, but the marriage didn't work. They went to Havana, a glamour spot then, some years later to attempt to reconcile—and Hobby was conceived, the last of their boys.

In his father's effects were found the ticket stubs and programs from all the baseball games in which his son had played.

On a questionnaire from Hobby's Law School, when asked for an essay or analysis of his life, I saw he once had written, "I have not much vision or imagination and temperamentally I am not much given to speculation. I have lived from day to day and done the job at hand. I am unable to present 'an analysis revealing and interesting' to anyone. Unusual as has been my career—" baseball, journalism, and the law—"I cannot estimate the impact that these years have made upon me or the extent to which my life would have been substantially different than anyone else's." You have to admit there may be a good deal of "denial" in this. So this was his aversion to being "sensitive" or introspective or self-interested in any way. So I must draw my own conclusions. I know that when he retired from baseball he wanted to be normal—to go to Law School, enter into a regular walk of life—he didn't want to play baseball until the end, and agonize over his retirement, and then have an automobile dealership in Atlanta, Hobby Ford. Not that he cast any aspersions on such a life. But I don't think the automobile dealership or beer distributorship that he said ex-athletes customarily lent their names to would hold enough interest for him. Instead he would keep his baseball personality somewhere else in life. He would be out there patiently smoking a fastball to left, as it were, when they called him up to bat.

He was a stalwart sort. An athlete, a newsman, a man's man, an old pro. Constant was simplicity, from the heart. Hobby was more gruff and suave in his devotion.

He had another quality that always strikes my heart. He had that slight touch of squalor. An aging fellow with a sweetness, however much he tried to hide it with his gruff exterior. In truth he was one who had suffered, and that of course had caused him to grow a heart. It is an old adage, but suffering had caused him to have compassion.

One thing about baseball that used to hurt my feelings, though of course my understanding is limited, was when they made trades. They kept making huge dramatic trades at deadlines in the middle of the night. They traded the handsomest player. They traded the one who had been there the longest. They made so many trades of sentimental favorites that the only possible consolation I could find for them was that the game itself is the only constant.

I found it to be poignant. But then again, I find a lot of things to be poignant.

14.

AFTER HIS SEASON in Atlanta, Hobby was traded to the St. Louis Cardinals (causing his father ecstatic joy). After an injury he was returned to the Carolina League. Upon recovery he was assembled into part of a big trade to the New York Yankees. But he never made it to New York —at least at that time. That was when he decided to retire from the game and pursue the law, and later journalism, in New Orleans.

The world went on in its customary way, among the palms and oaks, the green magnolia trees, when he left New Orleans. But at one time he and I were inseparable.

And I had not really seen him for some time when we were reunited in New York. Under the auspices of Mr. Underwood.

15. OUR OFFICE in New York was situated in Times Square, a neighborhood I favored most, because it was sleazy, and unpretentious, and a swirling vortex of chaos. There's nothing like a swirling vortex of chaos once in a while. There was always some sort of disaster happening, like an underground fire across from the office—busses and fire trucks and police cars careening through the streets; sirens, chaos, madness. Sirens, chaos, madness? Oh, that again. At the office that was nothing new. That tabloid mentality which they have in New York, on TV as well as in the papers, is something that we don't have in the South, but it pervades life here. Glaring restless disasters and crises that glitter with tragedy and sirens and loud lurid headlines—they don't have that in the South. For lunch I would go to the Godforsaken diner on Forty-fourth Street and Eighth Avenue. It was a sort of Godforsaken place. It was really what they call a Godforsaken place. Like a Godforsaken diner in a Godforsaken place. But all the waitresses fawn over me there so I like it. They fawn over me because I'm not a wino lunatic, their customary clientele. I'm the most genteel person they've ever seen in their entire lives. I would always be excessively gracious and polite and kind, to shock them. Everyone else was screaming epithets or quietly sobbing in their booths or having strained conversations with transvestites. And oddly enough, across the street, nestled between the Off-Track Betting and the Cuban lottery, was a church called Chapel of Angels.

Into this untoward setting radiated the fading splendor of the Majestic, now our office.

The Godforsaken diner was the type of place, so common in New York, where each person is alone, and yet each person is talking loudly to himself, making for an insane cacophony of conversation.

A lunatic would come into the middle of the room and start screaming, issue threats, engage in fisticuffs, the police would be called. You could easily imagine that a lunatic would come in someday with a gun. But so far that had not happened. There was a tall, lame black man who arrested my attention. He had an immensely kind face. He had a dignity. And somehow I saw in him, in the kindness in his face, that wryness or jocularity which is to me so Southern. Maybe I should have been scared of him. New York, Times Square, danger. Who knows?

A small flock of rabbis headed daily to the coffee shop on the other corner for the pungent Jewish food, amid, oddly enough, the obligatory mural of wrought-iron balconies in New Orleans that always seems to decorate the most maniac-ridden New York cafés.

Times Square was the most exciting part of town, in my opinion. That and the baseball stadium. A swirling vortex of chaos. But Times Square added to the swirling vortex of chaos the element of sleaze. Maybe it seemed reminiscent, in regard to sleaze, and lack of pretensions, to New Orleans. After all, when you take the sin out, the humanity goes with it. In such places you can contemplate your fellowman in a world of senseless desire and sleaze, standing on a corner lost in thought on Bourbon Street, for instance, with the screaming saxophones and old-time jazz, thinking of your memories and those held dear, as the gawking tourists lurch past.

In New York no one could care less about you. That's what I like about it. Somehow there is a hope in that. It is of course the anonymity, which a Southerner never finds in his South.

So at my lunch hour I went to the Splendide, the Godforsaken diner, where I listened to a Muzak version of the Brandenburg Concertos, and warded off born-again Christians. Often I got maniacal aggressive born-again Christians who screamed at me about it throughout my lunch hour. The kind where you start getting a migraine headache or think, "Okay, this is it, a maniac has monopolized me and now he is going to do something crazy." But so far it has always turned out all right. I calmly answer their questions about my religious views, and try to calm them down. But first these born-again Christians let me have it for an entire hour sometimes, screaming out, drowning out everything else in the place, "Do you believe in Jesus Christ as our savior?" or "Who do you think Jesus Christ is?" screaming defensively like you think they're going to clobber you if you say the wrong thing. No one in the Splendide would ever come to your aid while this was happening. That's not the kind of place it is. Everyone just has bored sidelong glances as if crazed religious evangelists are nothing out of the ordinary, which after all I suppose they are not. So I calmly state what I believe and try to calm them down. That is the key. Calm. You just try to calm them down.

Sometimes I would run into Cedric there. Cedric, too, worked at the paper. He wrote what he liked to call "color stuff" but what it really boiled down to was covering the recent beetle infestation of Scranton, a three-part series. A typical headline of a Cedric story was BLACK SPOTS FOUND IN WATER. He had a sort of science beat. Or when Mr. Underwood let him write about something human, a typical Cedric lead would be "The Senator jogged along the lake, retreating into the hidden caverns of his mind. Thinking thoughts known only to himself, concealed by his own brain."

He actually wrote that. And furthermore it was printed. But no one ever said Mr. Underwood's paper was highbrow.

"When the Senator drank, he drank scotch, and he drank

it on the rocks," wrote Cedric, in his color story about the Senator.

As for me, I was currently working on the Fun Section of the paper, which was actually rather ironic, since it's not very fun, in fact, it is driving me slowly bananas.

Actually, I think Mr. Underwood transferred me to the Fun Section because he always tells me to go out and have some fun, as he thinks I'm not having enough fun.

"Having Fun?" people would always ask me, passing by the Fun Section.

"No."

The Fun Section, sometimes known as the Home Decorating Section, was not what you would call a heavy-hitting type of assignment. Wallpaper, parking lots, bedspreads, and so on, that was my beat. Other aspects of the Fun Section included crosswords, acrostics, horoscopes, the comics, and a column called "Strictly Screwy" by a battered old former New York vaudevillian married to a cornball society columnist. They were always traipsing in with 1940s New York comedy routines and wisecracks to each other. "Whaddya, crazy? My husband is crazy. I married a crazy man." Then he would rejoin, "She married a crazy person. Okay. She married a crazy person and I married a doll. I married a doll. Maybe she's crazy!" They were sort of funny but not funny. It was mainly the New York lunatic old-time 1940s big-cheese parlance that was funny.

Mr. Underwood would come by my office sometimes or call me into his. "You're a kid! You're just a kid," he would scream, out of the blue. Or he might read a story of mine and make a baseball metaphor about it. "You're hitting with the bases loaded, kid." Or "Show them your curveball, kid!" It was ever more understandable why he was so enamored of

Hobby, owing to his past in baseball. Hobby had of course gone straight to the top—World Editor. I on the other hand had gone straight to the bottom—the Fun Section—where I smoldered quietly.

You might be asking yourself Why, if I have worked there for five years, why have I not advanced from the Fun Section. After all, let's face it, I am a Collier, I'm fairly brainy. The answer is that I've been demoted to the Fun Section, so it's not as if I've just been on the Fun Section for my entire five years there. I used to be on the Travel Section. Then I got to travel around and write feature stories. What happened?

Truthfully, I think the answer is that Mr. Underwood equates the Fun Section with Fun itself, and he thinks I'm not having enough fun. He always worried about me. And it is after all true that when I was on the Travel Section maybe I didn't always seem like the most fun-ridden person in the world, because even though I liked it, tawdry motels in Florida by yourself is kind of for the birds. See what I'm getting at? After a while it got to me, staying in tawdry motels in Florida by myself. I wasn't really sorry when he transferred me. Now I'm at the office all day with a bunch of nuts, or at the Godforsaken diner across the street, with lunatics.

It was definitely a contrast to the country. Between the Majestic, the Splendide, and the degraded elegance of the Grunewald, my apartment building, there was definitely a contrast to the country—arriving Friday nights to the green lawns of Orient.

Where a row of little children follow me, like a row of ducklings. They follow Hobby also. I take them to the playground, I take them on excursions, I rescue nameless tots completely unknown to me from near disasters on the jungle gym or from mad flips on the seesaw. I've noticed that you can't go anywhere near a playground without witnessing numerous hair-raising disasters. You're always rescuing some nameless little tot from a bloodcurdling fall from a chain-link fence screaming helplessly.

Huge waves of poignance waft toward me from all directions.

16. ORIENT POINT, Long Island.

The piercing cries of the children punctuate the night. Harry Locke, poor little fellow, his arm in a splint, chased after Hilary, the baby. She fled.

The love couple rowed in a small boat on the back lagoon among the swans.

"Storey, can I make a compinion?" said Al.

I figure Compinion = Comment + Opinion.

"Yes, Al?"

"Would you like to see my Styrofoam collection?" said Al, his little brow being furrowed in the utmost seriousness. Styrofoam plays a strong force in his life. Similar to that of cardboard.

Hilary, the baby, came along. "Hi," she said, to the Styrofoam. She says hi to everything. Also, she thinks everything is a duck.

"Is Dad coming soon?" said Al.

"I think so."

One always tries to sound very gay and positive and ceaselessly cheerful around children. So I attempted to elaborate on this remark. "I know he's coming as soon as he can. And I think it will probably be very soon. He'll come as soon as he can, my dear."

"We'll wait right here and keep an eye out for him. Probably, he's almost coming now. We'll wait right here, Storey, and keep our eyes peeled for him. Right, Storey?" he said in his piteous cheerful child's voice, with his Collier-like furrowed brow. My heart was in my throat, for I had spoken to Al's father this week. Although he would be at least in the vicinity, the doctors wanted him to go to a hospital up North for the remainder of the recovery. The psychiatrists were at him now. For some reason I had a vision of the place. It was a resort town on the sea, where people convalesce. There is an old hotel, a row of deck chairs on the porch, and everywhere a view of the mild blue sea. Or it would be Asheville, the green town ringed by mountains and stone angels, frequented by people looking for a cure. It would be a place with faded glory, like his own, in a strip of slightly ruined old hotels in what was once a gay town. It was once a jaunty town like Saratoga. There would be mysterious old architecture and old-time violins. Pleasure boats lit up on the lake. Sweet blue nights. A clouded moon.

He was a man whose self-denigration was so great that he was a singularly tortured individual. But the truth was his nobility, which he himself did not account for. That he had perseverance, courage, grace—he would not count his character that way. His later life had become a startling thing. A heartrending thing. From glamour boy to burnt-out failure— or so he saw himself—you had to realize it was only how he saw himself.

The difference between Hobby and Claude Collier, old cronies as they were, was that Claude was such a tortured soul, and time had made him introspective, and he did not like what he saw when he reviewed his heart—though I would say he did not take his quality into account—but Hobby had not allowed himself the look, it seemed. But one thing they did have in common was that both had suffered setbacks. Huge setbacks had befallen them. Claude had lost a brother ten years before whom he could not forget, and alcohol had been but a deceptive friend, and for Hobby, above all, his father's suicide. Such sorrows make a difference in a man. They had their dark

Southern glamour and dapper attire and dark Southern wit, but they had their sorrows. Claude was the more tortured and, in some ways, the more fascinating. But when you looked at him, a heavy mantle of responsibility would settle on your shoulders—for inextricably linked with his virtues was some devastating trouble or vice; alcohol, and others like it, dragged him down. Whereas when you looked at Hobby, you never felt that heavy mantle of responsibility settle on your shoulders —responsibility for a man's weakness. Of two hearts one is always the stronger.

When I was in the hospital that day with Claude, a crisis was definitely at hand. It was often so with him. When he last broke down it was in Europe, at the Venice Lido, when his wife saw before her a man in a suit and tie who seemed a normal man, yet from small remarks or signs it was ever apparent that he was in a crisis. Such as in the hospital that day. I remember the telephone was ringing incessantly. When he was in the hospital he got so many calls they had to disconnect the phone. But this step had not been taken as of yet.

"I understand, Judge," he had said into the phone, and wore a look of intense hopelessness.

He hung up the phone. He turned to me. "I am on probation in so many legal instances I can't so much as jaywalk," he said grimly.

What was that his father said to him, that I had heard him say? "I'm not going to tell you you're going to hell because you're already there."

I went to the racetrack with him the day before he was committed to the hospital. It was pouring rain. He won $700 —and of course walked away with $40 in his pocket, having taken his party, ever extending, to the clubhouse for a champagne lunch. But amid the mere sight of beauty, the huge oaks and the green wrought-iron chairs and the circle of white-haired gents playing cards in the men's grill. Inseparable, when I remember when, along the reckless glamour of the boulevards. Our fathers were brothers. There was that great bond, among others, between us. "Ever since I was born, my life was mapped out for me," he said. "I wanted to be different, but . . ."

He pointed to the garden, outside of the hospital window, the palms and oaks beside the river. "The world goes on without us," he said suddenly, and with a sweep of his hand to indicate the green, the lovely, waning afternoon, he looked at me with his deep benevolence.

He was suave in his suffering. Maybe I am drawn to people who are unhappy. I find them more interesting. So of course did he. He was, as I say, a singularly tortured individual. That is why I loved him.

I felt this same for Constant Fox. And if he loved me, it was for a similar reason, that he saw I was in trouble of a kind, that he thought problems were more interesting than normality, that he had a keen sense of pity.

Hobby was more guarded of his sorrows, or more crusty or stoic. He was one of six brothers who would hunt and fish and act manly. A sportsman, who could always be trusted to do a thing in the most sporting way. He would not show his emotions, for so he thought to be manly. It was an old code. But what people saw in him, the thing that drew them to him, or caused them to depend on him, was, despite a basic solitude, a concern for others above himself. That made the poetry of his life.

As it is noted on the Louisiana license plate, Louisiana is a sportsman's paradise. This refers mainly to hunting and fishing. My father was always off duck hunting at Grand Chenier or Bayou Barataria or fishing in the Gulf, like some kind of maniac. The same was true of Hobby.

He would listen to the baseball games ceaselessly, which on the one hand might drive you bananas, but on the other there he would be in his baggy khakis with a cigar and it would touch your heart too much, to get very mad.

He called his broker, smoked cigars, and read the baseball scores.

So I follow the sporting news.

17. "THIS REMINDS ME of Mississippi—old times—New Orleans," I said to Hobby in the moonlight on the bay and the green canal in Orient.

"What does?"

"I don't know, just you being here, and different things at different times in different places."

"Oh." He knitted his brow. "I guess I can see what you mean." He stopped. "Sort of." He stopped again.

"It's poignant," I suggested.

"What isn't?" he kidded me. But he looked at me slowly. "You worry me, sweetheart."

"I love it when I worry you."

"I'm worried about you, doll."

"I love it when you're worried about me."

There was a fleeting sorrow in his blue eyes. But he was a fellow who did not wear his heart on his sleeve.

Maybe he got that from baseball—as he explained to me for example why they act so stoical when they get a home run. It is to be gracious toward the losing team, not to gloat over the sharp misfortunes of individual opponents, such as the pitcher off whom you got the home run. So it is to be stalwart and gracious and courtly.

Another example. Of the restraint or composure that is involved. If you are in the batter's box and the ball is coming at you, you have to be a pretty cool cucumber to decide in two seconds whether it's a fastball, a curveball, a slider, a strike, a walk, or etc. etc. The whole thing involves the highest degree of composure, as he pointed out. Always to maintain your composure. And I admire that in many ways. I admire the player who behaves in that way, and is stalwart and stoic and elegant. When someone throws down his hat in the dugout when he does something wrong or throws a temper tantrum I prefer the man who is stoic, elegant, wry. Maybe it is because the type of man who throws a temper tantrum is the type of man who would fall apart in a crisis, say, whereas the other would not, and the other turns out to actually have the sweeter nature, mild and capable of being philosophical. However, Hobby regarded me in a certain wry, skeptical way because he and I are estranged. We are meant to be friends but we have not really reconciled. What is there between us now? Respect, and some skeptical dark Southern wit. But that is not a true reconciliation to me.

I see him at the office in the chaotic swelter of New York, I swelter through the summer crowds in Pennsylvania Station and find him then in Orient. But people say in love affairs there are no second chances.

"When I see you like this . . . I wish I could grab you, and hold on to you, and tell you not to worry," he said.

"Then why don't you?"

"Because I know what would happen."

"What?"

"The same thing that happened before."

"All right then, if we're meant to be friends. . . . I think you should spend more time with your friends."

He was tall and not hard to look at, wearing his quaint Southern attire, a seersucker suit and white bucks. A troubled silence ensued for some time, as we stood by the green canal.

When I look back, I find a fundamental ignorance on my part, not to have worked this out five years ago. I find a fundamental ignorance in my conception of what was good for me, when I look back to that time. It is a magnified version of the old adage, that you shouldn't go to sleep at night, if you are in a fight, without making it up before the sun goes down. In this case five years have passed, and I wonder if it can be reconciled. Into every love affair there comes a moment of dishonor. If you resolve it, then you may reach a deeper and more permanent agreement. If no, then on the ardors of your youth, on that the door may close.

My love for him was not a qualified one. Qualified loves are different—a different ball game entirely. Kindness, a kindness, must be the substance of the thing. If not, then I can only cherish my love at a contemplative distance. And recollect how it was before I ever met him. For before I met Hobby Fox the world was one way, and now it is strictly another.

18. Orient Point, Long Island.

The night is sweet and breezy. The night is sweet and cool. But I am filled with longing and unease, even in the beauty of the night, a pulse of beauty, the rustling of the leaves, in the sweet black night.

The TV was on in the distance. Ricky Ricardo talking to Fred. "She wants to do everything together, to show that we're not bored with each other in our marriage. It's like having a piece of gum stuck to your shoe."

"Well, you better scrape her off because it's just going to be me and you on that fishing trip."

I went to the dock at Port of Egypt, where I court solitude. There is the black night and a white sand island with green marshes, so white as though lit up, the tables and chairs on the water at the Arrow Inn, the breezy night, and Port of Egypt like Havana with boats in a cove with lights, old-time boats, some sailing toward a point out to sea.

I looked at the raging bay, the rustling of the leaves, this weather presages the fall, and saw the love couple run to meet one another across the lawn to the point.

Margaret picked up another shipwrecked sailor. She was sitting on the beach, just minding her own business, tending her own garden, when she noticed that a shipwrecked sailor in a small burnt wooden boat was floating up into the bay. It turned out that he too was a Southerner. Oddly enough, from Mississippi, floating up into our imitation antebellum Mississippi enclave. This place is a haven for lost Southerners.

Andrew, one of the Langguth boys, age four, told me that he wouldn't want to be a Southerner.

"Why?" I asked, incredulous.

"Because then I'd have to call everyone Sweetheart and Precious all the time," he said.

Nevertheless, I taught the children about the Civil War. I pointed out the Mason-Dixon Line on the map. I must say, they were riveted, throughout the lesson on the Civil War.

"What divides the North and South?" I asked Andrew, using the Socratic method.

"England?"

"Okay, buddy, it's called the Mason-Dixon Line, remember? Now, what is the difference between the Northerners and the Southerners?"

"The Southerners call everyone Sweetheart and Precious."

Mr. Underwood was on an important panel on television with other publishers, thinkers, and professors. In the middle of a fluent, comprehensive answer involving facts and figures, tax laws and public policy, Mr. Underwood suddenly said, "I've—uh—just lost my train of thought. I'll pass." A weird expression came across his face.

Everyone at the enclave was watching, and the place is alive with gossip.

Everything Mr. Underwood does is considered to be of major importance and is a source of ceaseless analysis.

Mr. Underwood's small troubled son, a pyromaniac, lit a bonfire in a corner of the enclave at Orient Point and accidentally blew up the laundry room.

Luckily, no one was in the laundry room at the time. If you ask me, the laundry room needed renovations anyway. Its chief function had become sex hideaway for the love couple.

No one was hurt, as I said, in the explosion. It falls somewhat awkwardly, however, to Mrs. Langguth, the mother of six, to attempt to discipline Mr. Underwood's small troubled son.

Margaret picked up an elderly Southern black man at a nightclub in Orient and brought him to one of Mr. Underwood's dinner parties—causing tongues to wag and eyebrows to be raised. There were many agonizing faux pas and gaffes. It turns out that he too is from Memphis. His name is Dollar Bill. He is a promoter or impresario for a Memphis soul singer by the name of Smokey Taylor who customarily performs at Green's Lounge on Person Street. But he got lost, called to the spurious allure of the North. Now he and Margaret are inseparable.

Another new person turned up, a broken-down, emotionally disturbed old flame of Margaret's. I noticed him because he exuded New Orleans, my hometown: he was an alcoholic pasty-faced unhealthy-looking young man with an elegant accent, making jokes, falling apart, destroying himself, lurching across the lawn in a trench coat.

I heard him whispering to Margaret.

"I just don't feel like going to a million bars," she said.

"That's a switch," I thought.

The house is alive with guests—blow-drying their hair, showering, making lists in the kitchen, reading the papers, fixing coffee, etc. etc.

Squalid. The squalor of proximity.

Plus it is raining so everyone is confined to quarters. A restive atmosphere prevails.

A Morale problem is developing at the enclave. Smoldering feuds, gaffes, faux pas, etc. Spy mania. Everyone jumps to the window when someone crosses the path, in order to see who is coming and going, and ceaselessly analyze them. Or if a crunch on the gravel is heard, indicating an arrival by car, everyone jumps to the window—the plot thickens.

Mr. Underwood had too much to drink again.

Grace Fox came by to make ominous predictions concerning the animal kingdom. Margaret has three stray cats, but according to Grace, the cats here are likely to get eaten by raccoons, who skin them alive, for they use the fur in their nests. It's the law of the jungle, she says.

Otherwise, the ferrets will get them.

These horrifying descriptions do little to aid the Morale problem.

I must describe this ceaseless din—among the houses of the Mississippi enclave—it's a good thing I don't mind a ceaseless din—I rather like a ceaseless din. Which is going on in the gardens—they're having parties.

But it is a restive atmosphere, due to the Morale problem.

Margaret spent the night in jail. Well, I have to say, maybe it's a good place for her. I mean, for the safety of the county maybe Margaret should be behind bars.

Jail is becoming a popular hotel among the members of our enclave. Mr. Underwood's small troubled son did time as a "missing person" but it is mostly Margaret who frequents prison. The Shore Patrol was influenced, however, in her favor by her sweet solicitude toward Mr. Underwood's small troubled son, and they set her free. It was a mistake. She went to Prudence Island to a dinner party and got into a fistfight with the ferry captain, who called the Shore Police. They were waiting when the captain docked the ferryboat in Orient.

"Where's Margaret?" Cedric asked, an old-fashioned in his hand. Maybe Cedric's visits seem endless because in his case the cocktail hour is twelve noon, sometimes 10 a.m., and just goes on from there. Since he met Margaret he has been drinking heavily.

"I'm crazy about that gal," said Cedric.

"She's crazy about you, too," I said.

"I'm just crazy about her."

"I'm crazy about her, too."

"I'm wild about her."

"I get the picture."

"I'm crazy about her."

"Cedric, I understand what you're telling me."

"Where is she?"

"She's in jail."

"What the—"

"She was imprisoned for disorderly conduct on the ferry."

"I knew that would happen," he brooded.

"How do you mean?"

"Look, I know she's been nuts about me since the first time she saw me. It's making her crazy."

I ought to take confidence lessons from Cedric. Jeez. On the other hand, of course, Cedric is completely oblivious of the fact that everyone deeply deplores him.

"She's so debonair," said Andrew's sister, wistfully, referring to Margaret, back from jail, collapsed in crisis, wearing a leopard-skin bathing suit and a huge bow in her hair, sitting on a deck chair by the bay, surrounded by several male admirers. It is true that Margaret has been acting rather Satanic lately. Obviously, she can't stay out of trouble even if she tries. And she does try. But it doesn't work. She certainly makes a startling contrast to the young couples, or the married women, who are in comparison sedate. Margaret, by contrast, is involved in Satanic frenzied socializing, often surrounded by beaux.

I feel sorry for her beaux. Often they become alcoholics or undergo startling personality transformations after knowing her.

But then again Margaret is from Memphis, which explains a lot. Memphis is definitely a town with a dark side.

She is always in crisis. But I love people who are always in crisis.

Margaret's old flame from New Orleans was standing on the lawn in the middle of a torturous group of screaming children. There was also a commotion emanating from Margaret's house—crashes, music, as if a number of people had just come in dancing.

"Is Margaret here?" said the old flame.

"Andrew, go get Margaret," said one of the Langguth boys.

"Speed, get Margaret," he, in turn, called to another.

"Tell Margaret to come down," Speed Weed said to Andrew's sister.

"Margaret," she called.

It was the domino effect.

The old flame looked hopelessly up to the window of her house, where crashes, music, and etc. could be heard.

"There are only four families in the Mississippi Delta, and hers is one of them," said Mr. Underwood.

"Sounds like he's been studying at the Birmingham Drawl Institute," said Hobby.

"The Delta is prettiest when the cotton is high," said Mr. Underwood in his new drawl with a faraway expression. Every once in a while Mr. Underwood will slip into a sort of Southern mode.

Cedric, in his turn, is in the kitchen at all hours making cornbread.

Cedric too is under Margaret's spell. Actually he has undergone a startling personality change since knowing her. Some of his previous personality traits have started to break down. His hair is all messed up and sticking up in tufts, he hasn't shaved for days. Formerly he was a square, with old-fashioned houndstooth suits and every hair in place, a cornball from some outmoded world. Now he is a madcap wreck who hasn't slept for days.

I remember when they first met. He asked her out for drinks. Actually he had about fifty drinks. Then he came back to the enclave and drank two quarts of gin. He was lurching along the lawn in a trench coat, suddenly transformed into this dissipated maniac. Purely from having one date with Margaret.

One date with Margaret, and the next thing he's lurching across the lawn in his trench coat like an insane person. I think she is driving him mentally insane. I'm talking about mood swings. Which Margaret seems to inspire in men.

Actually, Margaret gets kind of Satanic around Cedric, I have to admit. But she also gets kind of Satanic around John Peabody, aka Mr. Joviality, who also adores her. Let's face it, Margaret is rather Satanic. Or at any rate she's certainly acting Satanic lately.

I remember when John Peabody aka Mr. Joviality too met Margaret and returned to the enclave after that first date, suddenly a deeply troubled individual. His whole ordered, cornball world had crumbled. He came by my house and just started talking. He said there should be a solar crematorium on Ellis Island. He rambled on incoherently about a number of unconnected subjects—solar energy, God, immigration. Then he said there should be advertising in outer space, and it would pay for the space program. "Think it through, John," I said. "There's no one in outer space to see the ads, much less buy the products. See what I'm getting at?"

"Why are we here?" he said. "I mean, what's it all for?" etc. He leaned toward me confidentially. "One of these days I'm going to find out exactly who I am."

Jeez—I should have said, I already know who you are: a complete cornball who came from some cornball, outmoded world.

His apocalyptic behavior with regard to Margaret is definitely a lapse from the norm. Frequently he bounces back and pursues his ceaseless jollities.

Cedric was already troubled before he met Margaret. She has the opposite effect on him than on Mr. Joviality. Cedric is lovesick, and lolls about dolefully.

"That's a nice dock, kind of," said Cedric dolefully. "That's a nice swan, kind of," he added.

I remained silent.

"That's a nice pond, kind of," he said.

"Could you please tone it down a little?"

"I love when it's summer but it seems like fall," he said. "I love this place. I love this house. I love—"

"You love everything. Okay. I get the picture. I understand what you're telling me. I see what you're getting at," etc.

I have already mentioned that Cedric is talkative. And now Mr. Joviality too has become loquacious. After seeing Margaret in her leopard-skin bathing suit he often comes over to my house and starts talking in a maniacal fashion about the planets, the apocalypse, the Bible, Aristotle, Hollywood, outer space, and numerous other subjects in an unconnected manner. Cedric has become a born-again Christian.

It would be interesting if Margaret ended up becoming a born-again Christian. I mean since undoubtedly Cedric will try to convert her. And despite the fact that Margaret has been acting so Satanic lately, she is actually very impressionable, or at any rate, crazy, and I would not really be at all surprised if she ended up becoming a born-again Christian. On the other hand, it is equally likely that, under Margaret's spell, Cedric will lose his faith.

And become a devil worshiper. Or end up in a jail cell.

19.

I AM TAKING a two-week vacation. Remaining here in Orient to keep an eye on Al and his brother and sister. But I went in to the office for one afternoon, to instruct my protégé. My protégé, a twenty-three-year-old boy from North Carolina, goes out and gets drunk on a binge every night and sleeps in his clothes. He is sowing his wild oats. He goes out on wild bacchanalian binges at night with his friends from North Carolina or perhaps other young colleagues at the paper, weaving across rooms while waitresses stare and proprietors cringe, as he tells it, and then accidents happen. Then he gets home at five or six in the morning and the next thing he knows it is eight and time to go to work and he is lying there in his room fully clothed in his suit and tie from the day before so he just gets up and goes to work, as he is already dressed.

He looks surprisingly dapper, considering the circumstances.

I am trying to instruct him, as he is my protégé, but all I ever hear from him are wild stories about long masculine dinners with his cronies with bourbon and cigars and martinis and weaving across rooms while waitresses brace themselves and proprietors stare frozen while huge accidents happen. As he madly careens among the boroughs of New York, in his sleepworn suit.

He keeps running into people he knows in Times Square, which seems a little odd, since Times Square is populated by wino lunatics, pornographers, born-again Christians, public monologuists, insane maniacs, etc. Also he hangs out at African nightclubs that have names like Savage. He lives in Brooklyn in a place from which the Manhattan Bridge can be seen, and he says a steady stream of winos walk across the bridge every morning and walk down the off-ramp, just walking along into Brooklyn, for some reason.

He is related in some way to Hobby. This is another reason why I have taken an interest in him. I have to admit it is exciting having him for a protégé. But he has been my protégé for six months now, and under my tutelage he seems to have developed into some sort of bacchanalian god.

It has occurred to me that maybe I should matchmake him with Margaret. But I know that is a rather demonic idea.

Somehow through his channels of informants, Mr. Underwood learned of my protégé's behavior, and has quietly had him transferred to the Latin American Bureau, hoping that the assignment will instill in him a sense of responsibility, perhaps, as this is considered to be a plum assignment, dashing and glamorous, a foreign correspondent, showing Mr. Underwood's faith in him. For preparation, he is starting a crash course in Spanish. He has fallen in love with his Spanish instructress. Actually, since he has proven to have no aptitude whatsoever for languages, he has two Spanish instructresses, and he has fallen in love with them both. "Where is the American Embassy?" they say in Spanish, teaching him catchphrases. "How far to the hotel?" Meanwhile his thoughts turn only to love.

The Spanish instructresses are five or six years older than my protégé and so it was to my great surprise that he suddenly informed me one day that both of them had fallen in love with him and he was caught in a sordid trap, as each one of them planned to visit him in Mexico City at the Latin American Bureau at exactly the same time, and he did not know how to put them off.

His worries were short-lived. Mr. Underwood in his chaotic fashion has decided to keep him in New York after all, putting him back on the Metro desk. I can't say that I am sorry for the change. I can't conceive what havoc he might have wrought in Latin America—something similar to Margaret in Latin America comes to mind.

At times John Peabody (aka Mr. Joviality) would take me to the Harvard Club. Being a Southerner, I find that sort of stuff very quaint. I like to egg him on, his cornball joviality, his resounding guffaws, highballs, New York, the Harvard Club.

I frequently drive in from Orient with Mr. Joviality on Sunday night—Mr. Joviality singing "New York, New York" as I sit in the front seat with him while he, in his element, a huge

American rental car, glides along the Long Island Expressway to New York in the black night while I listen in a dream to the saxophones. Never has one person been so corny as Mr. Joviality. It comforts me. Put him in a room with some Frank Sinatra records and some Bombay gin, and he will be in his element. But maybe you're sitting there saying, Who wouldn't?

Ironically, he and I live in the same building in New York. So it is usually most convenient to ride into town with him. Only Mr. Joviality would have researched the matter of the name of our building—most large apartment buildings in New York tend to have names, indicating a certain grandiosity, for a building to have a name, a certain grandiosity that our building, however, did not actually possess. Perhaps it did once. It was called the Grunewald. It was attached to a sweltering Chinese restaurant, whose fumes wafted through the lobby. It was situated on a teeming street, in a teeming neighborhood comprised of wino lunatics, drug addicts, insane maniacs, etc. But to Mr. Joviality it was The Grunewald, as if elegance pervaded.

Everyone in the Grunewald seemed very furtive. The lobby of the building had once had furniture but it had been stolen shortly after I moved in, as witnessed by indignant memos posted in the elevator about security. Frequently the tenants posted indignant memos in the elevator about the lack of security because the building had no doorman. It did have, however, what were called porters—another throwback, like the name of the building, seeming to indicate some type of New York grandeur. Porters. You think of spruce-looking men to help you with your bags. But the porters were actually very furtive seeming. They seemed to be involved in a drug ring revolving around two wino lunatics who lived in the building and were sometimes seen sobbing or screaming in the hall.

Mr. Joviality actually contemplated having stationery made up, embossed with the swank legend "The Grunewald." Mr. Joviality had a way of somehow tracing everything back to his cornball world, no matter how far from it he had strayed.

I know that the Grunewald may sound grim. But it wasn't. You became accustomed to it, grew to thrive on it. It seemed to adhere to my Southerner's vision of New York.

You may think it grim. And yet to me New York is a plain American town, compared to New Orleans. New York was more normal to me, even at the Grunewald.

The windows of my apartment looked across dank inner courtyards and corridors to other people's windows, and no one had shades or blinds. You could always see what everyone else was doing. Usually they were hanging around in their boxer shorts, chewing cigars, opening the icebox. It was like the 1940s. Elevators, people in their boxer shorts, Glenn Miller music, New York. And everyone was always in a baseball craze throughout the summer, following the sporting news.

I kept the sports channel on in my apartment at the Grunewald all the time, for its comforting low masculine drone, droning on about the ball games in Chicago and New York. Storied names to me, a Southerner—Chicago, Philadelphia, New York.

Hobby gave me a subscription to *The Sporting News*. *The Sporting News*—you think of white-haired boulevardiers in suspenders and mustaches reading the racing form while strolling through the park. But no. It is sports-crazed baseball fans screaming at each other, nights of chaos in the Grunewald.

I have to admit that when I first moved into the Grunewald, I did not think it would be easy to adjust to my new surroundings. It was the most hideous neighborhood I had seen, a teeming swirling vortex of poverty and wino lunatics. In New

Orleans, there was the green avenue, that arch of venerable oaks and green palms. But I grew to love the very ugliness of the Grunewald. I grew to love my new surroundings.

It was better than the gleaming spires in more well-heeled sections of New York, it did not have pretension. It had lines of Cubans buying lottery tickets and lines of Cubans buying newspapers, the ceaseless din of salsa block parties. It did not have pretension. For this I loved it dearly.

That's why I like baseball—unpretentious, gutty, and dashing in its way. Or like New Orleans, on every corner a pool hall, a bar, and a church, no trends, no fads, only the unvarnished truth. Harlem is the one place in New York excepting maybe Times Square with seedy dives that reminds me of my hometown in the South, some broken-down old place that has jazz music. Unprepossessing bars populated by elderly black men and an old jazz band and politicians and preachers coming in from the rainy night. People in New York don't realize, but the Southerners can realize the familiarity, the similarity to Memphis or New Orleans or South Carolina, to a downtrodden place with seedy dives. Closer to Harlem, closer to God, among the sinned against.

In a broken-down old nightclub populated by a few elderly black men and an old jazz band.

Times Square was the other neighborhood I favored most. It was like Bourbon Street in New Orleans. Sleazy, seedy, and sin-ridden. At least it is unpretentious. When you take the sin out, the humanity goes with it.

Now of course the other main thing that a Southerner finds in New York is anonymity. It is the solitude among multitudes that many seek in teeming world capitals. And unlike in your hometown in the South, no one can point a finger at you in New York and say, What is she doing, she is drifting, why isn't she this, why isn't she that—no one in New York could care less, obviously. In New York you could sit in your room and watch TV and eat Chinese food for forty-eight hours straight on the weekend if you wanted to and no one would know or care. You could sit in your Lonely Splendor at the 4 Brothers coffee shop on Broadway every night for dinner. You could have plain American fun at baseball games with screaming sports fans chewing cigars.

New Orleans is very beautiful and very painful. New York is not that beautiful and not that painful. It is just a normal American town. Whereas New Orleans has a caliber of beauty among the massive oaks, at times a vision of paradise, but there is an unvarnished truth about it, and there are your memories and those held dear. I miss the society of my beloved father. I am pursued by my memories. I might be on the midnight train from Penn Station populated by wino lunatics on my way to Orient through the summer crowds, but in my mind's eye I must set my sights on that white house beside the palm tree in New Orleans, with its sweet gaiety. I must find my way back.

20. SOMEHOW it always seems that when something is sleazy in the North it is more sleazy than it is in the South, I think because the North with its Puritan heritage is meant to be the opposite.

And yet I must always see an innocence in New Orleans as the generations rise before me, for they stood in the same spots, a vision of my grandfather, say, in a boater hat getting his oysters at the Pearl.

New York—Fifth Avenue, the lights on the trees in Central Park—it does nothing for me. Actually it does one thing for me. It gives me mental stability. Because of its being more like a plain American town, with regular plain boring events like

opening nights at movies. But I hate how the people are pretentious and think that New York is the top of the world—
aside from their misapprehensions, they have no humility.
That is why I prefer the more unprepossessing parts of town,
with screaming lunatics. I prefer the chaotic swelter of the
Grunewald, in its unpretentious neighborhood of Cubans. Or
the world of baseball. It is true that Hobby bore his exile with
a better grace than I. Otherwise we are two misanthropes.
Misanthropy is a heartless pursuit, some might say. But misanthropy is the tonic of solitude.

21. I CAN SEE where being a pitcher epito-
mized a certain side of Hobby's personality, as I can see where
the pitcher has to sort of hold it all together. He has to maintain a certain composure. He has to face each man with courage and grace. If the pitcher cracks up or falls apart or goes to
pieces, then it's a catastrophe until they get another one. I
think that Hobby had an elaborate series of manners built up
to maintain his stalwart demeanor, a kind of repression in fact,
as though if he let down any one element of reserve then the
whole thing would crumble—which I am waiting for it to do.
For he and I had left something behind, in a seedy dive in
Baton Rouge while covering the legislature and the old sinner,
or on a stormy night in Biloxi, Mississippi, or at an old hotel
off the coast of Alabama, all before he blew out of town one
night in a seersucker suit on a midnight flight from New Orleans. My story starts in Orient, tame Orient, but pursues ever
to the South, to the green palms on a raging sea. For I had left
a part of myself there—and there it must remain.

But I have to admit that I take a perverse satisfaction in the
nights of remorseless Puerto Rican dance rhythms in the
Grunewald, amid the occasional scream of agony, sirens,

chaos, madness coming from the street, and the sports radio program on twenty-four hours a day in its comforting low masculine drone. This is a phenomenon worthy of speculation: the announcer keeps reassuring the listeners that the line is open twenty-four hours a day—so they can call to agonize over their Feelings about sports. Do you see what I'm getting at? They are not going to agonize about their Feelings about personal emotions, only about their Feelings about sports. But they do need to agonize over something.

So it seems that every time I go to Hobby's house we always end up watching a tape of the sixth game of the 1986 World Series where the New York team came back as underdogs to make the dramatic win. Then we just watch the tape of the Series all the way through to the very end, where the sports announcers go into the clubhouse and all the players are throwing champagne on each other. They interview the heart and soul of the team—the one who always was referred to as the heart and soul of the team. First he says this sexy thing about how they just kept throwing him pitches that landed in a certain place "right where I like it" plus he is modest about getting the hits. Then later—the tape Hobby has goes all the way through from afternoon to the eleven o'clock news— they're still in the clubhouse throwing champagne on each other, except now they're totally succotashed, and they interview the heart and soul of the team again, asking him about one player who got the winning hit. He goes into this endless soliloquy about how that player is the unsung hero of the team, and people may call him the heart of the team, but it is really this other guy who is the real heart of the team, and he just keeps rambling on about him, shaking his head in bemusement, fondly, giving endless and kind of drunken superlatives about him. Then some other players come up and throw champagne on him, they also douse the announcer, and then they throw champagne on the camera, and the newscast gets cut off.

He also has a tape that is the "history of the franchise," with a lot of white-haired gents at podiums at press conferences talking about baseball as if it were World War II. I mean you'd think they were talking about World War II, considering the seriousness and the level of agony being used in their talks. But they are talking about "the franchise." Its future, its past, its hopes and dreams. A great pitcher retires. He stands at the podium. He tries to give his speech. He breaks. He steps back, he brushes away a clandestine tear. Talking to another old sports hero, who breaks down when he says good-bye or is honored. Like the one on the World Series tape, who defended his friend, who does not need defending, but that is the cast of the man, to defend. Like honor, and probity, and the sword, the battlefield, the old heroes.

On certain Fridays since this April Hobby started taking me to the baseball games. Our entire relationship revolves around baseball. As he is an athlete and ex-jock, etc., and now I am a sports fan even though I used to hate sports, like many a woman, I don't doubt. But now it's like I'm glued to the radio —"Don't bother me, the football game is on." Football. Not only baseball but every other sport in existence. Though of course baseball is the most elegant, has the most grace, is the most quaint.

The baseball game last night was truly a metaphor for the human condition, it seemed. They had two rain delays, one half an hour and shortly thereafter an hour. It was raining lightly even when they played. It was a night game and unseasonably cold. In short the conditions for the fans were terrible or could not have been worse, and yet a lot of people stayed in the stadium until two in the morning. It was like a small dinner party, as the announcer said. It was the diehards. They were like feisty old-timers who just wouldn't quit. They were a metaphor for the h. condition. They were in it for the long haul, not only in perseverance, but enjoying it. You have to love the attempt, even if the attempt is a failure. Anyway they were sitting there with umbrellas in the stands at two in the morning like maniacs.

I tried to talk to Hobby about our Feelings and he was receptive but the only problem is my talk was excessively lame. Feelings, I murmured, I have Feelings too, I'm a Human Being—I mean, Jeez, for pity's sake, what am I talking about?

"What do you think is going to happen?" I said finally.

"I think you're going to drive me crazy," he said, and looked at me sideways, askance, with those dazzling blue eyes.

So we're just two jocks sitting in the stands at two in the morning watching a baseball game. Plus in New York, up North, how strange.

Why is it that I cannot reconcile the past?

It reminds me of Gary Cooper and Marlene Dietrich eye-balling each other world-wearily in Morocco. Why is it I am pursued by my memories, with my heart broken by them.

As often in baseball, there were some late heroics. Someone saved the day at the last minute, "eking out a last-minute victory" as the announcer says. How can they always eke out these last-minute victories? Maybe it could be the same for us. Maybe it is not too late for us.

Some people think baseball is slow. But not only do I dis-agree with that, I like it when they have rain delays, extra innings, and any other thing that can stretch it out even more to be as long and slow as possible.

My whole life revolves around sports now. As time wore on Hobby also introduced me to the basketball season as ex-emplified in Madison Square Garden, which is like a smoldering Babylonian prison. I mean you'd think it would be plain American fun. But Madison Square Garden is more squalid than the baseball stadium. In taking the subway you go through Pennsylvania Station, where many lunatics convene. Each person is alone and yet each person is engaged in a loud conversation with himself, making an insane cacophony reverberating throughout the place. One thing about New York, in the subway or on any street corner, any man feels free to just start spouting his philosophy. A woman spoke in tongues on the Thirty-fourth Street platform, also a Jamaican evangelist. Everything is shrouded in smoldering iniquity and teeming squalor. New York, the Grunewald, the sporting news.

But it is actually plain American fun. Because I have found that when you are in a theatre watching a movie, say, I find that you still think about your worries, while watching the movie. You can't get away from your worries, even while watching a movie. If you are depressed you will be even more sad in the theatre. Whereas if you are watching a baseball game, or listening to the sporting news on the radio in the ceaseless low masculine drone, or at a basketball game in Madison Square Garden, it is truly relaxing to the mind, and for that time you forget your worries. You are all in it together— lunatics, screaming sports fans chewing cigars, scuzzy men in checkered jackets with hacking coughs—you are all in it together, and in something innocent.

Sometimes I hang around with the Carolinians and Virginians who have reunions at the North Carolina Club. It is for people who went to the University of North Carolina or the University of Virginia. The girls wear pearl earrings and cashmere sweaters and pearls and handbags and headbands and obsolete hairstyles and kilts or other outmoded genteel Southern clothing. It touches my heart compared to the New York girls in miniskirts or some other faddish attire. The Carolinians and Virginians escape fads. They don't follow trends or fashion. They are caught in some obsolete genteel moment, and they will not change. This I find indescribably endearing. Or comforting. But I don't really hang around with them. But they have the secret. They cleave obliviously, unknowingly, abandoningly to their genteel outmoded Southern ways, as the young couples in Orient pursue their summer pleasures boating on the bay, dinner parties, bridge, etc. They are as serious about their pleasures as the sports announcers on the radio or the nuts who analyze it are about baseball when I listen to the baseball games with Hobby. Or as Mr. Collier is about his hobbies. And that is the secret. To be so eminently serious about something so trivial, Virginia girls talking about clothes, the Carolinians about basketball, the young couples playing bridge and wearing silly sports caps at a card table set up on the lawn.

22. ORIENT POINT, Long Island.

Music emanates into the night. Old jazz saxophones and violins. "I Put a Spell on You," "One Night of Sin." Old saxophones and black crooners with soul ballads. "Inseparable" and "Reconsider Me."

"That music hurts my feelings, Storey," said Al.

"Why, Al?" I said.

"Because every time I leave a place I love, it hurts my feelings, and that music reminds me of New Orleans."

"Oh, Al."

Dollar Bill sang a soul song in the garden. That certainly was like New Orleans. It was indescribably beautiful. He sang without accompaniment. He snapped his fingers and made heartfelt gestures. The song had something to do with rain.

He just kept singing about the rain. It was a ballad, but it had some dark jazz aspects, to which he snapped his fingers and made sad gestures. It was the most breathtaking thing. Dollar Bill walking out in a flashy white suit with white patent-leather shoes, his costume at once dignified and old and elegant, however flashy somehow. He must be in his fifties. He has the air of having been around the clubs in Memphis singing hard on his luck. His face is immeasurably kind. Despite the signs of all he has been through. Or because of them.

At the end when he had finished, he made a sort of jaunty sign at Hobby, who was the one that had found out he could sing—the kind of jaunty sign that you would think he'd make to the piano player in some seedy club in Memphis, after bringing ten ecstatic people to their knees—and then shook his hand and walked off with a spring in his old step.

He was like an angel that came down specifically from heaven. He has angels in his brain. Everyone at the enclave was completely overpowered, and now he and Hobby are inseparable—ordinarily Hobby keeps to himself. Save for two constant companions, basic attachments, Dollar Bill and Al.

Hobby gave me a baseball autographed by Darryl Strawberry. He gave me a subscription to the official newspaper of the New York team. He gave me a wristwatch of the New York team. It has a miniature version of their helmet on it—you flip the helmet up to see the dial.

I find these presents to be poignant. It seems that baseball is the only way we can express ourselves. He and I have been estranged for some years now, but perhaps a reconciliation is being achieved through baseball.

Romance always ends, but love, love is different, as Mrs. Collier used to always say. And great things are achieved by perseverance, in the face of repeated failures, and this is what distinguishes a strong soul from a weak. And few great things

which were desired, it is often the case, were achieved on the
first attempt. A girl could do a lot worse than to set her heart
on something, and be faithful to it.

23. MR. UNDERWOOD'S secretary called

again. Mr. Underwood wishes to have lunch with me. Of
course it is possible he is concerned about my column. Maybe
he has heard the talk. I write a column about Feelings in the
Fun Section, as per Mr. Underwood's latest command, and it
is not going well.

We went to the 21 Club. At the time, its decor was red
plush and cobweb. It was filled with New York lunatic big
cheeses and statues of black Southern jockeys.

"What makes you tick, kid?" said Mr. Underwood.

"Sports?"

"Hah!" screamed Mr. Underwood.

There was a long silence.

"You've taken an interest in baseball, I see," he said. "Pass
the salt for Chrissake! You kill me, kid. Jesus Christ!" He
lapsed into silence and dined.

"What exactly is it between you and Hobby Fox?" he said.

"I'm not sure . . ."

"You'll never be sure. You just have to make a stab in the
dark, kid," he said. "Now, about Overton" (my protégé).
"Tell him to come into my office when you get back." He
rose. "Lot of memories in this place," he said, looking around,
rocking on his heels. An acquaintance passed. He nodded to a
few other big cheeses. "A lot of people know me in this town,
kid," he said. He went into one of his reveries, standing there
with his cigar with a brooding expression. We brooded silently for several moments before leaving.

. . .

You kind of know you're in trouble when Mr. Underwood takes an interest in you in the first place, because he always takes an interest in people like retired sports players, troubled prizefighters, and washed-up Southern bandleaders. The broken-wing contingent, you might call it. He likes people who have a broken wing so he can scrape them up off the floor and paste them back together. So if he takes an interest in you, it kind of means you are the equivalent of a washed-up Southern bandleader.

It seemed as though Mr. Underwood tried more ardently than another man to believe in things, and that yet, in his heart of hearts, he could not believe in them. In another man, it would not be a noteworthy, or may I say, uplifting trait, but in Mr. Underwood, taking him all in all, it was the key to his character.

Meanwhile Overton, my protégé, as you recall, has been wearing the same suit for days, careening madly throughout the boroughs of New York, sleeping in his clothes. He is beginning to look a bit well-worn. But he maintained his composure, straightened his tie, and forged forth to Mr. Underwood's office.

Mr. Underwood sat him down, and then stared at him in dead silence for five minutes. Finally he spoke.

"You're a kid, and you're having fun," said Mr. Underwood finally. "You're just a kid!" he screamed. "Now how would you like to come to Atlantic City this afternoon, kid? I want to have some fun!"

So they went to Atlantic City, which is like a smoldering monument to human degradation—no—a sweltering mecca of human frailty—and in the oddly comforting air of desperation in the modernistic red plush casinos populated by the dregs of humanity, they smoked cigars and lost their shirts, returning that evening on the train for big cheeses to Penn Station.

This week there was more of the same at the office, a bouquet of torture in Times Square, then at the Grunewald, careening sirens, yelping mongrels, sudden bursts of salsa music after midnight. At night one slept to ceaseless salsa dances pounding in the street below. The pounding staccato of the Cuban heart. Remorseless gaiety. Colored lights madly strung up in the streets, chairs set outside on the corner. It reminds me of Havana. Only missing are the palms.

Irritating Lucille Ball reruns being played at four in the morning by my next-door neighbor. An occasional obtrusive accordion. Sudden screams. Sirens, chaos, madness. The baseball games. The sporting news. It's a good thing I enjoy a ceaseless din. Luckily I happen to find a ceaseless din relaxing.

Mr. Underwood called Overton and me into his office. Another big cheese was there, some politician. After he left Mr. Underwood said, "He used to write pornography." He shook his head. "Pathetic."

According to Mr. Underwood, everyone used to write pornography. And now everyone was all washed up.

"He's washed up. Pathetic." Sighs of disgust. "Losers are losers. They're losers!" he screamed. Then he dismissed us and went off to one of his clubs. He loves clubs. Clubs with white-haired gents with mustaches and suspenders.

I think someone has a crush on me in the office. Someone keeps leaving flowers on my desk.

A cheesy-looking man with thick black-rimmed glasses and a checkered shirt stuck his head in my office.

"Are you Naomi?" he said.

"No."

At least once a week, some scuzzy-looking guy sticks his

head in my office and asks me if I'm Naomi. That's New York
—someone is always sticking his head in your office and asking you if you're Naomi. No one knows you and no one could
care less about you. Not only that, but they think you're
Naomi.

Thence to another night in the Grunewald, accompanied by
pounding, remorseless rumba music from the street below.

Some time ago, Mr. Underwood transferred me again on
the paper. He has given me a column. My column is called
"Strictly Personal." It is in the Fun Section. Unfortunately,
the column also carries a photograph of me. I mean it's bad
enough to have "Strictly Personal" with my byline, Storey
Collier, but then to have a picture also, of me smiling inanely,
how will I cope with the embarrassment?

All right then. "Strictly Personal." What is my column
about, you might ask? My personal feelings or something? No
—the personal feelings of others. It is a sort of advice to the
lovelorn column. "How can I give advice?" I asked of Hobby.
"Journalists give advice to the world," he stoutly allowed. "So
you'll be good at it." But actually I'm not good at it. For
instance, the letters I get are all from weirdos, and members of
the rejected and despised. Every day all day long I get letters
from weirdos. Like this poor kid from Memphis who a black
woman came up to him in a nightclub and said, "You is a
fool," and it deeply depressed him. My advice is, Listen to
her, she speaks the truth, and abject self-loathing is what you
ought to have if you are wise, and to face the truth. But this is
not the type of advice I am meant to give.

The Fun Editor, who edits the column, is coaching me, but
I'm not sure he is the type of person who should be giving
advice either.

The Fun Editor collected accessories of Scottie dogs as a

hobby. I mean he collected little china Scottie dogs and little knickknacks that had to do with Scottie dogs, like tartan scarves. Whenever I saw anything connected with Scottie dogs, like those little tartan hats they wear, or some china figurine, I would buy it for him. For Christmas I found for him a figurine of a jockey holding a tray with liquor bottles and martini shakers on it and then at the very top of his head there was a little Scottie dog. Obviously, the fellow was a lunatic, and frankly, I liked to encourage him.

The Fun Editor may have sent me the flowers, I suppose. He loves me. You'd love me too if you were obsessed with little Scottie dogs and I spent two years needlepointing you one. I can't deny I like to egg him on.

For him it's little Scottie dogs. But for me it's old gents on the sports channel reminiscing about the Brooklyn Dodgers and their old heroes, agonizing over their memories.

One old gent has a program on at noon that takes place at a restaurant owned by a great former baseball player. You can hear the clink of martini glasses in the background. The old gent moderating the program talks to people who are coming in for lunch, or has special guests come on the show, and they reminisce about their sporting memories, in baseball.

"Philadelphia is not going to make it. Philadelphia is through. Finished. It's over for Philadelphia!" screamed the man. There was a long tortured silence. Collecting himself, he then resumed, in a tortured strangled voice. "I've been saying this all along, Frank," summoning his dignity, "there is very little hope left for Philadelphia at this point in time." He sounded as if he had just been let out of a mental institution for the day. The nuts on the radio were analyzing the pennant race, and who would be in the World Series.

The screaming sports analyses were always droning on

throughout the office. But to me it always was a sort of old-time world. Historical, in fact, and memoried of men in suits and ties screaming at the Polo Grounds in older times.

There were a couple of big-cheese political columnists. They too made an odd pair. One spoke in baroque elocutions as if he were in another century. He was courtly and Victorian, a white-haired gent. If you saw him at the elevators, he would graciously greet you and inquire into your well-being, and miss about ten elevators out of simply being too courtly to walk away. The other big-cheese columnist was his diametric opposite, hard-bitten, streetwise, vulgar, screaming out cuss words, though he too was a white-haired gent.

Many of the old-timers in the office such as the cornball society columnist and her former vaudevillian husband, I might add, were not shy of Mr. Underwood, whom they had known for fifty years. Often they would traipse into his office, yelling at him. I found that people who had known Mr. Underwood for a long time or were his contemporaries gave him back his own medicine. His secretary sometimes yelled at him, I noticed, the doormen sometimes did, the electrician, and once when I was walking in the lobby downstairs, I found a strange intruder yelling at him.

The one person who was not a lunatic, of course, was Hobby. He was unpretentious, for instance about being the World Editor in the grandeur of the old Majestic, at a storied firm, on top of the world directing his dominions, but he was calm and workmanlike and stalwart, unlike seemingly most others there. He did not have one ounce of pretension. He was completely dedicated, but he made light of it. He was wry. He took himself lightly. What a relief to sometimes see a normal person there, not acting like a lunatic.

He was a man with a purpose.

I tried to chide him for working too hard. But then he

leaned back in his chair and said, "Storey, one thing you have
to understand about me. I am a very dull, unexciting, unro-
mantic type of guy."

"Oh really? White Slavery is dull? Baseball is dull?"

"Very dull."

He was reading the stock pages and smoking a cigar. Dolores brought in some papers. He sighed. Some tortured messages started coming in over the computer from the Asian
bureaus.

"I seem to be in a vortex," he said.

"Great!" I said. "You're speaking my language."

He smiled. His smile was like someone who kept a grand
old Rolls-Royce in their garage and every once in a while
broke it out and took it for a ride.

He started reading the stock pages.

"You, reading the stock pages, it's poignant," I said.

"It is?"

"Don't you think it's poignant?"

"No."

"The World Editor, baseball, stocks and bonds. . . . It's
poignant."

"It is many things, but one thing it is not is poignant." He
looked at me slowly. "It strikes me that you're not the brooding misanthrope you think you are, my dear," he said.

But in a rare instance of leaving the office early, he came on
the train to Orient with me that night.

It was a sultry evening. A light rain fell. New York played
Chicago.

24. ORIENT POINT, Long Island.

Mrs. Langguth, the serenely calm mother of six, has developed an interest in Hobby. As jazz music penetrates the night.

"It was a sad night in Harlem. . . . There was no moonlight in Harlem. . . ." Old-time saxophones and violins. She sits in a deck chair on the lawn at night by Hobby's house from which the music emanates, smoking cigarettes. The jazz-crazed mother.

"Are we being gracious enough?" I said to Hobby.

"We're in a vortex of graciousness," he said.

Al stood before me and dramatically announced, three feet tall, "I'm in love with you so I'm going to marry you." He then reiterated his point of view to Hobby. "I'm in love with her, so I'm going to marry her, and get her life in order." Hobby knitted his brows.

Jesus Christ! as Mr. Underwood would say. A three-year-old gentleman caller.

However, his real interest at the moment is in bees and wasps. If not bees, wasps. They frighten him, but he loves them. He takes an obsessive interest in them.

The somnambulists are upstairs, resting.

Perhaps I should explain.

The somnambulists are this couple whom Mr. Joviality invited to the enclave as his guests. Apparently he met them in the tropics on a yacht. They were sailing around the world as yacht captains for people taking vacations. Mr. Joviality befriended them, as it turns out they went to the same school; often, he found, they were napping, below, until finally they explained that they were somnambulists and had to rest often. They gave up their yacht to return to the East Coast and take banking jobs, which seems to take a lot out of them. Mr. Joviality ran into them in the banking world and befriended them again and now they are visiting him here. Margaret keeps trying to make them sail in regattas and help her with her boat since they once were seasoned ship captains; but every

time they go out on the boat with Margaret they stagger
back to the house and pass out. Then they have to rest for
hours.

Margaret was on a ladder on her boat fixing the mast this
afternoon when a speedboat came by making waves, causing
Margaret to fall and collide with a water skier. They have been
inseparable, since. It turns out that he (the water skier) is from
Memphis.

People are divided into three categories here. Misanthropes,
gay blades, and somnambulists.

"Here comes trouble," Hobby said as Margaret walked up
from the bay. It is true that Margaret is constantly getting into
trouble. But she also has a very big heart. She's like St. Francis
of Assisi, in fact. Cats, dogs, ducks, ducklings, birds, you
name it, she takes pity on it. Her house is like an animal farm.
Her house is like a haven for the animal kingdom. She refused
to go into a restaurant we frequent in the next town over
because she said she saw a dead goldfish there once, in the
aquarium. Her bounty is not alone reserved for animals. She
seems to have a soft spot for strays. Stray people, too. She
often picks up stray people, members of the rejected and despised, shipwrecked sailors, wino lunatics for all I know. It's
like *Miracle on Thirty-fourth Street* at her house. All the towns-
people are acquainted with her, and she is constantly bringing
them pesto or tomato sauce. I mean Margaret walks down the
street and the next thing you know she's toiling over a hot
stove fixing pesto sauce for the entire neighborhood, while
Puerto Rican children trail behind her and every wino lunatic
comes up to tell her his philosophy. Margaret is the type of
person that if she's just sitting on the stoop, every wino lunatic
or neighbor passing by will feel that she is a forum for philosophy and he must stop and just start telling her what he feels

about his life. Then the next thing, of course, she's fixing him pesto sauce and taking it over to his house while Puerto Rican children trail behind her, carrying small wounded birds. Her table is set for the rejected and despised.

"She literally has no time in a twenty-four-hour period for anything except lunch and dinner because it takes so long to get ready and agonize over the arrangements," said Hobby, referring to Margaret's penchant for agonizing over which dates to accept and which beaux to accompany to which functions, etc. This is one reason why she is a sort of old-style Southern belle. She might spend hours agonizing over whether to get her hair colored, and if so when, and where. Hobby seems to be the one person on the entire island who has not fallen under her spell. I mean he likes her, he finds her bemusing, but he is not lurching across the lawn in a trench coat with his hair sticking up in tufts and gazing up at her windows remorsefully, etc. This is an observation that, naturally enough, fills me with hope and satisfaction.

25. GEORGE COLLIER, Speed Weed, and Harry Locke were caught smoking cigars in the attic. They were punished by Mr. Underwood. This involved being frisked for firearms, cigars, and implements of ignition, and then banished to what was once the laundry room for several hours with nothing but a printed lecture on World History, which Mr. Underwood prepared.

Margaret stole in intermittently bearing refreshments. They must not have had such a bad time, the boys, whatever they did in there, for hilarity emanated from their quarter. Harry Locke had fallen off the dock and broken his leg; he was in the hospital when the misdemeanor occurred. Otherwise, no telling what would have gone on in the laundry room.

The enclave is enflamed with gossip. Mr. Underwood made
a series of startling complaints. He gathered together the of-
fenders—Margaret and her band of shipwrecked sailors and
catastrophe-ridden friends, his small troubled son, and the
children, whose piercing cries have disturbed him. First he
acted very calm.

"I just have one thing to say. I know that it's summer and
this is the time to have fun. And I'm all for the Young People
having a little Fun now and then. But I just want to say one
thing." He paused. "THE GAME IS UP!" he screamed in a
maniacal fashion, while everyone trembled in fear. Then he
made a series of startling complaints, and posted a list of rules
on the laundry room. He said that from now on we would
have what he liked to call Town Meetings once a week at the
laundry room to be attended by all members of the enclave
under the age of twenty-five.

I took a brisk walk to Port of Egypt with Margaret. We sat
on the dock. We had a drink at the Arrow Inn, outside in the
back at tables and chairs looking to the different fishing boats
and pleasure boats skimming out into the bay. Then we had
fried clams at Port of Egypt. Margaret cried. I tried to paste
her back together.

Sunday night everyone returned to New York excepting
Margaret and me. After dinner we roamed around the garden
in the moonlight, nothing to do, innocent, sweet, in the country, etc. It was just Margaret and me. There was nothing to
do so we broke into Mr. Underwood's house and looked at
his stuff. Then we sat on his porch in the moonlight.

Then we came home and the telephone rang. Who could it
be? A source of ceaseless speculation. It was ringing as we
crossed the garden. It was Mr. Underwood, calling to check

on something. "What did you do tonight?" he asked politely. We cowered in fear. Can't you just see it? "Oh—well, first we broke into your house and looked at your stuff. Then we trashed the place." We concocted a gracious fabrication of innocent doings.

26. ORIENT POINT, Long Island.

Uneventful week as I recall. Hung about the dock with the children, observing the swans, whom they have named George and Martha. Of their three children, Huey, Dooey, and Louie, only one remains—rechristened Georgetta after her father—I believe the rest were eaten by otters. It's the law of the jungle, unfortunately.

I was pursued by my memories. I took the ferry from Orient to New London and the train thence to Providence—a godly town, hence the name.

On return the talk of the enclave was still the pathetic fate of the ducklings.

"Sick," said Al.

Margaret sailed to Paradise Point for a party, drove to Orient for another, went to the carnival in Greenport and got hit by a car, and then took the ferry to Deering Harbor for a dance at the hotel to hear a Dixieland band. She traipsed in around one in the morning and cooked Raspberries Flambé. Who knows what keeps Margaret going? She is the live wire, needless to say.

Margaret got a police summons in Greenport the next day for not being registered.

"Officer, I'm from Tennessee," she drawled. "I know it's against the law, but I'm from Tennessee and I didn't realize." He let her go. Later she was accused of hitting a singer in a nightclub and so ended up at her ordinary destination, that old haunt, the Orient prison.

The enclave is being overrun by the animal kingdom. Horrifying toadfish were seen in the bay; they look like prehistoric dinosaurs. Varmints are digging a virtual subway system in horrifying dirt holes seen by the side of everyone's houses.

Mr. Joviality arrived in a hydrofoil on the beach and leapt off the pontoon in triumph, hoping that members of the enclave would be there on the beach to witness his dramatic advent. But he leapt off the pontoon, and no one was there.

Mr. Joviality pursues his ceaseless jollity, that hollow construction I take him to be, which seems so precarious to me, but so well kept up. Someone made a brilliant character analysis of Mr. Joviality—that he is like a TV dad—the father of the family next door on TV. He's like *Leave It to Beaver*'s dad. See? Resounding waves of enthusiasm and jollity surround him.

"Storey, you're an original," he bellowed. "Ho ho ho! So it's hard for you! Ha ha—" Every phrase of his is followed by strange laughter. "Wow—look at that—" referring to Margaret at work on her mast, wearing a leopard-skin bathing suit and a huge bow in her hair. "Whoa! What a gal. What the heck? Hey! Very creative."

Huh?

"Whoa! You gals are something else!"

Gee, am I being gracious enough, I wondered?

I have developed a new personality trait: cowering fear. I am cowering in fear of him. I'm on pins and needles. I feel I should be doing his laundry, fixing him trays, walking around on pins and needles. While he plays the genial host, forcing liquor on everyone, fixing solitary nightcaps when there are no comers, and trying to keep the somnambulists awake (a losing battle). Now he is drinking gin—a bad sign—and leading a rather riotous game of croquet on the lawn.

I am not sure that I am being gracious enough. My attempts at entertaining, lately, seem riddled with smoldering faux pas and gaffes. Awkward agonizing moments, etc. At my last dinner party, for example, Margaret cried, Cedric told sad pointless tales, and the champagne-soaked authors became engulfed in melancholy. Then at my last dinner party before that everything seemed hollow, and no one called to thank me. At the end they all went to the Seven-Eleven. Fearing that agonizing faux pas and gaffes had been committed, I asked them when they returned, "Okay, now tell me every detail. The agonizing moments. The awkward silences. The embarrassing gaffes."

"But we only went to the Seven-Eleven."

"You mean, nothing happened?"

"Of course not; we only went to the convenience store."

"But what about the agony, the torment?"

"What agony? What torment?"

"Let's analyze the party," I said to Hobby. "What did you think of it?"

"Smoldering," he said, puffing on his cigar. "One faux pas after another." He thought it over. "Everyone was in crisis."

"Now you're speaking my language!"

"And you, sweetheart, are losing your mind."

But the thing is, someone is always going to pieces, in a situation like this. Take me, for instance. Sitting in the den on a clear day watching the baseball game on TV, chain-smoking, alone, then tuning in on the radio station afterward to hear the other obsessed people analyze it ceaselessly—when Hobby introduced me to baseball I doubt that is the picture that he dreamt. Or take Cedric, who has formed, in his own right, an

obsessive interest in golf. Every day he plays golf from 11
until 8 p.m. and then comes home and studies his score card
all night, and makes mayonnaise. He makes homemade mayonnaise constantly, obsessively. These people are snapping, in
my opinion. I was discussing it all with Hobby.

"We're having a crisis in our souls," he said.

"Now you're talking."

The morose overweight fellow with the handlebar mustache
was standing near. He seemed doleful.

"There certainly are a lot of Yankees here," I remarked,
innocently attempting to draw him into the discussion.

"Oh, do you feel out of place?" he asked. Then he threw
back his head and laughed maniacally.

What did I tell you? Another smoldering, agonizing
faux pas.

The place is riddled with them.

"He's cracking," said Hobby, and looked at me gently.

Mrs. Langguth, the serenely calm mother of six, sits in a
deck chair on the bay, with her aged mother. The morose
overweight fellow with the handlebar mustache, otherwise
known as her husband, sits in tragic isolation some distance
away, wearing plaid shorts with his stomach hanging out of
them and reading *The Wall Street Journal*.

He is a bonds broker. This winter his partner committed
suicide. I guess that gives you some idea of how the business
is doing. But his wife is a hopeless optimist. She always speaks
in euphemisms. "The stock market crashed," she says. This
is a euphemism for saying that her husband is out of a job.
"The stock market looks bad"—a slight variation, with a
melancholy gaze directed at Margaret, indicating that Margaret also is out of a job, that she was fired. "She likes to
have a good time," says Mrs. Langguth euphemistically, of
Margaret.

"She's taking it easy." This means she has a hangover. "She has joie de vivre." Meaning ditto, etc., she is constantly dancing her heart out in bars and getting in nautical accidents and her life is a ceaseless series of insane disasters, etc.

"Is that her boyfriend?" asked Mrs. Langguth. I couldn't tell if she meant Dollar Bill or the old flame from New Orleans.

"Who? Which one? What is he like?"

"Sort of dilapidated-looking," she admitted, doubtfully. "Today they're taking it easy."

Of the love couple it is perhaps impossible to be euphemistic in the sense that when Mrs. Langguth says, "They're in love," it could not be denied; but it could be viewed as a euphemism for their engulfing sex life, of which everyone is aware, having each in his turn surprised the love couple at one time or another, coming on them unexpectedly in the laundry room, for instance.

When it happens to Mrs. Langguth she smiles brightly and then rushes off. Her husband, in his turn, looks on morosely. Mrs. Langguth rushes off, perhaps fearing that her husband will get ideas, and that she will get more children, being devoutly Catholic.

Like many women who have many children, she is vague, distracted, deeply kind, rather elegant or witty in a certain way, and above all, has a dignity.

"What does Hobby do?" she asked me.

"He's in the journalism game," I said. "Do you work?" I asked her.

"She's in the social-work game," chimed in her husband morosely.

"It's been so kind of you to help keep an eye on Al," I said.

"Al is wonderful," she said, and stopped to think. "He will be a good man," she said—and I found a tear came to my eyes.

"Thank you so much for looking out for him," I said again.

"Is his father coming soon, do you know?" she asked. "I've heard so much about him."

"I'm not exactly sure . . ."

"He's resting," she said euphemistically.

27. CEDRIC SAUNTERED into Hobby's room, his customary practice, to suggest story ideas for the World Section. He sank into an armchair, as if dazed. "Two words," he said. "A word and a date." He paused. "Europe. 1995." Dramatic silence. "It's a series," said Cedric.

"Good idea," said Hobby.

"It's a series," said Cedric.

"I know. I got that. I like it," said Hobby.

"What do you think of it?" said Cedric.

"I like it," said Hobby.

"What do you really think of it?" said Cedric.

"I'm telling you, I like it. I love it."

Etc. etc., then he would keep sitting in Hobby's room and start talking about everything under the sun.

Even in Orient, where we're all supposed to be on vacation, when Cedric sees Hobby he doesn't say hello or make a normal social greeting, he just glares at him for a few minutes and then says smolderingly, "Three words. Latin American Democracy."

"I'll keep that in mind."

"It's a feature story."

"Good. Fabulous."

"It's a think piece."

Typical to his stoic demeanor Hobby always hears him out, betraying no emotion, I mean of irritation or rudeness. The only slight show of emotion he may make, if you could call it that, but it's really more like just a motion, would be to maybe loosen his tie. He would maybe loosen his tie and look a little nervous. But in my opinion the last thing he needs is to go to the country for the weekend to try to relax and have Cedric come up to his room and settle into the armchair and sink into a moody silence staring off into space in a daze, and start saying, "The Tanzanian Rebels. Who are they? What do they want? What makes them tick? Why can't they get it together? Compare and contrast them. Diplomatically, militarily, politically."

"That's a good piece of thinking. It's a fine idea. I'll keep that in mind."

"The Omar of Sultoon. What makes him tick? What does he want? Why does he—?" etc.

Trying to get Cedric to stop talking is like trying to ride a hog to Memphis. It would be easier to swim to Borneo than it would be to get him to stop talking.

Although he is a misanthrope, Hobby performs an integral diplomatic function at the enclave involving everyone. His house is like the Central Bureau.

Mr. Underwood was in the hall of Hobby's house, on his way to Hobby's room.

"Hah! Jesus Christ!" said Mr. Underwood—often his customary mode of address.

"Likewise I'm sure," said Hobby. Truthfully only an old pro like Hobby knows how to deal with Mr. Underwood.

The U.S. Navy "accidentally" shot down a passenger jet in Micronesia, causing an international crisis. Mr. Underwood would have to leave and forgo the planned jollities. He went in and talked to Hobby about it for a minute. Later I asked Hobby what was happening.

"How are things in Micronesia?"

"Tense."

"Will you have to go there?"

"No, I think I can work on it from the office. Saffron-clad monks . . . riots in the streets . . ."

"Saffron-clad?"

He was reading the wire stories on his computer. While listening to the baseball game on the radio. Plus supervising the boys. George Collier, Speed Weed, and Harry Locke. The boys are like diabolical demons from hell and require constant supervision. Al watched forlornly, as they are in the vicinity of ten and he is three and is usually considered to be too young to be included in their diabolical adventures. Hobby picked Al up and held him on his lap, while reading the wire stories, talking on the telephone, and correcting galleys of an article. Al looked up at him, ecstatic.

28. MARGARET RECEIVED a catamaran in the mail that had to be assembled on the lawn with inflatable pontoons, etc. She put everyone to work on it after making them sail in regattas all weekend. It took about six hours to assemble the catamaran, and when it was finished she found out that the mast was on backward and the entire thing had to be taken apart and redone. She batted her eyelashes at Hobby, who acquiesced on her behalf and fixed the entire thing while smoking a cigar in a hard-boiled manner. He's a soft touch, all in all, though preserving his strong silent type tough-guy demeanor.

The young couples were in a rare bad humor—I think because Margaret made them sail in regattas all weekend.

Much observation of swans, who tried to eat jellyfish in the canal, causing diabolical mirth among the boys.

The smaller children too are growing restive. They call each other names. Banana brain, screwball, picklehead—the harshest cut of all.

29. "I THINK I am going to take off and go to Wyoming," said George Collier. "I want to worship American Indian gods and live in a debris tent. Is that okay?"

"No, it's not okay," said Hobby.

"Can we go down to the beach now?" Al asked him.

"No, you may not."

"Don't you think you're running a sort of a tight ship around here?" I said to Hobby.

"No, I do not. Look, I adore you, but just sit there and be quiet. And that goes for you too, mister."

"Give me a martini," said the baby—her first words—she has come too much under the influence of the Southern contingent.

"No, sweetie, don't say that. Say 'Bye-bye. Bye-bye, Hobby'—"

"Give me a martini."

"Cut that out, young lady."

She requested again for the highball.

"The answer is No," said Hobby.

He pulled the little girl onto his lap.

"I have to go and pick up John at the hotel," I said. (John Peabody aka Mr. Joviality.)

"He's still at the hotel?"

"He had to stay at the hotel on business, halfway between New York and here, nowhere else to stay. I stopped there on my way in the other day. It was his birthday. I gave him a football. He was so ecstatic that he started throwing it around the hotel room and broke the chandelier."

"Oh, broken chandeliers are very common in hotels. Very common, don't worry about it. Broken chandeliers and tidal waves, those two are very common in hotels."

"He's hyper. That's one Yankee thing about him."

"He's pathetic, Storey."

"You love people who are pathetic, Hobby. That's what is so great about you."

"Pathetic," said the baby, with relish, imitating Hobby.

"Sick," said Al.

"Come here," said Hobby. "I want to keep an eye on you, Storey."

His brow was furrowed in some concern, and he held my wrist, as if to check my pulse. He looked down at me askance, with some amusement, but with some solicitude, and held my wrist, and took my hand, with his brow furrowed; and in this I found his love for me, which gave to me that rare thing, peace, unworried and unafraid. Perhaps it was a dream, that peace, the green lawns and gardens, the old houses, old verandas, the old clubhouse of white wood, looking to the raging bay.

"Are you going out dancing?" said Al.

The concept of dancing has usurped the place of cole slaw and mustaches.

"Dad used to go out dancing," said Al. "He danced so hard that he cried. He danced so kindly that he cried."

But we do not have any plans to go out dancing. I don't know what all the commotion is about dancing. Maybe he got it from Margaret. Margaret certainly goes out dancing quite a bit. But usually ends up in a jail cell.

30. THE BOYS were caught smoking cigars again, in what was once the attic. They were discovered by Mr. Underwood, who was incensed. Together with his small troubled son they have also lit several bonfires in the remains of the laundry room, and the pyromania aspect is becoming a problem.

. . .

There was an explosive dinner party. Literally explosive. The theme is pyromania. Margaret boated out to the sandbar and built a bonfire—the boys were ecstatic; pyromania is something they live for. She constructed a fuse of gasoline leading from the sandbar across the water to the garden, through the yard, and up to the porch, from which point it could be ignited. Even the somnambulists were roused by the explosion. To the boys it was a night of joy, from the diabolical mirth they found in the spectacle of the lobsters being boiled for dinner (you'd think most children would be frightened) to the bacchanalian midnight boating excursion they took after dinner, from which they showed no signs of returning. Hobby had to swim out and rescue them.

Afterward the saxophones from "Stormy Weather" emanated from the radio in Hobby's room.

"My life is like that song," he said.

"Well, it's a good song," I consoled him.

31. GEORGE COLLIER sat at his desk. It was Sunday afternoon. He was ten years old. George Collier put a piece of paper into his typewriter.

The Dawn
A Poem
By George Collier

The dawn is over
I see the clover

Deeply dissatisfied with this effort, George Collier took the paper out and crumpled it up into a little ball and threw it in the wastebasket. He began anew.

The Dawn
A Novel
By George Collier

My thoughts are filled with brooding anguish as I contemplate in agony the

Uncertain as to how to continue, he sat perplexed.

brooding agony which I tragically suffer in the chamber pots of my mind.

Chamber pots. No, not chamber pots, he thought. Chamber closets? As he sat in his brooding agony, his little sister, age four, came unsteadily into the room and asked her brother for her daily swimming lesson. With the grave air of responsibility and protectiveness often seen in older brothers, George Collier resigned himself to this interruption of his labor, climbed down from his chair and took his little sister by the hand.

George Collier was teaching his little sister how to dive. However, the pupil continued to revert to her previous method of immersion and proved unable to advance beyond that stage known as the belly-flop, which she executed in a rather torturous, histrionic way unique to her.

Although it could not be said that the siblings found no cause for mirth in this, George Collier's basic attitude toward his sister was that of a mentor for a promising protégé, and so he conducted his lessons with gravity and perseverance.

Boldly stifling the hilarity that his little sister never failed to rouse in him, the mentor persisted in his attempts to help his wayward pupil.

32. GEORGE COLLIER sat at his typewriter.

Ode to my Father
by
George Collier

Thirty-six years ago today
A new twig was born on the family tree
And that twig grew into a branch
And now it has its own twigs
And today that branch is 36 years old
And his name is Claude Louis Collier
And he is married to Louise Brown Collier
And his children are George Collier
And Anne Collier
And Albert Collier
And

Uncertain as to how to continue (as there were no more children in the family), he fell into an artistic reverie.

And he is the leader of this family
And we look up to him as a great man
And he is very noble
And it would be noble if I wrote an ode
Because it is our duty to be noble
And

The nobility of it all began to make him feel somewhat uncertain, and he put on his baseball cap and went pensively out to the backyard to play.

Al followed his brother into the backyard. George looked kindly at the boy.

"Wait for me, George," said Al, "wait for the little boy who loves you."

"Poor thing," said George as Al walked unsteadily across the lawn.

"I'm not a poor thing, George," said Al. "I'm not pathetic."

That's what you think, buster! These little fellows break my heart.

Anne Collier dictated a letter to her mother.

Dear Mother,

George is swimming out very far into the bay, as he has learned how to swim very well.

Yesterday George said we should pick up driftwood on the shore because it would be noble. So we picked up all the driftwood on the shore, but I know that grandmother loves him more than me, and I think that grandmother is more proud of him than she is of me. But I know you are not, my mother.

Love,

the late Anne Collier

The appellation she unwittingly attached to her name, an expression she had heard, she used for the vague air of pathos it seemed to carry.

33.   I took the children on an excursion to an old estate with a ruined mansion.

"This mansion was destroyed by arson," said the guide.

"What's arson?" said Anne Collier.

"It's when poachers come and set fire to the property."

"What's poachers?" said Anne Collier.

"Men who maliciously trespass on the property."

"What's maliciously?" said Anne Collier.

"Someone who deliberately—"

"What's deliberately?" said the little girl.

"I'll explain later, sweetheart," I told the little girl. "Now it is time to just listen."

"Why is there tinfoil?" said Al.

"There just is, mister. It's a kitchen appliance."

"What's appliance?" said Anne Collier.

"I told you, sweetheart, now is just time to listen."

"I want to sit by Speed," said the baby. "Speed, will you help me?"

"All right, children. Line up quietly now in front of me. We've seen enough now."

"Why do we have to line up quietly now?"

"Because we're getting ready to go home. Now line up, and don't make a single noise."

"Why do we have to not make a single noise?"

"Because I said so. Now come on. We're going home *now*."

"Why are we going home *now*?"

God give me strength, I whispered to the ceiling (I have created monsters).

Mr. Underwood was in "one of his moods" and walked around the enclave saying, "I can't get a moment's peace no matter where I go."

Then he sat at his kitchen table with his head in his hands.

We were seething and writhing in fear in corners.

I had to drive him into Manhattan, leaving Orient at about noon, driving into Manhattan with two and a half hours of his wrath, straight through midtown to the office in dead silence.

I had to wait for him there—this was a Saturday—while he conducted his business—and then drive him all the way back.

There was a slight chill in the air, oddly enough, although it was August. There was a clouded moon. There was a softball game on the lawn. The women were dainty and spastic, the men jocks who hit the ball hard. Meanwhile the boys, in their continuing obsession with fire (Man has always been mesmerized by fire), lit a bonfire in Mr. Underwood's library, severely damaging an Oriental rug.

Mr. Underwood called a Town Meeting at what was once the laundry room, where he held a "discussion group for the youngsters." He handed out mimeographed instruction sheets.

POLITICAL/CULTURAL/SOCIAL DISCUSSION GROUP
Calendar
(by invitation)

PLEASE NOTE THAT THIS LIST COVERS ALL OF THE
DISCUSSIONS PLANNED THROUGH THE SUMMER

We will attempt to remind you before each discussion.

PLEASE BRING:
(1) An interesting fact/idea UNRELATED to the main topic for a 15-minute presentation to the group.
(2) A snack

PLEASE COME PREPARED TO ACTIVELY
DISCUSS THE ISSUES.
Bring any notes, articles, etc. as references

INTERESTING FACTS until 5:00. DISCUSSION until 6:10.
SNACKS until 6:25.

CALENDAR OF DISCUSSIONS

US-SOVIET RELATIONS
THE DEMOCRATS

HUMAN RELATIONSHIPS
PREMARITAL SEX
FUTURE OF THE ECONOMY
THE MOOD OF THE COUNTRY
WORLD OUTLOOK

NO SMOKING PLEASE

The Town Meeting was not a success. The small children's minds wandered, nor could the older boys maintain an acceptable attention span. Harry Locke lit a cherry bomb, and the whole thing degenerated into a swirling madhouse of chaos, despite Mr. Underwood's stern command that there would be "no monkey business."

The boys were caught lighting bonfires in what remains of the laundry room, causing a small explosion, and Mr. Underwood made them spend the afternoon at his house while he tried out on them his speech entitled "Outlook for the Democrats." As for the laundry room, there is very little left of it.

What with Mr. Underwood's small troubled son having blown it up a few weeks ago, after which a few small repairs were made, and then the latest explosion, I don't think we will be able to have any more Town Meetings held at the laundry room. There's nothing left of it. A pathetic shredded remnant of Mr. Underwood's mimeographed schedule for World Outlook discussions lies atop what was once the laundry room.

Mr. Underwood had a dinner party and I asked a ceaseless stream of questions of my dinner partner, as per instructions, in order to be gracious. Mr. Underwood had mood swings again. He sat at the head of the table with a mesmerized grin plastered across his face. He is given to sudden fits of beatitude.

It was stormy and cold. There was an accident on the ferry

today in the storm. I was scared. But the captain laughed. A
manly fellow.

Margaret was thrown overboard in a gale. She was nearly
drowned. The captain had to dive in and rescue her. Of
course, when we returned to the enclave she decided it was a
good time for wind surfing. We sat on the beach in lawn chairs
and sweaters and mufflers like invalids, for it was cold, and
observed her progress. She was capsized. Hobby had to rescue
her in a motorboat.

The young couples are downstairs fixing hampers, lighting
a fire, playing bridge, etc. They comfort me as ever.

"I'm getting married soon," said Al.
"Who are you marrying, heart?"
"I'm marrying Mom."
"But she's already married, Al."
"She is?"
"Yes, she's married to Dad."
He looked pensive.

All discussing traffic disasters Friday afternoon and evening
on arrival. Margaret left New York at 10 a.m. and claims not
to have reached Long Island until 5 p.m. She was caught in a
traffic jam of such huge proportions that it began on Fifty-
seventh Street in Manhattan at the morning rush hour and was
bumper to bumper from there until the exit to Orient, Exit
70, the last stop.

I too experienced gridlock from Fifty-seventh Street in
Manhattan until Exit 70.

The love couple came in on the train. They had an "intimate
dinner" in the parlor car.

Mr. Underwood takes a hydrofoil, whatever that is. He is
the big cheese.

Vernon doesn't have to cope with the traffic disasters because, being retired, he never returns to Manhattan at all, remaining at Orient throughout the week in an ecstatic condition. Conducting the madcap revelries to which the elderly, I find, are often prone.

Margaret reminisced about her experience of traffic disasters. She had to go to the bathroom while trapped on the Long Island Expressway. She had to get out and go behind the guardrail. She cried.

Anne Collier dictated a letter to her mother.

Dear Mother,

I can't concentrate on anything because I am in love with Beeper LeMoyne.

The two youngest children here are my brother, Al; and a little girl next door. My brother Al loves the little girl but the little girl loves Speed Weed. But Speed Weed plays with Beeper LeMoyne.

I feel sorry for Thomas Underwood. He tried to run away.

I love Storey Collier. But Storey Collier loves Hobby Fox. Hobby Fox had to leave.

Love,
the late Anne Collier

After describing these torturous emotions, Anne Collier went out to seek her heart throb, Beeper LeMoyne.

"Hilary!" called Al to the baby. She fled.

I lay in an exhausted stupor while Al cavorted about me in a hyperbolic manner. But my love for the little fellow. And even his love for me.

"How did you get to be so cute, little fella?"

"Because we came to the train to pick you up!" he said.

Often Al actually took care of me, not the reverse. "Go to sleep," he said.

Al stood on the dock with his fishing pole, and then trudged home across the lawn—a poignant figure. Everyone is currently obsessed with fishing and spends hours at it, but has never caught a thing. Everyone is obsessed with things nautical—except the baby, who is immensely unconcerned with things nautical.

34.

MR. UNDERWOOD is planning to go into politics. That is why he keeps going on all those debates and panels on TV. He has made the announcement that he intends to run for Senator from New York.

In the middle of a comprehensive answer about tax laws and facts and figures on another panel, Mr. Underwood suddenly "lost his train of thought" again and said, "I'll pass," with an expression of perplexity. It happened right in the middle of his delivery, making a stunning effect. Or at least a startling one.

The main source of scandal in the town of Orient emanates from the liquor store. The town of Orient is very small, the main street containing a general store, a luncheonette, and a liquor store. Whoever is seen in the liquor store frequently is considered to be at the heart of the scandal, and the person mainly seen in the liquor store lately, or coming in and out of it, carrying heavy gallon jugs of vodka, is Mr. Underwood.

Yesterday his secretary called me up and said that Mr. Underwood wished to have lunch with me and arranged a time and a place. Needless to say, I was cowering in fear. The big cheese. Lunch with the big cheese? Why me? I thought it might be a demotion or getting fired. At the least I naturally assumed he had some specific thing in mind that he wished to discuss. But then on the appointed day—today—we went to lunch and he simply rambled on about a number of unconnected subjects, such as telling me his reminiscences, or sounding off about what burned him up (the trade deficit), and then it was over. The trade deficit was what burned him up the most. "I've had it with this trade deficit," etc. etc.—as if I had the slightest idea of what the trade deficit even is or was in some way connected with it—Mr. Underwood was obsessed with the trade deficit—slamming his fist on the table, practically tearing his hair out, etc.

Mr. Underwood was the type of person that would write sixteen-page letters to the President about the trade deficit. He would send copies to the Cabinet. Once he went to some dinner party at the White House where he tried to talk to the President about the trade deficit and later wrote an account of their conversation, ten pages, of which he sent copies to all members of the Cabinet. He had buttonholed the President, as he described it, to talk to him about the trade deficit. He asked the President if he had been reading his letters. He seemed crazed. The President wasn't listening. His mind wandered. He wasn't interested. Then Mr. Underwood looked at him and noticed he was wearing an unattractive brown suit. It looked as if he had slept in it, he said. He told the President that he didn't know how to dress. The President started calling, faintly, for help. Some Secret Service men came up and took him away. All this Mr. Underwood recorded in the crazed ten-page letter. "I've had it with this trade deficit," etc. etc.

Being with Mr. Underwood was hair-raising. That is the only way I can describe it.

Then he began to reminisce about when he was "in the nut house." I guess that kind of explains it all. According to Mr.

Underwood, he spent a good part of his youth in the looney bin. He loved to mention it, for some reason. It seemed to make him very happy. Then he talked about other things that burned him up. A lot of things burned him up.

A lot of things burned him up in sports, for one thing. In baseball. He followed of course the old New York team not the new one. He followed the droll quaint antiquated one, because he was an old-time New York person. Apparently the old teams in the older league are more like chaos. Each game of theirs is more like chaos because the hitters are sluggers and the pitching is bad and also the owners are more crazy and make snap decisions all the time and everyone hates them and they make too many trades. The sports channel on the radio, however, is centered around the other team, the new one. Favoring the new team as the sports channel does, they only have one person who covers the old New York team, and this person is the sole female announcer, for some reason. She is always at the breaking point, harried and upset. She can never get into the press box. She's always calling in from the pay phone in the bathroom or on some lonely corridor, filing her reports in despair. "Bob, I'm calling from the parking lot. I couldn't get into the stands. It's chaos here. We're in the third rain delay. We are trailing fifteen to nothing. I'm going to try to get into the press box. It's eleven o'clock. They've been playing since five, with the rain delays. And we're only at the bottom of the third. They just put in Bonano [relief pitcher] and as you know"—sigh of despair—"Whitey Hershfield [the owner] announced earlier today to the New York media that he has fired the manager." Etc. etc. in a long recital of disasters. But this is Mr. Underwood's team because it is the old-time New York team, and I have to say that the style of the old New York team seems to somewhat resemble the style of the New York *Examiner*.

. . .

The obligatory born-again Christian came up to me, outside the Godforsaken diner, this one snappily dressed in a blue serge suit and broad yellow tie, and began to harangue me. He had a jaunty step, as if he had just come out of an evangelist's tent at a circus fifty years ago in a small Southern town. He told me that unless I believed in Jesus Christ I could not be born again. "DO YOU HEAR ME?" he screamed. Oh, here it comes, I thought. Why do they always have to be so defensive, and make you feel like they're about to go insane on the spot or clobber you if you say the wrong thing? "Do You Hear What I Say? Don't look at me in that tone of voice!" he warned. That's a good one.

Then he degenerated. "Goddamnit, I believe in God!" he raved.

35. I LOOKED into Hobby's office.

The World Editor sat at his desk, at dusk, watching the lights go up on the city. He was alone in the office. He was responsible. He would have to work late. He looked out the window at the lights in the city. He reviewed his heart. Tortured messages from all over the world came in on his computer.

TO HOBBY. Fact One. Night falls in the desert. Fact Two. Famine to the South. Fact Three. Bombs in Baghdad. Fact Four. A city in flames. Fact Five. Trouble on all fronts. Copy to Underwood. What do you think? FROM CAIRO.

TO HOBBY. Trouble in Cairo. President under attack at reception. Bodyguard killed. Front-page story. [Long tortured analysis followed.] FROM CAIRO.

Hobby smoked a cigar, called his broker, read the baseball scores. If you had asked him his reaction to the job, he would have said that he was giving out a daily slice of world events, and tomorrow he would serve up another slice.

I was late in the office that day. I had the column. I was listening to the old gents on the sports channel reminiscing about the Brooklyn Dodgers and their old heroes, agonizing over their memories.

After listening to that for a while, I went by Hobby's office. He had his sad blue eyes. We both had magnificent restraint. We chatted for a few minutes. It was Friday night. I would go on to Orient. As I was leaving, he came around from his desk. "Here. Take this," he said. He slipped me a hundred-dollar bill. That was like old times. Some link to the past, some remembrance of his company and that of his family, his father. On occasion at their house years ago when his father was living, he would slip me one of the famous hundred-dollar bills. It touched my heart because I think it was his way of expressing emotions.

He pressed it into my hand. "Call it mad money."

Mad money. Sounds like something from another era, of cornballs, and men who call you "doll" and say they might get fresh, stuff like that, phrases from a black-and-white movie before I was born.

So I strolled home from the office. A light rain fell. The sky was a rinsed cobalt grey. Leaving the office with its name lit up dashingly in bare bulbs above the old arcade. At the news-stand, the tobacco store, the restaurant, on the way home, the music of a hundred cultures—Indian, Tunisian, Cuban, Puerto Rican—issued from the doorways of the neighborhood of the Grunewald.

Fire engines raved in the vicinity, sirens, chaos, madness—

the usual cacophony of sirens, fire engines, and car alarms—
and as I came closer, I found it all revolved around the Grunewald—whose street was roped off with a banner saying, Do
not approach within 20 feet of this truck, and there was a giant
sort of combination fire and police truck—policemen loitering
and finally, on my approach into the building, a procession of
firemen in their full regalia carrying a yellow hose came troop-
ing out—the elevator had been on fire. A comely homecom-
ing to the Grunewald!

A wino lunatic came into the elevator on the fourth floor.

"Greetings!" he remarked. "I'm on the last plane to Paki-
stan. See you in Baghdad. Good-bye, everyone!"

He exited on the fifth floor, after his brief appearance. No
one batted an eyelash, of course, in the elevator. Wino lunatics
were sometimes getting in the building, wandering around
from floor to floor. The tenants of the Grunewald often held
indignant meetings about it but could never seem to conquer
the problem.

It may sound a bit extreme. But they're not exactly wearing
top hats and tails in New York these days.

There was a truck parked permanently it seemed in front of
the Grunewald piled with steaming refuse being carted out of
the building by philosophical Southern black men every day.
One day I asked, "What is going on here? Is it an eviction?"

"Unfortunately, it's a demise," said one of the philosophical
black men working on the crew.

That kind of sums up the mood at the Grunewald.

I had a message at home from Mr. Underwood. It filled me
with nameless dread and anxiety. Why? Because if I feel I have
incurred his displeasure or disgust, then I am filled with nameless dread and anxiety.

Weird.

Often Mr. Underwood would call me into his office, taking me under his wing.

Before going in I would stop at the Godforsaken diner across the street, or the Sordid Café next door, to get ready.

His wife, the Charleston girl, with her high-society gaiety, was not much in evidence, either in New York or Orient. At that Southern hotel—that was different, on her own turf, in the South, amid the swaying palms or in the Magnolia Room. Perhaps in New York she secluded herself.

His office was adorned with pictures of her, in Southern settings, standing beside palms and oaks—mixed in with the photographs of prizefighters, baseball players, and other champions that also lined his walls. His love for the South, after all, that may have originated with his wife, and he had a soft spot for the Southerners, as I've said, including me.

"Why haven't I heard from you lately?" he said. "Speak up."

"I'm shy."

"I'm shy, too," he said.

Then he would get a phone call and say to me, "Close the door."

So I closed the door and he said into the phone, "I adore you."

"How is that column coming along?" he said to me when he hung up the phone. But he was not interested in the column. It is hard to say what he was interested in. It wasn't personal, it seemed. He played the 1940s New York lunatic who looked like Central Casting had just sent him over. However, it was personal to the extent that I think I was somehow a reminder to him of Constant. Who was never present, but was constant in my heart. With my father, those gents from another era, who stood for a courtliness that did not exist in New York that Mr. Underwood dreamt of. "Now what seems to be the trouble?" he said. "Why haven't I heard from you lately? Do you have any problems?"

"Well . . . I guess I have a few problems."

"What are they?"

"Well . . . a friend of mine, actually a member of my family, has a serious drinking problem, for one thing," I said.

"Everyone has that problem, babe! A lot of people have drinking problems," he said blissfully. It seemed to make him very happy.

"Oh. Well, another problem is . . . love. Boy, girl."

"Well, kid, that's a lifelong problem."

"Sometimes it feels like I'm losing control," I ventured.

"Kid, everyone loses control. You can't keep control."

Then he lapsed into silence, just staring at me in dead silence. We brooded silently.

"You eat like a bird, kid," he said. "Whaddya, a bird? You eat like a bird?"

After another lengthy silence—the Latin American Dictator routine—his feet up on the desk, smoking a cigar, staring at you in dead silence—I said I would take my departure.

"No, no, don't leave me, don't leave, kid, just sit there and be quiet." He gave me a book to read.

"Now come on out with me and I'll put you on the bus." We walked to Fifth Avenue. We went to Brooks Brothers to exchange a tie for his small troubled son. "How many children do you have?" I asked.

"One. One living. Had two."

Perhaps it explained a lot.

He took me to the bus stop. Then he ran into an acquaintance. "I was at the office today," he said to her, "and who do I see skulking down the hall? A certain someone who is betrothed to you."

After exchanging pleasantries the acquaintance moved along. "A lot of people know me in this town, kid," he said.

"Now, are you all right? Have you eaten? Will someone take care of you?"

It was not the case and he divined it. He said I did not eat right and he did not know what made me tick. He offered to take me to the grocery store. He was crashingly handsome. He wasn't a flirt—as a Southerner would be, I think. Like even Constant, he couldn't help it, he just had a drawling, jocular, flirtatious way of dealing with you, courtly, you might say. But there wasn't an ounce of that in Mr. Underwood. An interesting difference.

He put me in a taxicab. "Now go out and have some fun, kid. That's an order."

The taxi driver said, after we drove on, "Was that man your father?"

"No, he's my boss."

"He's looking out for you."

And as I looked back at the bright lights of Broadway, and the landmarks of Forty-fourth Street, the Rialto, the Barry-more, and the New York *Examiner,* I thought, Jeez, this town's getting under my skin.

Across the street from Pennsylvania Station on Eighth Avenue was the all-night Post Office with its grandiose Corinthian columns and the legend NEITHER SNOW NOR RAIN NOR HEAT NOR GLOOM OF NIGHT STAYS THESE COURIERS FROM THE SWIFT COMPLETION OF THEIR APPOINTED ROUNDS, which arrested my attention. Thinking lewd thoughts in the Post Office, for some reason, and of the ancients, virtue, courage, love.

Then I sweltered through the summer crowds to Orient.

36.
THE ELDERLY are closeted in their rooms drinking vodka, a ritual which they practice religiously every evening beginning at five o'clock. Elegantly attired, im-

maculately coiffed and groomed, white gloves, black sunglasses, dapper, dark, and glamorous. The atmosphere in which they exist is sumptuous. Often they discuss their ailments. But in a strangely debonair yet somewhat feebleminded manner. Maybe they are just being gallant. It is hard to say. But they represent to me a courtly world. I am enraptured by their glamour. They are the glamour element at the enclave, even at their age.

"How is Batty?" inquired Mr. Collier.

"Don't you remember we had a conversation about him today?"

"We did?"

"He's not well at all."

"It comes back to me now."

"Grace told me. She claims to be his sister."

"She *is* his sister. Sully is his brother."

"Do you believe all that?"

"He has a wife?"

"No, he has *my* wife."

"Suited to his heart, eh? Let him rejoice in her."

"He already has a wife."

"But he didn't get along too well with *her.*"

"He keepeth my wife, the darling of my heart."

"What you say about her isn't very nice."

"What did I say?"

"You've forgotten?"

"How's that?"

"You've forgotten," he said, plainly triumphant.

"My dear, I don't know if you plan to live as long as I have, but I don't advise it. I am ninety-eight, and I go nowhere. And, my dear, if I go somewhere, I don't even know where I am."

Thus they continue their strangely debonair yet feeble-

minded conversations, Mrs. Legendre in the background with
her cigarette voice, wearing black sunglasses though it was
night, glamorous, chain-smoking, etc.

"Well, babe, are you ready for this, kiddo? It's congestive
heart failure!" she said in her jazzy way, imparting new information on Batty's condition. She always talks in a jazzy way
as if she were about to give a party. Always she has been so.
In New Orleans in her day every afternoon at five the women
would put on dressing gowns and start drinking cocktails until
dinner, having profoundly animated discussions about how to
hang curtains or fix the oyster stew. Mrs. Legendre's husband
was then in India—womanizing?—they were often separated
—and the wildly crestfallen expression that came to be im-
posed upon the beauty of her face had even then begun to
show—theirs was a stormy marriage. She had a defiant gaiety,
a jazzy way of talking, calling everyone "sweetheart" and
"baby doll" and "precious," playing jazz records with screaming saxophones, a glamour girl.

The white-haired gents were sitting in a row, with the devil
in their eyes, with their baggy khaki pants but cutting handsome figures for an athlete's grace is seen, even in these white-
haired gents, sitting together talking incessantly, conducting
their feeble-minded or incomprehensible conversations.

Batty Legendre, the subject of discussion, was standing outside of his house in Bermuda shorts holding his rifle—for
some reason—and screaming to his sister, Grace Fox, four
houses down, "GRACIE. BABY! DID YOU HEAR WHAT THE
DOCTOR SAID?"

"I think we were just discussing it."

"Yes, and there was something I wanted to show you. But
I forgot what."

"You've forgotten?"

"What's that? Eh?"

"Forget it."

"I've already forgotten, my dear."

"Well, good night."

"What's that? Eh?"

"GOOD NIGHT."

37.

"I'VE BEEN MARRIED to that girl for forty years and I've only seen her pass out from liquor once," said Mr. Collier, looking at his wife. "That was forty years ago, at my cousin's wedding, from champagne. She hasn't touched it since."

The elderly were sitting in the garden. Not all were as abstinent as Mrs. Collier. Batty Legendre sat in his wheelchair with a portable bar and ashtray attached to it, chain-smoking, drinking his head off. Actually he had two seizures at the party. Later he called from his car phone.

Everyone at the party suddenly turned to me to tell long-drawn-out tales of their family divisions. Mrs. Collier later described it as "harrowing."

"There are a lot of nuts in the world," she says, "and it's hard to separate the nuts from the non-nuts. But now there's this whole influx of new nuts who you can't screen and protect yourself from."

A penetrating old girl.

"He's going to pieces," observed Mrs. Collier, as we watched Mr. Underwood's strange performance on the latest TV panel. "His hair looks funny," she continued. Actually it was true his hair looked sort of messed-up on the TV panel and was sticking up in tufts. "He looks very peculiar," she said darkly. "He's going to pieces," she repeated.

"You think everyone is going to pieces," I commented.

"Storey, darling, he's a doomed person. Anyone can see that," she said.

"You think everyone is a doomed person," I said.

"Storey, darling, do you want to be like Cousin Malcolm?" she inquired. A silence ensued. This was a conversation stopper.

Cousin Malcolm sat in the lobby of the Hummingbird Hotel in New Orleans all day and lined up outside the Ozonam Inn, where wino lunatics got bread from a priest. In short, Cousin Malcolm was a wino lunatic.

Mr. Collier chuckled softly. "Cousin Malcolm is a little unreliable," he said. It was the first time I had ever heard him say anything bad about anyone. Vague optimism was Mr. Collier's credo.

His wife's was the opposite. She regarded me tragically.

"Aren't you even going to use a coaster?" she asked, in despair.

"A coaster?"

"A coaster for your drink," she said, her eyes boring into mine, as though if you didn't use a coaster for your drink you might as well go out and blow your head off. Like it's a huge gigantic tragedy if you don't use a coaster. Like it was the most huge tragedy she could think of. She sat staring at me penetratingly, as though if you didn't use a coaster you were right in line to be the second Cousin Malcolm.

"Storey, darling, this playgirl life you lead . . ." she pleaded.

"What playgirl life?"

"Pass the salt for Chrissake," screamed Mr. Underwood, who had appeared and seated himself at their luncheon table.

It was New York big-cheese parlance.

"Ha ha, that's grand," said Batty Legendre, confined to his

wheelchair after the accident. "Just grand." He polished off his Bourbon old-fashioned.

"What are your feelings about these rugs?" I said to Mrs. Collier regarding some floorwear I picked up at the local emporium to enliven my place of residence in New York.

"Storey, darling, that rug," said Mrs. Collier, pointing, "that rug says 'I Believe in You.' "

"What? I Believe in You? You mean *you* believe in me, or what?"

Hobby and his pal Mr. Collier walked up.

"What do you think of this rug?" I asked them.

"*These* rugs, you mean," said Mrs. Collier. "You have to choose between *these* rugs."

"Okay. *These* rugs. What are your feelings about these rugs?"

"This rug has more motion," said Hobby, pointing to the left.

"More emotions, right," said Mr. Collier, puffing on his cigar. "That's very true. This rug has more emotions."

"But—"

"More emotions," said Mr. Collier, tipping his ashes. "But the other rug is more sincere."

"Sincere?"

"This other rug is immature," said Hobby. "It may be sincere, but it's immature. The other rug says, 'I've been around, and I've seen something of life. I know something of life.' "

"I can't believe you're getting all that from these rugs," I said. "I mean I can't believe you can get all this out of a rug."

"*These* rugs. Not *a* rug."

"Okay okay. *These* rugs."

"Storey, will you marry me?" said Al.

"Ally, sugar, I'm too old for you."

My little Al, though, understands everything. He has a thorough understanding of other people's sorrows and concerns. "When you're sad I'll keep an eye on you," he said. "Don't go in the street, Storey. You might get run over. Stand near to me, Storey." Also, he is shy and studious, as when he reads quietly in bed. Brainy. That kid is brainy. "I have to calm myself," he said. It was bedtime. "Now, Storey, it's your turn to try to calm me down. Others have tried, and now it's your turn. I have to calm myself."

"I LOVE YOU," Al screamed, at the dinner table.
"God, he is sweet," said Hobby, smoking his cigar.
"I LOVE YOU TOO," Al screamed.
A veritable bath of emotion.
"I love you, Storey," he said at a normal decibel level. "Don't move. I'll be right back." He toddled off.

After dinner Mr. Collier showed us the perplexing "key lot" bordering on Grace's property, behind the enclave. It was a thing we had ceaselessly studied, because it mystified or fascinated Mr. Collier. As he too was getting on in years, like some other members of our party, I did not know exactly if he had forgotten how many times he had discussed it with us, or simply found it so fascinating that he could never look at it enough.

The "key lot" was actually bordered by four different pieces of property, except the puzzling key lot did not belong to any of the four owners. It was a ceaseless mystery to Mr. Collier.

We stood in feigned bewilderment and wonder, marveling at the key lot. Gazing at it. Being fascinated by it. Hypnotized. I don't know. Mainly gazing at it.

A lost-looking couple idled by. They stopped.
"May we help you?" said Mr. Collier.
"We're looking for Adrian."
"Adrian?"

"Thomas Underwood is having a birthday party and there's supposed to be a trampoline around here somewhere for the children."

"Where's Adrian?" said Mr. Collier.

"Well, that's what we want to know."

`"Sorry. Haven't seen her."

We walked back to the house.

George Collier, Speed Weed, and Beeper LeMoyne were in the garden.

"Where's Adrian?" said Mr. Collier to the little boys.

Speed Weed offered a shrug.

"What have you done with Adrian?" said Mr. Collier.

The lost-looking couple followed forlornly at a suitable distance, looking sheepish.

In a corner of the lawn, Mr. Underwood was unsuccessfully trying to discipline his small son. There was no sign of a trampoline. Mr. Underwood was wearing an apron with a martini shaker and a daisy embroidered on the front, making him an object of ridicule, and saying in a dazed monotone to his small son, who stood aloof and aimless on the lawn, "Help Daddy. Come here, son. Help Daddy with the hose."

Mr. Underwood ducked awkwardly through some bushes at the corner of the lawn, trying to gain access to the child, who stood with the same unruffled demeanor next to a hedge, regarding his father thoughtfully. He held the end of the hose in the recesses of his mouth.

"Come to Daddy, son," the poor fellow said in his monotone, awkwardly grabbing through the bushes for the child— who then withdrew.

"What say, old man," Mr. Collier said to Mr. Underwood. "Where's Adrian?"

"Who's Adrian?"

"What have you done with Adrian?" said Mr. Collier.

"Who is she?"

"That's what we want to know. What have you done with her?"

Mr. Collier bent down and regarded Mr. Underwood's small troubled son, seated on a knoll. "What have you done with Adrian, you rascal?" he said to the child. The child was overtaken with a sudden fit of mirth. "That man is crazy," the child said to his father, pointing at Mr. Collier. Mr. Collier regarded him solemnly. He puffed on his cigar.

Mr. Collier was in a sort of fog—that was his personality.

Mr. Collier was well versed in a wide variety of esoteric subjects, but was completely in the dark when it came to the modern conveyances of ordinary life. If you took a walk with him, for instance, something deadeningly ordinary would seize his interest every few paces, such as a car, and he would take out a notepad and start making notes—a garden, a tree, a little boy, a car, whatever it was would stop him in his tracks for at least five minutes while he puffed on his cigar, taking it in.

"This is a driveway," he commented, looking at same. "I've never seen a driveway like that. Is that a driveway?"

"That is a driveway," I confirmed.

"That is a driveway," he mused, and puffed on his cigar.

Mr. Collier stopped slowly at a hedge, to ponder it. To regard the hedge. To study the dendrology. To see if the hedge was blooming. To note the progress of the hedge.

He proceeded to the bay. There he regarded the water with a look of great concentration. He was studying the tides.

The sea rises and falls during the tide with a variable rate. You can calculate the height of the tide at any time by using the tide .tables and applying the rule of twelfths. It takes roughly six hours for the tide to come in and six hours to go out. When the tide is coming in, the water rises, in the first hour, one-twelfth of the total marnage; in the second hour two-twelfths, and so on, as Mr. Collier duly noted.

He was a man driven beyond endurance, I believe, by the sorrows of life, though you would not know it on the surface, for his dignity and calmness. But since he had lost a son, I believe that he sought desperately, in the tides, the dendrology, and be it what it may, to solve the mystery of life.

Mr. Collier procured a supply of his beloved Havana cigars in Europe. He gave Hobby a small supply. In return, Hobby went to the Seven-Eleven and purchased for Mr. Collier a novelty item called Slime, as a joke. It was a rubber-like green liquid-like substance in a plastic jar. Sure enough, this offering seemed to hit the spot with Mr. Collier. It seemed to endlessly fascinate him. What is it? he wants to know. Mr. Collier didn't keep up with anything modern or with contemporary consumer products, like Slime. "Let's fry some," said Mr. Collier, "and see what happens to it." He came into the kitchen with his beloved Slime and said, "Let's test it," and poured it out onto the table. Meanwhile Hobby looked on, stalwart, expressionless, trying not to smile (reminds me of the baseball players when they get a home run), as they puffed on their cigars.

"Why do you think it is," I said, "that men show less Feelings and Emotions, less than women, or mainly, that men don't like to discuss Feelings and Emotions?" I asked the two deadpan fellows. "Men don't like communication," I said.

"Well, what about you, old man?" said Mr. Collier to Hobby. "Do you like communication?"

Hobby looked doubtful.

"He can take it or leave it," said Mr. Collier, happily, and went back to testing his Slime.

"Louis, you're such a nut," said Mrs. Collier. Mr. Collier

was a nut, it could not be denied, as his wife was frequently known to observe. Also my father was a nut, but they were very different kinds of nuts. The differences between my father and his brother were as I say quite wide. Mr. Collier often went on lengthy European trips and had obscure, pedantic interests. Whereas his brother's chief haunt was the Mississippi Delta, or the Bayou Barataria Duck Club. But one thing they had in common was the stony grandeur that they came from, of the Collier family in New Orleans.

The brothers were noted for their brains though also for their eccentricity, of which both were the source of wide remark. One might wonder how they got any work done, considering the wide and rather quixotic exchange of memos that took place between them in the office.

"In preparation for going to Lafayette today," wrote Mr. Collier to his brother—sitting in the next office—"I was reluctant to get my trousers wet walking to and from the Whitney Building. Accordingly, I parked in the Place St. Charles garage, entering a few minutes before nine, and it took approximately six minutes to get to Gravier Street from a parking spot on the tenth floor."

Several days later—a mysterious time lapse—the response: "I am sure you are correct. I have taken to parking in the Place St. Charles garage when I have to come down on Sundays, because (1) It is free, and (2) You can always get a space on the first floor. P.S. May I remind you, that in response to your inquiry on Sunday the 3rd about whether or not there were ever palm trees next to the swan boat in Audubon Park, the answer is No."

To make a conservative estimate, ten memos on similarly less than earth-shattering subjects shot back and forth per day between the brothers, sometimes with the time lapse in terms of chronological answers. Together, they tackled many subjects. My father did not know much about many of his brother's interests, such as the Partial Diluvian Heresy, for example, whatever that is, in which Mr. Collier took an interest bordering on obsession; but on the other hand, my father was able to fill him in on the many subjects of a modern consumer-type nature of which Mr. Collier was completely in the dark. As I said, one might wonder how they got any work done, considering the wide exchange of memos and Mr. Collier's heavy files on esoteric subjects. But the answer is simple. They were brainy. Plus, they adhered to a rigid routine of work at the office involving a nine-to-five day on Saturday as a matter of course, sometimes also spending Sunday afternoon there. It was as if the law was easy to them, but the memos and the ceaseless particulars of life were not.

Once I came upon Mr. Collier in his office conducting an elaborate procedure for gaining the exact time. Other people would look at a clock for this purpose. There was a box of static on his windowsill—a small black box emitting static and, every so often, the remote sound of a bell. Mr. Collier would take out his pocket watch when the bell occurred, then take out a file, listen for the bell, and then mark it in his file.

"Don't you think that's taking it a bit far?" I said. "You're certainly living up to your reputation as an eccentric."

"You have to keep time," he defended himself.

"But not like that!"

"Girls today are so casual," he remarked, in his deadpan.

His files were on pedantic subjects often related to theology, such as the Partial Diluvian Heresy or Bilocation Miracles. His interest in theology was perhaps his most pressing interest. It was a little odd since unlike Constant Fox, who had such faith, Mr. Collier's interest in religion seemed purely pedantic. Perhaps it was a cover for his faith.

In Orient he would set up his desk after dinner while everyone else ceaselessly socialized and fell apart, and start smoking
cigars and studying obscure church statistics. Maybe that was
his version of falling apart. Though it was actually his method
of holding himself together. Others of his files were similar,
including Patriarchs of Babylon, Occasions of Sin, and The
Meaning of Life.

In the afternoon he set up a card table on the lawn and
studied his beloved ancient Greek.

I used to go to his Greek class sometimes in New Orleans.
Walking through the night was very stunning, with the palms
and oaks and architecture, and the air was sweet, being sometimes less humid. You crossed the Avenue and walked
through the Catholic quadrangles and something in the evening and the night was stunning there, and as ever the peace
and quietude, among the green, as compared to New York.
Mr. Collier's tutor in ancient Greek, Father Boudreaux, was a
Jesuit priest, and the class was held at the university attached
to his quarters. "Child of grace," he would call me. "Good
evening, child of grace." "But, child of grace, don't you
see . . ." if discussing some point of religion. Father Boudreaux would be sitting on a quiet bench alone in the evening
contemplating a nearby spire, Mr. Collier would come strolling down the walk in his olive-drab suit and bow tie. Father
Boudreaux commented there was a certain breeze at that hour
of the evening, which he chose for contemplation. Mr. Collier
arrived, cigar in hand, the two men, the quietude, the peace,
the sweetness of the setting, walking through the sweet black
night. It was a Godly place. With scenes of arresting beauty,
the green Avenue, the huge palms in the night with a slight
chill in the air when it was less humid. You could always see
the moon.

Their study was called Rhapsody, for a Rhapsode is a person

who can recite the entirety of Homer in the ancient Greek. Father Boudreaux took a more abstract view, but Mr. Collier aimed to be a Rhapsode. Once Mr. Collier heard of a man in Europe who was also a Rhapsode. Mr. Collier tracked the man down and wrote him a letter. They commenced an ardent correspondence. The man had committed to memory the first fifteen books of the *Odyssey,* which took him seventy hours to recite. He said it would take him forty-five years to memorize the rest. He wrote to Mr. Collier in a piteous scrawl, "Could you please next time remember to send me a copy of your forthcoming term paper on the Phalaecean and other hendecasyllabic meters, if convenient to you?"

Mr. Collier of course was all too willing to comply. So they conducted their unintelligible correspondence in their childlike scrawls.

The Rhapsode from Europe always calculated things down to the exact fraction, for instance, he never mentioned 70 lines of Homer, he memorized 72.5 lines; to calculate the time it would take him to publicly recite, according to the speed of his hexameter, it would take him 32.75 hours, etc. etc.

At last they met—in person, I mean. The Rhapsode came to America for the express purpose of meeting his beloved Mr. Collier and Mr. Collier's tutor, Father Boudreaux.

The Rhapsode's name was J. P. S. Smith, originally of Arlington, Massachusetts. Rhapsode Smith, they called him.

The Rhapsode said that he had become interested in Rhapsody through the mellifluous recitation of a drunken miller, but Mr. Collier through that of a very sober priest.

It developed that there was yet another Rhapsode living in the world today. He was a professor at Harvard University, and hearing of the Rhapsodes in New Orleans, the professor, unable to control his native professorial impulses, compiled a lengthy and elaborate exam for what he believed to be the wayward if enthusiastic Rhapsodes in New Orleans, to test them on their true knowledge.

Mr. Collier, Rhapsode Smith, and Father Boudreaux took the test and promptly sent their copies back to the professor to be graded. Then in turn he sent back the graded tests. Study of the graded tests occupied at least three full nights of emotional outpourings and protests.

"Not only were her knees loosened, but her heart was loosened," translated Mr. Collier, studying the graded test. "That's a zunga."

"How could it be?" said Rhapsode Smith.

"He thinks it's dative," said Mr. Collier with unutterable scorn.

"He's wrong, of course," agreed Rhapsode Smith.

"It's a trap to catch the unwary," quoted Father Boudreaux.

"It certainly caught *him,*" said Mr. Collier.

"Let's protest," said Rhapsode Smith.

"Oh, certainly," said Mr. Collier. "And look at this." He pointed to another question on the test. "He thinks that's genufactive." Hilarity ensued. A good joke was had all around.

"I protest Question Three," said Rhapsode Smith.

"What would the second person imperfect middle be?"

"It's imperfect."

"I can't support that."

"It's an asthigmatic."

"He thinks it's dative."

"Do you agree with that?"

"No, I do not."

"Should we protest?"

"It's a majority protest. Not a unanimous protest. The Father doesn't protest."

"Okay, I'll protest that," said the Father.

"I would never have thought that would be a contracted disjunctive zunga," said Mr. Collier. "Maybe he's right."

"He can't be right," said Rhapsode Smith.

"That can be settled, gentlemen, outside of class," said Mr. Collier.

"By a duel, of course," chuckled Father Boudreaux.

"I protest," said Rhapsode Smith.

"Does everyone agree that this is a disjunctive zunga?"

"Not everyone," said Rhapsode Smith morosely.

"Well then, let's protest," said Mr. Collier.

"It's not a majority protest," said Father Boudreaux.

"I think we should protest," said Rhapsode Smith.

"I disagree," said Father Boudreaux.

"I protest to this," said Rhapsode Smith.

"But we don't want to protest everything," said Mr. Collier. "He'll think we're cranks."

Cranks, eh. How could he think that, I wonder? Jeez. I can only wonder what the Harvard professor's attitude was to the small protesting band of Rhapsodes in New Orleans.

Father Boudreaux found Rhapsode Smith to be disrespectful. His hexameter was shockingly abrupt. Its speed was grossly fast.

"Test me on any hapax," said the Rhapsode. "Any hapax in the *Odyssey* at all."

"We'll have to test him on his hapaxes," whispered Mr. Collier to Father Boudreaux dolefully when they met for weekly lunch.

Sometimes I would see the three men in the elevator arguing in ancient Greek, heckling each other over their hapaxes.

The last time I went to Greek class, they were translating Pericles. It was a passage pertaining to gratitude. "Gratitude is a noble emotion," I said, contending with Pericles.

"That's because you have a clean soul," said Mr. Collier.

The remarkable thing was that such a man had produced such a son as Claude Collier. I mean that a man with such pedantic, cerebral interests, with such a stern conception of innocence, had bred such a wild-hearted boy.

But I was impressed by Claude's frailties. That he was a failure at this moment, couldn't make a go of his business ventures, or whatever else he tried, and drank. Alcohol was the worst of his frailties to me. But his children idolized him. They were too young to understand his troubles. They were spending the summer away from their parents but they did not know the cause. Mr. and Mrs. Collier had had to struggle, at various times, to keep the marriage of Claude and his wife together. It was a wild scene, a town in a haze of alcohol— New Orleans—but the Colliers had an odd formality, emanating from Mr. Collier in that branch of the family, a stony dignity, an ordered household, even amid Claude's troubles. These things were kept strictly apart from the children, as witnessed by their total removal from the scene, to Orient.

What the children felt in their hearts, I cannot say. But I guess it is possible that in a case like this one, the children notice at a young age that one or both of their parents seem to be traumatized, or troubled, or upset in some way frequently, and that they take on a sense of responsibility for them, even at their young age, instead of the customary reverse, and they acquire a strange sixth sense of noticing suffering or trouble, and the wish to comfort the sufferer. I think this explains Al's courtly behavior, even at the age of three, his frequent desire to take responsibility for others, his consideration for them, and wish to console them.

38.
AL AND I were sitting in the sandbox. The sandbox had a crack in it that bothered him, and he washed it with a hose.

"Why does it bother you, Al?" I asked.

"Because it's so pathetic."

I didn't realize his compassion extended to inanimate objects. But he did have a pity emanating from his heart, which reminded me of all the great men I have known. It reminded me of Constant, of whom I always had thought this: not only is it rare in life to make what is called an actual "connection" with a person in the first place, but for that person to be essentially kind, so kind as to notice and seek out a sufferer, or someone in trouble, and then extend to him his aid, seems to me the most hopeful thing I can think of in life, and of course, also the most rare.

Al's thoughts turned similarly often toward others, to a remarkable degree. "Hobby could get your life in order, Storey," he mused.

"But, Al, there's problems."

"Then you can marry with me, Storey," he said, "and I'll get your life in order. And we can live on Mars," he added, bright-eyed.

I called him "doll" and he said, "I'm not a doll, Storey," and I explained that it was a turn of phrase or a term of endearment and that Constant for example always called me "doll," and as Al understands everything, he then said, "Constant is a doll." Because he understands everything—including my love for Constant—whom he met once, but once, and Al was one at the time. "I love him very much," I said, and shed another tear. "Don't cry," said Al. "You love Hobby and Hobby is a doll also. It's all right, my dear. Don't be sad." And that he calls me "my dear"? Lord knows where he got that from. The Southern contingent, no doubt.

Talking to a three-year-old who has the grasp of the English language and of understanding that he does is of course an unusual experience. His thoughts are very pure. A very gallant little fellow. A definite Collier. My little one, my heart.

39. THERE IS a biographer of Constant hang-
ing around the enclave asking us questions. The biographer
has sex on the brain. I mean he keeps trying to give sex inter-
pretations of Constant. No doubt he reads his Bible. Desire is
the tree of life. It must be odd for the biographers, talking to
people who know Constant. For when a man is distinguished
by great accomplishments, I find he does not often have much
personality left over for his personal life, and it seems to me
rare that a man could be great in his accomplishments and also
great in his personal life, so much beloved as a character. But
with Constant, he was of course the type of person that, even
if you only met him once for an hour, you would remember
for the rest of your life. And I of course am the type of person
who treasures the mere examples of his handwriting when she
gets his letters, and packs them if she goes on a trip. People in
life will often tell you not to have hero worship. Don't let
them. If you worship the ground someone walks on, then go
ahead and do so. People will constantly tell you not to. Don't
let them. It is the world's dark magic, which as I have concluded, is the only thing. He was an overpowering thing in
my life, but one could do worse than to have an overpowering
thing in one's life.

40. I RECEIVED the following mysterious if remarkable missive from Al, dictated yesterday.

Dear Storey,
When I woke up this morning I thought about being in
your life. I wanted to send you three postcards from my
book. I slept with my book to be ready to do this in the
morning, but it slipped off the bed and onto the floor but

I found it. I love you, Storey. I would like to be invited to your house when it's your birthday to eat some cake. I would like you to buy some balloons. I can play with them when I am outside your house at the sea. I want to be in your life. Because I want to visit your life. Carousel. Merry-go-round. The sea is in Storey's life. That's it, my dear.

Dad used to go out dancing. He danced so hard that he cried. He danced so kindly that he cried.

Start out with love, dear Storey. That's all of what I wanted to say, because it's the most important thing. I want you to buy a cake.

Love,
Ally

This rambling discourse he delivered to me by hand, with a look of Collier-like concentration and concern, adding, "I think you should move to New Orleans, Storey. Because I know how much you like to ride the streetcar. And if you are sad, we will rescue you.

"I want to be in your life," he keeps saying. "Are you in Dad's life?" I asked him. "No, I'm in *my* life," he said. "He's in *his* life. But I want you in *my* life."

This kid is like some sort of world leader.

It seems I am spending my time with the very old and the very young, with nothing in between. Not that I have anything against the very old and the very young, on the contrary, I find them beloved, beloved and closer to God.

41. GEORGE COLLIER was writing a book of essays, *History and Its Heroes*. At the time, his hero was Ulysses S. Grant, and George had personally given himself the middle

name of Ulysses. George Ulysses Collier. Thus be began his
new tome.

History and Its Heroes
By George Ulysses Collier
Chapter One

Robert E. Lee

Robert E. Lee, so noble, so brave, facing North to
ward off invaders. We all can learn from his great life. A
hero, real, was he. There has no greater ever lived than
Robert Edward Lee.

The Civil War seemed to be a theme in the family. It was a
theme in the family.

In her desperate bid to be as noble as her older brother, Anne
Collier composed her version of the historical events.

History and Its Heroes
by the late Anne Collier

History has had many heroes. I found a butterfly. I asked
my grandmother if I could call up Chester and ask him
did he see my butterfly. She said I could but I said, What
if he's not at home. But she said if he wasn't at home,
then no one would answer.

THE END

Her conception of the events was as yet a little sketchy. The
mind of a four-year-old finds it difficult to concentrate on the
phases of history.

42. ANNE COLLIER DICTATED her daily letter to her mother.

Dear Mother,
    I wrote a poem because George said it would be noble.
        I had a little Christmas tree,
        It was so very little,
        I sent it to the market
        To buy a pound of fiddle.

        It was so very green, my dear.
        I ate a fig newton.

Love,
the late Anne Collier

43.

My Grandfather
by George Ulysses Collier

My grandfather is a nice man. He taught me how to go crabbing on Bayou Barataria. In New Orleans they have a thing called crabbing. My grandfather teaches the most sporting method, because he says it gives the crab a sporting chance.

44. I TOOK the ferry to Prudence Island with Margaret to hear the black jazz singer at the American Hotel. Margaret cried. I would cry too if I were Margaret and my life was such a ceaseless series of nautical disasters. Or if life ran

as high in me, perhaps, as it does in Margaret. Or if my
life depended from one nautical crisis to the next, and I was
constantly dancing my heart out in bars or getting in fistfights, etc.

The past two days the weather has been sweet, mild, and
balmy, like old New Orleans, among the green leaves, the
rustling of the leaves, at night. I had many visions. Amid the
clink of glasses and martini shakers. Also amid the bloodcurdling shrieks of the children now emanating from the garden.

"Wait for me, George. Wait for the little boy who loves
you," Al called to his brother. "Because I love you, George."

I went to the soul nightclub in Orient with Cedric. He
bugged me.

But of course that's not exactly news. That's not exactly
headline news. That's not exactly surprising. That's yesterday's news. The soul nightclub was good because it was humble, pure, unpretentious, the real thing, the true thing,
completely uncorrupted.

Here is the difference between Cedric and me. We were
discussing the sand bars of Florida. The sand bars of Florida
are these bars with sand on the floors and open to the sky that
frats, squares, and other Southern jocks who are square go to.
These are the type of people whose attire and demeanor describe a time whose moment has since passed—kind of like
Mr. Joviality. They describe an era of madras pants and pink
shirts and jukeboxes with songs from the sixties. In certain
pockets of the South this type is often found, comprising a
sort of time-warped gentility. In the North I have discovered
that this type also can be found—at Princeton football games.
But that is neither here nor there. Cedric said that he came to
New York because he didn't want to spend his life going to
sand bars in Florida populated by frats, squares, and people

with frosted hair. But Cedric is wrong to think he is any better than squares in sand bars in Florida. I wish I were at a sand bar in Florida right now. Why? Because then I wouldn't be too grand. I wouldn't think I was too grand.

As I sat in my Lonely Splendor, I began to be alienated from my very self. Personality, memory, regret—alienation—these are my themes. I was thinking it might be a good time to write my column, since Mr. Joviality, the only other person around, had gone to the South Fork with his friend to a party. But then I began to be alienated from my very self. So it's a good thing Margaret decided to take the boat out to watch the fireworks at Prudence Island. I might have thought twice since it was Margaret. I was right to worry. We got lost. The night was black after the fireworks and we entered many coves thinking each was ours and none was. Unfortunately it looked as though we had drifted to the other side of that slender riotous island that lies east of New York and might be floating out to the Atlantic Ocean.

However let me start from the beginning, when we drove down the boat canal toward Prudence Island. The bay was filled with speedboats gliding past, the harbor looked like Monte Carlo. It was unspeakably glamorous, the night, the boats. Margaret said this was why Gatsby had that green light —when we got lost. If we had had that green light it would have saved us. But the night, the moon, I love the sea—it was unspeakably beautiful, with a Northern chill in the air. Then the boaters in the night were courtly not Yankeefied and helped us find our way.

Vernon and Batty Legendre invited me to take a turn with them after dinner across the garden to have a nightcap at Vernon's sunken bar, which is a thing that he built into his house. Vernon fell asleep, as is his wont, and Mr. Legendre sat staring in a dazed manner at the fire. Mr. Underwood came by and also sank into a daze. Mr. Legendre sat brooding silently into the fire, perhaps thinking of past conquests, brooding. I sat with my nightcap wondering how it would be proper to conduct myself. I decided it would be most proper to brood silently. I mean being as there the old gents were, silent as tombs, brooding on their past misdeeds or something. Vernon suddenly awoke and made some flirtatious comments to me. Then he lapsed into a stupor. Mr. Legendre continued to stare menacingly into the fire thinking about his amorous conquests. Eighty and still flirting. How it breaks my heart.

45. THE ENCLAVE is enflamed with illness. Everyone is beset by physical ailments. Little wonder, what with the complaints of the elderly, no doubt exacerbated by their alcoholic intake and late hours.

I too am beset by a dazzling array of physical ailments.

The house is deserted. I watched *The Best years of Our Lives* —I have a fascination with Myrna Loy. She always is so knowing, and always such an elegant wife. She always is so knowing about the flaws of her husband. Yet she loves him dearly. He ought to get off the sauce, though, see. And by the way, if those are the best years of our lives, please give me the worst ones right away.

"I want to kiss a Chiquita banana," said Al.

"What's that supposed to mean, mister?"

"I want to kiss a Chiquita banana," he inexplicably repeats. "I'm from Brazil where the nuts come from," he said.

Hey, I get it—he's been watching those Carmen Miranda movies I rented. Well, I guess it can't hurt him. It's better than *My Little Pony,* the children's video I had to watch with him seventeen times in a row. I've memorized the sound track.

I guess Carmen Miranda's okay—unless he gets a complex that everyone ordinarily goes around with huge bananas on their heads.

There was nothing to do so I watched *Born to Dance* and *Wife vs. Secretary* on TV. The latter haunted me, because neither the wife nor the secretary had any personality. It haunted me because I don't have any personality either. Where is my personality? This is the Big Problem. Myrna Loy had a bit more personality than Jean Harlow but Jean Harlow had no personality. That was too bad. She was accommodating and that was all. She never made a single wisecrack. Who wrote the script? Then in Havana (a torrid plot twist) the moment came when, even in this Hollywood of the 1930s, they had the opportunity to do it. Clark Gable and his secretary Jean Harlow in his hotel room in Havana. He looked at her in a certain way. It was very plain or marked. Lust. Pure lust. No concern or anything else, just lust. Hobby had that look. Actually Hobby had that look in Havana—as it happens—but he had more—as when in the private booth he suddenly said, Storey, don't worry—with extreme concern as though I had some look of anguish, and reached across and touched my mouth. It was there that I first met him.

He was on some immigration business during his White Slavery days, something secret with the FBI so that I do not know too much about it, but as a prosecutor in New Orleans, which was once the "gateway to Havana" and the Latin world and certainly the closest thing to it in our country; and I was on a story for the *Southern Democrat*.

The night was very steamy, the green hot night. I stayed at the Nacional, with its faded grandeur. The old hotel was situated on the sea, with a tawdry ruined garden, and a teeming lobby, and long corridors on the upper floors. Ceaseless salsa parties at late hours below. Every night one slept to ceaseless salsa dances, among the leaning palms below, and in the morning drills for construction work began—many tried to change their rooms—some succeeded—their nerves being frayed.

Havana reminded me somewhat of Cairo—crumbling colonial Beaux Arts architecture and green palms. The very green, the variety of palms, a historical elegance among the crumbling mansions as of my New Orleans. The green of paradise, among the leaning palms.

Constant Fox had given me his nephew's name, as he knew he would be there. He was staying at the Habana Libre. As I was falling apart I found a girl with the AP Wire who agreed to help me find him, as she had fluent Spanish and had been in Havana many times before. I remember we were standing in the lobby, after she had called him in his room and he had said he would come down. A few minutes later she said, "I think this is your man."

Laconic, gruff, a white summer suit on his lanky frame, he ambled up and shook our hands in the crowded room and for a moment the whole crowd receded, for the sake of his sad blue eyes.

We went into the bar, which was crowded with international intrigues. The walls had ears, if you catch my drift. In Havana I was falling apart, as I always fall apart in Communist dictatorships in Third World countries, see? Get the picture? He calmed me down, being a plain manly sort. Called me Sweetheart. Pushed back my hair. Kidded me in the elevator.

He saw immediately what kind of nervous wreck I was, and he bore it or was kind.

There was a tropical storm in Havana. The Gulf Stream goes from Key West and Havana up to the Carolinas—treacherous,

I think. It was like something out of Pago Pago, that town in the South Seas where they stay at the seedy hotel and everyone has rumpled white suits under ceiling fans and it constantly rains, and they can never leave the hotel because it always rains. The lights went out at dinner. The power went off. Candles were lit. An hour later the transformer exploded.

I can remember he called his father, who was living then. They must have been very close—though you wouldn't have known it from the conversation, which sounded like Greek to me:

"Owen Illinois is up five."

"The Mets dropped two to the Cards."

"Merrill is at forty."

They only talked about sports or stocks. His father died later that year. I had lost mine also. We had such things between us. With us it was Havana, Cuba, later the Governor, always a story that was bigger than we were. Then there was the dashing figure that he cut, with his dark sunglasses and long hair, old suits, and manly frame, a strapping fellow. He had the strange solicitude of Constant. When there was a spot on my glass he got me another, looked after me, made jokes. I kind of thought that he would go for the girl from the AP Wire, who had been with us when we met. I had no confidence. But he looked at me the way a man looks at a woman. I was surprised, to look into his eyes and hold his gaze I was surprised to find such lust there, like looking into a very world —until I had to look away—yet a sweetness or an innocence there. I had no confidence—he drew out my soul instead of my drawing out his, though I would have wished to—he was more gracious and more kind than I.

In the morning when I woke up he was just sitting on the side of the bed holding my hand.

"I was worried about you," he said.

"I love it when you worry about me," I said.

"I'm not as nice as you think," he said. "I can give you an example of how I'm not as nice as you think. Do you want to hear it?"

"Go ahead."

"I've been having impure thoughts about you."

"That's okay."

"How does it make you feel?"

"It makes me very happy. But I hope I never do anything that disturbs your peace," I said.

"I can think of one or two things . . ." He looked at me with those blue eyes whose sudden love made me feel better and calm and my nervous stomachache go away and then he kissed me on the mouth. When suddenly he pulled me over, and what I felt to be in his arms. It was a sweetness but an innocence, stunned, that you could hardly believe. It was a truth of something.

But sooner than later came our moment of dishonor, and the thing was lost.

Thus the World Editor sat at his desk in New York years later, at dusk, watching the lights go up on the city. Often he had to work late. He bore the weight of the world, and did not show emotions, for so he thought to be manly. But he silently reviewed his heart. Like Lee at the surrender, or Grant at the victory, whether sorrow at defeat, or gladness at the end of the conflict, no one could tell, for the way they would not show their emotions.

New York was playing St. Louis. This could be heard on the radio. Hobby called his broker. Then he lit a cigar.

He turned his attention to the tortured messages coming in over his computer.

TO HOBBY. Re the General's fate. Paris is in with a report from *Le Monde* that the General will probably seek political asylum in Algeria. FROM BAGHDAD.

A MESSAGE TO HOBBY. Just sent you take two. It's about 260 lines. I haven't spent enough space on the war narrative, maybe. Maybe you should take out the first 100 lines. If you could get me any more than 600 lines, I could fill whatever I get with no padding. FROM CAIRO.

A MESSAGE TO HOBBY. Just a reminder that the 4 text blocks have to close by 4:30. FROM CAIRO.

TO HOBBY. You have the fifth decisive moment. The fourth and last, Hail Mary, is next. Sorry about the delay. The General is back. Moscow had some screw-up with this query and apparently it didn't get through, but given that we have enough to fill the two pages I presume that doesn't matter. FROM BAGHDAD.

A MESSAGE TO HOBBY. The text for the map are in EDIT for review. The General is threatening to make an appearance in every lead paragraph of every story in the special section, judging by your early edits. What does Underwood think? FROM CAIRO.

A MESSAGE TO HOBBY. The problem is that every time I do this story I end up with about 35 lines to address each topic which means I only have space to spell out the most basic situation. What do you think? CAIRO.

HOBBY. Do we want the French moment from Uganda? Otherwise we only have five lines, though that may be enough. TK the Uganda file on the Hail Mary play if the General decides to call off the war. CAIRO.

CAIRO seemed to be having some problems. CAIRO sent a lot of tortured messages.

I would look in at his office. He would be swiveling back in his chair, blowing cigar smoke up to the ceiling. The AP Wire would be coming in over one of the computers. His was a large separate office, away from the others, with a full view to the lights of the city. Like Mr. Collier in his law practice, Hobby made no show of grandeur about his work, which made him suave, that he made so little of it, and yet performed it so efficiently, as if effortlessly, or suavely. It's no joke being the World Editor, and bearing the world on your shoulders. I was wondering if he would ever crack, but I wasn't altogether sure that he ever would. But I would be waiting if he ever did. To reconcile the past.

In reality he was as much of an exile as I, but he bore his exile with a better grace.

He had what the sports announcers call a high threshold for adversity—something that distinguishes a great pitcher. My father would have called it four o'clock in the morning courage—which meant that if you woke him in the middle of the night with the news that the enemy was charging he would still be cool as a cucumber. After all, bravery on the field. And at the surrender, when some of the Union boys started to cheer, Grant bade them be quiet and said, Do not exult at their downfall, and told them to maintain a stoic demeanor. This was also the exact principle of baseball—or at least of the most sporting way.

46. ORIENT POINT, Long Island.

George Collier has a motto, which he has typed up and nailed to his door. It is a line from "Invictus" by William

Ernest Henley. "Under the bludgeonings of chance / My head is bloody, but unbowed."

Al's motto is "I'm from Brazil where the nuts come from."

Anne Collier's motto, or rather the message attached to her door, written in a laborious scrawl, is "If you want to come in, knock 3 times. But do not disturb."

A budding misanthrope, perhaps.

A succession of nurses, who seemingly hover between mental twilight and morn, have been imported to look after the Collier children in lieu of their parents, who are still believed to be arriving later in the summer. The succession of nurses has at least caused Anne Collier to widen her circle of acquaintances, though perhaps raising the question in her mind whether it is better to have one good friend or a host of acquaintances.

47. BATTY LEGENDRE and Margaret are in that popular hotel, prison. Margaret was picked up at the Arrow Inn evincing "a depraved indifference to human civilization"—which is a misdemeanor citation, and Batty Legendre received a police demerit for Refusal to Move Along. Bail has been posted, but not paid, at $5,000—obviously they are trying to keep them there, in jail. They are being held for psychiatric observation.

An army of psychiatrists were called in to evaluate Margaret, and have deemed her to be "a menace to society." Batty Legendre was analyzed and diagnosed as schizoid split-personality type exacerbated by alcoholism and he was released with a detective assigned as his tail. An FBI file has been opened on Margaret.

A policeman has been hanging around the enclave, snoop-

ing. He actually entered several of the houses—and I sincerely
doubt that he has a search warrant. After going through one
of the houses the policeman came back to speak with the occupant.

"Your house has been ransacked," said the policeman.

"No, that's just the way my wife left it," said the man.

Margaret called from jail. "Wait," she said, "hold the phone
—they're knocking at my door." I heard crashes in the background, irate screams, lurid threats. Then there was a long
silence. A dull thud was heard. Then another long silence,
followed by honeyed apologies in a female drawl.

48. MY COLUMN, "Strictly Personal," is not
going well. One woman wrote in about how her father-in-law
was a slob and he lived with them and what should she say to
her father-in-law to tell him he was a slob. I feel that we are
not meant to judge one another, so I gave her a huge lecture
on that. "Who am I to be his judge? For who are you or any
person who condemns your father-in-law to be his judge? Unless you are as wise as Socrates, which you are not, because
if you were you would despise yourself and know you were
not wise."

My column is too apocalyptic.

A woman wrote in about her womanizing husband, and
what should she say to him? "Your husband, needless to say,
is unconstant. He may be the dark side, but he has his points,
and it is not for me to be his judge."

I mean, I'm not Ann Landers. Or maybe I am. I mean I
obviously am meant to be. I mean since I write the column.
So then I tried to give more regular answers.

"Get yourself some plain old-fashioned spunk," I advised.

"Don't turn your back on life," I wrote.

"Live life to the fullest."
"Don't take any of his guff!"
"Life is meant to be lived."
(What does this stuff mean?)

Strictly Personal
by
Storey Collier

Dear Alaska,
Life is meant to be lived. Don't turn your back on life. Live life to the fullest.

> Regards,
> Storey Collier

Dear Jilted,
Don't worry about it. Plus, there's a lot of other fish in the sea. Live life to the fullest.

> Regards,
> Storey Collier

Dear Texas,
It's a big state. With big dreams. Stand tall.

> Regards,
> Storey Collier

Yesterday at the grocery store I overheard a conversation taking place about my column, "Strictly Personal."

"Do you know her?" said a stranger.

"No, but I've seen her three times and every time I've seen her she's bombed."

I don't get it! I tried to write regular stuff like Ann Landers. Maybe I should go back to Socrates. A woman wrote in describing the character flaws of her boyfriend and asked if I thought she should marry him. I answered, "Some people I take to be good, even if they are not—I take them to be. I take them to be very good indeed. The honest reality is I think it is possible they are sleazy—but I take them to be good, and—how can I say it—I take them to be better than myself. Who am I to be their judge? Let them make their own peace, for I am not their judge, and would not presume to be. The dark side, do you understand, is good, the badness AND the goodness. We are not meant to embrace only half. Remember the Godly man came from the town of Desire. 'And therefore, let no one frighten or flutter us by saying that the temperate friend is to be chosen rather than the inspired, but let him further show that love is not sent by the gods for any good to lover or beloved; if he can do so we will allow him to carry off the palm.' Does that answer your question?"

Maybe not.

Strictly Personal
by
Storey Collier

Dear Doubts,

Anxiety, solitude—familiar companions. Reconcile yourself, and then forge forth. The key is that one has to be resolved. Single-hearted. It is a matter of application, at that point, and faith. And when you cannot shake your faith, then you know you are in business. A girl could do a lot worse than to set her heart on something. Be faithful to it. No matter the result. You have to love the attempt, no matter the result, even if the result is a failure.

Regards,
Storey Collier

Dear Troubled,
You have to learn to "appreciate the situation," as they say in the army. Ceaseless analysis, that's my motto. To advance your vision, much is required, even beyond perseverance.
   Does that answer your question? Maybe. Maybe not. But I tried.

Regards,
Storey Collier

Strictly Personal
by Storey Collier

Dear Nervous,
You are, like me, a hypochondriac. Try to calm yourself. Peace is a thing that is not easily to be found in this world. A place where you can find peace is so rare that it must be a Godly place indeed, and ordered well, and better far than all your babbling Ninevehs.

Regards,
Storey Collier

"I saw her at the Arrow Inn," the stranger said, in the grocery store. "She was succotashed."
"Succotashed?"
"Plastered."
I was not! Now wait just a cotton-picking minute. I wasn't drinking. I was listening to the nuts go berserk on the sports channel on the radio analyzing everything. The girl reporter who covers the old team was filing one of her hair-raising reports where she is always harried and upset and everything is in chaos.
"Bob, there's a fight going on on the pitcher's mound. Bonano threw to Jones, and the ball hit him in the small of his back. He ran to the mound and threw Bonano onto the

ground. They came in from the dugout. The—uh—they—
what's that thing called? The bullpen. They came in from the
bullpen. And from the dugout. They've thrown out Bonano.
They've thrown out Righetti. We're waiting to see who else
they'll throw out. It's thirty degrees and looks like rain. The
stands are almost completely empty. I'm calling from the
parking lot. I couldn't get into the press box. I'm hoping to
get into the stands. It's a nasty night in New York and there's
a nasty fight going on in the bullpen now. It's—"

"Okay, Janie, thanks a lot."

The announcer always cuts her off right in the middle of
some huge disaster, and just goes on to the next thing. They
seem to treat her very badly. One time they had her on a talk
show—not in the ball park, but in the studio—and then she
seemed more relaxed.

But I wouldn't be relaxed either if I were her. It's too heartbreaking. Like the old adage. I don't care whether or not they
win the pennant. I don't even know what the pennant is. I
don't even know why it is heartbreaking. I only know that the
other night, as it is nearing the end of the season, they had a
music video of the highlights, and my heart was breaking so
badly I was in tears. Why? It was just one fellow hitting a
home run, one fellow catching a fly ball, a handsome one
running the bases, with soppy music in the background, and
there I was, weeping. Weeping. But I hardly even know why.
It is my love for Hobby. Or at least connected with it. They
were heroes and their season is short.

As I have noted, the New York manager is very listless, and
his personality may affect the team, and this may be why they
often lose, they don't have a real spirit of determination, perseverance. And this listless manager, I do think it would be
better if they had a crusty old gent with a lot of personality
who screams at the umpires and is a terror, like Mr. Under-

wood, sort of. However, with the manager they have, the one who is listless, the team has an elegance, as they are nonchalant, effortless, stoic. I care that they have an elegance, but this is not the type of attitude to go over in New York. It's more of a Southern attitude, where if you have honor and grace it doesn't matter if you are the underdog or struggle always with defeat. To advance your vision, much is required, even beyond perseverance.

In other years they might have had less talent, less perfect athletes, but more of a spirit to win. But whether they win or lose it must break your heart just as well, everyone carried away by sports metaphors, the announcers comparing the old ball park in Chicago to a stately society dowager in basic black and pearls, with fading grandeur, etc., or everyone agonizing over the imminent departure of the aging heroes, with their aging grace, from the world of baseball. They remind me, of course, of Hobby.

Some people say it is a more antiquated, droll or quaint sport than football, say, being more representative of a sort of bygone era. Football for its violence is more beloved in the South, where they don't have baseball. Whereas I would think that baseball would suit the South, being rather courtly. But it is more mental or cerebral, than football, say, and that does not suit the South. But even if baseball is more cerebral, everyone is certainly an emotional wreck by the end of the season, agonizing over it all.

I like the older players, debonair, with their aging grace, agonizing over when to retire. They give a last curtain call, sometimes they might even gruffly brush off a clandestine tear. The crowd goes wild.

Now the players have to learn how to control their emotions, but the manager is allowed to have emotions. It may be that the New York manager, the one who is listless, remembers too well how he learned to control his emotions as a player, for he is still quite young. I guess it's mostly the crusty old codgers who put on a big show—like Mr. Underwood, no doubt.

Then there is the manager of the old-time New York team. He sits in the dugout chain-smoking, occasionally chuckling bemusedly at the antics of his drug-crazed pitcher; it's as if it doesn't occur to him to coach, only to spectate while wearing dark sunglasses, chain-smoking, presenting a rather satyrlike figure. He too is quite young.

But he of course is the pawn of the owner. Mr. Underwood is a friend of the owner. I sometimes think that Mr. Underwood is his only friend. Not only does everyone despise him, the owner of the old-time team, but they experience heartbreak and trauma due to him because he makes too many trades and thinks he knows everything. It's like a one-man show—he runs it. It's the Latin American Dictator routine. But his is the old New York team, with everything cloaked in tradition, the old pinstripes, glamorous capes for the pitchers when it is cold, a storied name, and white-haired gents in trench coats musing in the stands.

New York is supposed to be the favorite, always the favored team to win, and yet they can't even beat Pittsburgh. I don't think they could beat Cincinnati. I know one thing for certain. They couldn't ever beat Oakland. This team has a romance with failure.

I am listening to a game taking place in Chicago. My head is in Chicago but my heart is in New York. Chicago has the prettiest ball park in the league. Everyone is always agonizing over it. Everyone is always agonizing over everything, in sports. Except for the players. You see them sitting in the dugout, watching sorrows, agonies, sometimes miracles, not even talking. Where are their feelings buried? And yet as ever I admire them. I like them that way, especially the debonair seasoned veterans, who show the least emotion of all, compared to the callow youths just starting out, who don't interest me at all. I like the ones who have been through something. I like the ones who have suffered.

There is one fellow who is twenty-nine but he has been in the minor leagues all his life until now. He was voted the most valuable player in the minor leagues for the last ten years. But not good enough for the big leagues—until just now—and he is crumbling, already. He has just gotten up to the big leagues. He is not a callow youth, at twenty-nine. But the poor fellow can't get a hit. He always strikes out. I was wondering, what if his sad career finally just got to him, and after a strikeout, he stood at the plate and just broke into tears. Just broke out into agony, tears. What would happen? It would be an unimaginable thing. It would never happen, of course. But if this fellow from the minor leagues suddenly broke down, there would be a heck of a lot of people in the dugout who could feel for him. As they are all constantly checking into alcohol-rehabilitation treatment centers, getting picked up by the police, experiencing agony, and going through slumps. But it is their damn manly code to be stalwart on the field.

Suddenly happiness welled up in my throat. The kid got a home run. Then others got hits. They were winning. They were suddenly, suddenly winning. My heart was in my throat. Happiness rose in my chest.

"Sunday-night baseball on ABC is going to ruin a lot of marriages," chuckled the announcer. Mine it would save.

I know I go overboard but I think it is because they didn't have baseball in New Orleans. That is one of my basic philosophical tenets. They don't have baseball in New Orleans. Leave this plain American sport to the North.

Actually they did have baseball in New Orleans once. It was about fifty years ago. They were the Pelicans, a minor-league team. Hobby's father used to go to the games as a boy. His uncle would take him. Hobby's father was shocked because in the box next to theirs was a priest who smoked cigars, drank beer, and cursed. Mostly, he cursed.

The listless manager got fired and I've been all broken up about it. The level of agony being achieved in New York, and on the sports radio channel where the nuts call in, is unparalleled. The sportswriters in the tabloids complain about the nuts who call up on the radio to analyze everything—they say that these people don't have a life. Quite on the contrary, I would say that these people have the secret of life. To be so dead serious about something so eminently trivial. So I joined along. In despair over missing the New York manager (I did not agree that he should have been fired), I joined the Rotisserie League. What is the Rotisserie League? Well, it is this thing that men who are nuts who call up the radio sports talk show to complain, protest, and analyze everything in baseball do—you pretend that you own your own team, and you compose it of existing players in the two existing leagues, you make your own trades, you form your own statistics—in short, you drift into a fantasy world of insanity. Because you are driven by despair over the trades and problems etc. in your real team.

Nuts call up on the sports radio channel and they say, "Chris, I've had it. But I'm in the Rotisserie League, and I've made a trade—Strawberry, McReynolds, and Darling for Tim Raines." Then the announcer says, dead serious, "Really? How's it working out for you?" etc. etc. and they get in long conversations about it.

So what is going on in my Rotisserie League? Well, I'll tell you. My team is the New York team, with the listless manager. In my team, he was not fired. Listless, but stalwart, elegant, not a coward, can do the job. Then, a player from last year who agonized over his retirement because he was aging, thirty-six, and then was traded away, who had been known as the heart of the team, who was dashing and glamorous and dark, with a mustache, came back as the first-base coach—we are grooming him to be the manager. The players are elated about it. Strawberry talked to him for hours. As they chain-smoked in the dugout. My dugout is vice-ridden but I like it that way. And I'm the owner, see? Everyone chain-smokes, they play cards, they drink bourbon, they're allowed to, it's fun, my manager doesn't enforce discipline, he doesn't have to, because the players respect him, like a father, and he may be listless, but he is stalwart, and gets the job done.

49.

"THERE IS a light rain falling," said the announcer. "Well, we have that light rain falling." He paused. "You just can't depend on the weather in Chicago."

"No, you can't depend on the weather in Chicago. Can you, Bob?" said the other announcer.

"Chicago is a town that has a lot of weather, Frank. You can't tell how it's going to turn out in Chicago," the other opined, as they droned on in their lamebrained conversations desperately trying to fill up the silences in calling the game, having plain American fun.

Hobby had to visit the Paris Bureau. He was gone for five days. Then he had to tour the Eastern European bureaus. He was absent for another six days. I received word that he arrives in New York tonight. He said he might come out on Sunday. So I was whiling away the time in Orient listening to the ceaseless baseball games on the radio.

Someone called up espousing a torturous mathematical analysis of why the New York team would not make it to the World Series—if they played .500 ball in the next 23.5 games, and Chicago did something (all in numerical equations) compared to Philadelphia, with all these torturous mathematical equations, then—but the announcer simply disconnected him before he could finish—"Gotta go, Chris, good call"—click, he had to go to a commercial. I found this to be poignant. It was like a Byzantine code or mystical equation to build the pyramids in ancient Egypt. These people are in agony, agonizing over their feelings about baseball. No doubt they are under stress. Stress at the office or at home, and they have to formulate these Byzantine mathematical equations about baseball as if to solve the mystery of their lives. What is the stressor in their lives, I wondered. I was discussing this with Al. Or what is the stressor in my life, listening, crazed, to these nuts on the radio analyzing sports for twenty-four hours a day with a cigarette hanging out of my mouth and my hair all disheveled, in a darkened room. Maybe Hobby is the stressor, to me.

"Hobby Fox is not a stressor," said Al firmly. I never know if Al understands or not the things he says. Mrs. Langguth, something of a matchmaker, has ideas about me and Hobby. Rising out of her accustomed vagueness, she questioned me extensively. She even asked me, "Would you like to spend the rest of your life with him?" I was riddled with anxiety, embarrassment, and stress. . . . I was at sixes and sevens. "I would like to spend the rest of my life with her," Al said shyly, to Mrs. Langguth, looking at me from the side, causing my heart to break into a number of small pieces.

Speed Weed gave a party for four girls and four boys. The parents went to a dance. Leaving Cedric and me as chaperones. At a quarter to ten one of the mothers came to call for her daughter (age twelve) and found her in the cellar with the lights out under the ironing table with one of the boys (age ten). It developed the rest of the children were closeted in darkened parked cars in the lane. It goes without saying I was deeply, and horribly, mortified. I questioned the host, Speed Weed. "I was so excited that I had three bourbons and three crème de menthes," he said happily. God give me strength, I whispered to the ceiling. "Look, I'm not your pal. I'm your chaperone," I said sternly. "Come with me, mister. You're all going home right now. This is not a bordello!"

"What's a bordello?" said Anne Collier, trying to keep tabs on her hero, Speed Weed.

"Give me a martini," said the baby.

God give me strength, I whispered to the ceiling.

"Children, a bordello is a place for grownups. A martini is a drink only for grownups. So is bourbon, crème de menthe, and *get that cigar out of your mouth, mister. The game is up here, buddy. This is not—*"

Mr. Underwood slowly walked up. Everyone cowered in fear.

"What have we here?" he said mildly. "Wasn't there a shindig here tonight for the youngsters?"

I elected to tell him the whole story. I told him.

He rocked back and forth on his heels. "Well, I think the young people are entitled to a little fun now and then. Am I right, youngsters?"

What is wrong with him? He is having a personality breakdown.

50. MR. UNDERWOOD must be taking lessons from Southern evangelists for his delivery, so it seems lately. He has developed a sort of drawl. On his television spot he comes on and the first thing he says is, "New York, I'm mad.

I'm mad at the mayor. I'm mad at the governor. And I'm mad at the politicians of this city. New York, it's up to you. Take my hand. We'll do it together. We're on a team. We're in this together. Together, we'll do the job right. Help me, New York," etc. etc. delivered in a slow and ceaseless drawl with a mesmerizing stare.

He had to read from a typed page his name and age, but could recite or recollect the remainder of his views and information.

His performance is extremely odd, needless to say.

He says the reason why he wants to be the Senator from New York is because he is sick of reading about problems in the newspaper and appears to think that therefore he'll just mosey on into the legislature and be Senator. He's got this Southern thing now. He doesn't walk, he sashays. Like he's just going to sashay on in and turn things around. He may as well wear a ten-gallon hat. I don't know where he got it from. Something is wrong with him, plainly.

Also, he has a ceaseless thing called "The Underwood Report," which is a comprehensive plan for the state, comprised in a huge stack of papers, handsomely bound, which he keeps holding up during his television commercials and giving out a toll-free number to call for.

Mr. Underwood had another television spot, in his bid for Senator. "Hi. I'm Stokes Underwood. And I'm mad," he drawled. What does he think this is, Texas? He thinks he's in Texas.

Mr. Underwood was on a call-in talk show for an hour on a New York radio station. People called in and told him what they were mad about and what made them mad and what made them tick and asked what Mr. Underwood would do about it. He played the raconteur. Sometimes he would get off the track, and play the rambling Southern raconteur. "I married my sweetheart in 1948 in Charleston, South Carolina," he would say. Totally unrelated to the question. He would go off into reminiscences. "But we met in New York, at The Palm." Then he would brood about his memories for several moments. Then he would slip back into his New York big-cheese falling-lunatic mode.

For his opponent in the Senate race Mr. Underwood had a passionate disgust. If Mr. Underwood had one foot firmly planted in the lunatic fringe, his opponent, in Mr. Underwood's words, was "deeply disturbed." Whenever the newspapers asked for his comment on his opponent, Mr. Underwood would always say that his opponent was "deeply disturbed." Those of us following the campaign would often speculate which is worse, "crazy" or "deeply disturbed." We concluded that "deeply disturbed" was worse. And Mr. Underwood was only crazy.

Mr. Underwood flew into Orient on Saturday night on a hydrofoil. At dinner he went off on a weird tangent about men who wear necklaces. They were terrible, they were horrible, they were taking over. But I've never seen any men who wear necklaces. I've never met any. Except sometimes I've noticed that baseball players wear necklaces and the umpire makes them take them off. Then it turned out it was all because Mr. Underwood's opponent in the senatorial race wears a necklace. "He's a very disturbed individual," said Mr. Underwood. "If I may be very candid with you."

The somnambulists struggled to maintain consciousness. Cedric led a pointless discussion on the makeup of the universe, ending with morose observations about its lack of meaning. Margaret listened with rapt attention and then wept, and the somnambulists could barely stay awake. But the somnambulists can never stay awake. They are always falling asleep in the middle of dinner parties, dozing off, struggling to maintain consciousness.

"She makes my blood run like lava. Lava," said Cedric, after Margaret had run sobbing from the table. "She makes the blood in my veins run like lava."

"Lava. Okay. I get it. Lava."

I am surrounded by a dazzling array of insane maniacs. But I guess that's not exactly news. That's not exactly news. That's yesterday's news.

The Southern bandleader who is Mr. Underwood's campaign mascot is visiting for the weekend. He has been put under the jurisdiction of the Southern contingent, appropriately, since he is constantly sozzled.

Eventless weekend except waves of anxiety caused by newspaper reporter who came to do a story on Mr. Underwood's campaign, in which Mr. Underwood was portrayed, it was generally felt, as an insane maniac. The Southern bandleader, of course, did not help, but Mr. Underwood has this love for the South. A television crew briefly appeared and made a tape. "Help me, New York," the Southern bandleader would cry, in front of the cameras, espousing Mr. Underwood's campaign motto.

51.

MR. UNDERWOOD had a party for the Governor at which he engaged a country-music band as the entertainment. The band played the "Tennessee Waltz" and the "Mississippi Winter Waltz" with violins that were so beautiful it made your heart break. Mr. Underwood went to the microphones to sing a number with the band. The crowd sat in stunned silence—he sang a country-music song, completely off key, with a highly dramatic delivery, but I mean the man can't carry a tune. When he would dance with a woman, he would stare straight into her eyeballs, making his eyes like smoldering coals.

"Here comes that old country crooner, Stokes Underwood," said the Southern bandleader who is Mr. Underwood's campaign mascot, when Mr. Underwood approached the microphones again. "I dedicate this song to Grace," he histrionically announced. "Put your sweet lips a little closer to the phone," he sang, "And when your boyfriend comes along, just tell him he has to go."

"Oh, Lord, now what," responded Grace, in her unimpressed drawl, being a sarcastic Southern girl.

It was another lugubrious night in society with everyone forty to fifty years older than me.

Perhaps God is testing me. It almost seems hardly else than that. It is not a specific desire, really, that I have. It is a generic desire. It is desire in the abstract. Is that all right? How come people never ask questions like that in my column?

"The oldest member of the Senate" (he was ninety-five) "has asked me if he may say a word," said Mr. Underwood, during the toasts. "As we know, he is prone to long speeches, but he promises he will be brief."

The fellow stood up and said loudly, "My doctor told me to give up women. So I gave up the doctor."

Then he sat down abruptly and lapsed into an elegant stupor.

Speed Weed asked Mr. Underwood if he could make a toast. Mr. Underwood said, "Of course, my boy," and gained the podium to introduce the little fellow. Mr. Underwood explained that Speed Weed's father was a noted lawyer and that he had coached him some on public speaking. With that, Speed Weed gained the podium and said, "Ladies and gentlemen, it is a great pleasure to address you, since I cannot undress you—" which brought down the house, especially among those aged under twelve, and the speaker was so overcome that he could not go on.

Mr. Underwood took from the speaker, who was weak with mirth, a glass of what he thought was water, which the speaker had held, and drank it. What he thought was water was of course straight vodka. Intending to confer punishment, Mr. Underwood took the young man to what was once the laundry room only to find George Collier and Andrew Langguth wryly puffing on what were once Mr. Underwood's priceless Havana cigars.

Margaret chartered a fishing boat to a dangerous area called Death Gulch. It must have been a rough passage. She returned to Orient in the middle of Mr. Underwood's campaign rally or party for the Governor or whatever it was, weeping and hysterical. She was sopping wet and ran to the microphones and was nearly electrocuted.

The incident did not dampen the gaiety of the atmosphere. The swans were on the green lagoon. Peacocks were in the meadow. Mr. Underwood had imported these famous chefs from Paris, for some reason, to cook the food. I mean they were famous French chefs who were now, I believe, the chefs at famous restaurants in Connecticut and New York or food critics for *The New York Times*. The chefs had all this French *joie de vivre*—ruddy complexions, blue canvas aprons, exuberant gesticulations, torrents of French *joie de vivre*. Kooks. They were kooks. Mr. Underwood directed everything, and spent a lot of his time screaming out Southernisms to me, as I ended up closeted in Vernon's sunken bar, alone with Mr. Underwood, who kept screaming out things like "She was in love with your granddaddy" or "Your mother was in love with my brother" until finally I practically carried him home.

"You're a born sucker, sweetheart," said Hobby.

pic Sailing Team. But of course Margaret knows a lot of nautical types. If you want to find Margaret, just look on a sailboat. Or in a nightclub. Otherwise in a jail cell.

"Let's stick together tonight, kid," Mr. Underwood said to me, chomping on his cigar, in a conspiratorial tone. Jeez—the big cheese—why me? However, then he ambled on and I was instead closeted between an elderly couple, the Baumgards, with whom it was extremely hard to make conversation but I was desperately trying to be gracious as per instructions so finally I had the all-purpose solution: asking Mr. Baumgard about his World War II experiences. Because when you ask a man in his sixties about his World War II experiences, then you don't have to say anything for a long time. So now I am an expert on Rommel, the Desert Fox, forms of bombardment and interdiction fighting in Africa, etc. etc. from listening to Mr. Baumgard talk about his World War II experiences.

I find an interesting difference between Northerners and Southerners in this regard, as when you ask a New Orleans man about his World War II experiences it always turns out to be dancing beneath a tent in Biloxi, or taking the night boat to Havana.

Whereas when you ask a Northern man, it is forms of interdiction fighting in the North African desert, or tapping out intelligence codes from a Quonset hut in the Pacific.

On the other hand, my father was Southern, and he did the latter.

The guests were circulating in the gardens of the different houses in the enclave. It was a pretty sight. Leading to the bay there was a rose garden surrounded by a path with black wrought-iron chairs and tables, around a long court planted with peonies. I haven't seen peonies since I was in Alabama. And how often I think of Alabama—Point Clear, Mobile, the miles west of Savannah," he resumed. "About sixty miles south of Atlanta," he said. He lit a cigarette. I nodded vigorously, attempting to indicate stoppage. "About a hundred miles below the Mason-Dixon Line," he mused. He blew a smoke ring. "Forty miles west of the Atlantic Ocean." You kept thinking it was over because he would stop and ruminate for a moment after each description. I thought that I had died and gone to Purgatory.

Quickly attempting to change the subject, I asked him another question—making certain it had nothing to do with measurements or calculated distances. I asked him where he was staying. He was staying in a hotel.

"It's about three miles down the road," he said ominously. Oh no, I thought. So I quickly tried to change the subject and asked him if he was alone.

"I'm meeting a woman later, at the hotel," he said. I recollected that he had a reputation as a ladies' man. "Do you think that's wrong?" he asked me in a very deep suggestive voice, looking at me with his eyes like smoldering coals.

"No, I think it's grand."

His eyes burned into mine menacingly.

The party was populated not only by the Governor, some Senators, the Memphis contingent, etc., but a troubled prizefighter, the Olympic Sailing Team, and many of Margaret's old flames. Causing many smoldering faux pas and gaffes. Memphis, Montgomery, New Orleans, and Latin America were all represented as geographical points of origin of her old flames.

Margaret was seated at a table with the Olympic Sailing Team; the guest list seemed rather eclectic, but when you're the big cheese, plus in politics, that's how it is. Retired sports players, troubled prizefighters, washed-up Southern bandleaders—Mr. Underwood loved that sort of stuff.

Leave it to Margaret to get hooked up with the entire Olym-

"Thanks a lot."

"Pathetic," aptly said Al.

Al and Hobby walked across the garden to the dock, as if to be alone. "I am very close to Storey," I heard Al say to Hobby, "and she is like a second mother to me and she tells me all her problems and I give her advice and help her out and it shows I can be close to someone because I'm very close to Storey."

My close companions are the very young and the very old. But I think that hanging around with the very young and the very old, with nothing in between, may be the sign of someone who is about to crack up.

It is true that among the elderly, the best time was had, as they certainly were cutting the rug on the dance floor, or putting on the Ritz, I believe it is called. This was also true of course for the New Orleans contingent. But I must say that the Memphis contingent was even more riotous. Or scandal-ridden, you might say. The New Orleans contingent conducted their strangely elegant bantering conversations and knocked back their cocktails, collected in a corner of the garden in deck chairs; whereas the Memphis contingent actually danced, despite any claims of age and infirmity, and seemed to be instigating various scandals. There were many smoldering gaffes and agonizing faux pas. Some of the white-haired gents were cutting the rug, and others were fuming in corners.

My dinner partner was the oldest member of the Senate. He seemed to be obsessed with measurements. "What is your town near?" I asked him, innocently attempting to be gracious.

"It's about thirty miles north of Augusta," he said. "About fifty miles west of Charleston," he added. "About forty miles south of Macon." He stopped. I nodded. "About twenty-five

Bay—is another matter. How one is tempted to compare everything in the world no matter how far to what one knows best—especially this for a Southerner, who more readily admits his love for his native place than the Northerner, is more unashamed, and also is more conscious of his love for it—especially when he is so often parted from it as I am, unable to kill the intolerable love of a place.

One girl sat at a table still. When the night was drawing to a close. There was something in her exhausted, somewhat glamorous air that gave the dark hint of nightclubs. This of course was Margaret. In truth there was something slightly depraved about her. There was plainly a vortex of chaos represented by her exhaustion and tears and the dark hint of nightclubs. But she was full of life. A young man from Memphis among others yearned for her—he had come all the way from Memphis to see her. But her heart was simply, thoroughly broken, by something in the past—and like all people whose hearts are simply, thoroughly broken by something in the past, she had left her heart there, in the past—some part of her personality—she had left a part of herself behind—in this case, on a flight of stairs one night at some cotton plantation in the Mississippi Delta.

Her heart is Delta-bound, like the song that sometimes emanates from Hobby's room, or from the vicinity of Dollar Bill, with its dark inexorable beat, darkly glamorous and eternal.

> I'm tired of roaming.
> And so I'm homing
> I'm Delta bound . . .
>
> I'm in a hurry,
> My heart's a flurry,
> I'm Delta bound;

Every time I close my eyes
It seems I see Louisiana . . .

I've been a rover,
But now that's over,
Knee deep in clover,
I'll soon be found,

I'm on my way now,
Most any day now,
I'm Delta bound.

Hobby helped her to her house when all the guests had gone. He helped people who were troubled, and in fact liked them better, for in them saw God's grace.

52.

52. IT IS SEPTEMBER. The temperature is brisk. It doesn't of course bother the Yankees. On the beach the morose overweight fellow with the handlebar mustache is attired in bathing trunks and flying a kite, though the temperature can't be much over fifty degrees.

People are allowed to stay at the enclave for as long as they can stand it.

"What do you mean, for as long as they can stand it? You mean they just keep coming out until one weekend they sit in the living room and just start screaming, 'I can't stand it anymore!'?" said Hobby.

But no. It refers to the weather. It refers to climatic conditions. People can stay as long as they can stand it, meaning until it gets too cold, as the houses aren't heated. But it doesn't bother the Yankees. They come out for romantic fall weekends with autumnal chills in the air, collecting firewood, building a fire, sometimes even still swimming. Collecting chestnuts, flying kites, acting like maniacs. Flying kites while wearing bathing suits, collecting chestnuts, looking at the foliage. I myself am not that wild about foliage. Fall foliage, I mean.

"Aside from your enmity to foliage," said Hobby, "maybe you and I can go for a drive sometime," he said.

Vernon walked along the beach with his paramour, his beret cocked at the usual rakish angle, a cigarette hanging out of his mouth.

The love couple found a new hideaway—the lumberyard. Of the laundry room no trace remains.

Margaret had to appear in civil court. I accompanied her to trial. The entire courtroom seemed to be under Margaret's influence. Oblivious of the bedlam around her, the judge sang soul songs to herself and wore a blue chiffon dress. The court seemed never to convene, and one after another the cases were postponed or dismissed. Occasionally some lawyers were able to confer with the judge, by capturing her attention among the Total Chaos. You expected the judge at any moment to stand up and start belting out gospel songs, and the spectators and witnesses to sing as the choir. Meanwhile the judge sang soul songs quietly to herself, snapping her fingers at the bench, while the bailiffs brought her trays with cold drinks. She had an immensely kind face, and looked at Margaret with immensely kind eyes, and dismissed the case.

53.
Hobby sat on the porch with Dollar Bill by the garden in the night, from which saxophones of jazz songs emanated. "One Night of Sin," "I Put a Spell on You," and "How Come My Dog Don't Bark When You Come Around." Dollar Bill knows all these songs that have names like "Guess I'll Get the Papers and Go Home."

The boys were in the garden, up to no good. Anne Collier

watched the boys forlornly and with some longing. Like Al, she longs to be included in some of their diabolical adventures, but unlike Al she is never once included in their diabolical adventures, as girls are strictly excluded from their mischief-laden world. If anything, they attempt to torture her. The closest she gets to inclusion is if they try to torture her—with frogs, snakes, etc. Hobby scooped her up and held her on his lap. She looked up at him, ecstatic. She is actually a gallant little creature; she misses her mother more than her brothers do, or needs her more. Her mother's arrival now, however, finally, is imminent.

Mr. Underwood was riding around the enclave in his campaign truck, which has one of those loud recordings of his speeches and campaign mottos coming out of a loudspeaker; Hobby had to go over and wryly ask him to turn it down.

Two dark-haired beauties sat in lawn chairs nearby—the champagne-soaked authors.

We were discussing the latest problem with Margaret, which is that she has formed an attachment to a Latin American peasant who can't read or write. I myself don't cast asperpsions on this alliance. If she is happy, that is what counts. It's physical, I think. Their relationship, I mean. "It's physical," I said.

"Me Tarzan, you Jane," commented Hobby, while reading the paper.

A bloodcurdling cry issued from the vicinity of the boys—Hobby was there before I even thought to check—Harry Locke crashed his bike into an oncoming car. Hobby had to take him to the emergency room.

54. "WHERE'S HOBBY?" I later asked the populace.

"He has a migraine. He's in his room in bed."

They gave him a migraine. The boys, Mr. Underwood, the young couples—the whole combination.

I heard the strains of swami music coming from his room, as in an old Hollywood movie. He was locked in his room watching *Quo Vadis*. "A thrilling saga of the collapse of civilization!" ran the advertisement that preceded the picture. He also had *El Cid*. I've watched it about seventeen times. When I was seven years old my father took me on a boat to France, and the boat had a movie theater, which was playing *El Cid*, and I watched it continuously about twenty-three times. I spent the entire boat ride in the theater. Watching Sophia Loren in *El Cid*. I memorized it. I can recite the entire thing. The climax is at the end when Charlton Heston leads the army even though he is dead. He is actually dead, but he died with his eyes open, on his horse, as he was stabbed while riding, and he just keeps on, even though he is actually dead, giving hope to the army, who continue to follow, ignorant that they are following a dead corpse. I think he becomes a saint.

We were discussing if Charlton Heston became a saint. "You idealize these people, Storey," said Hobby. "They're not so great. Just read the lives of the saints. You'll find out they're not so saintly."

"But maybe they *are* so saintly."

He looked at me sideways, askance, with those blue eyes. "You worry me. Look. Nine out of every ten people are crumbs."

"Crumbs?"

"Sure. Your trouble is, Storey, you don't call a spade a spade."

"But they're supposed to be saints."

"But maybe they're crumbs."

A silence ensued.

"Okay, crumbs. But you love these crumbs, Hobby. I know you. You help crumbs. People who are sleazy you love. Like the old sinner, the Governor, you loved him. You love people who are sleazy."

"True. But so do you. Crumbs, sleazeballs, and people who are pathetic. That's what you love. That's why you can be a good reporter. Or columnist, as the case may be." He looked at me sideways. "But you idealize them. They're crumbs, even if you love them. That's what I'm trying to tell you. Like the Governor. I like him, but I know he's a crumb. There's a difference. And, sweetheart, once you pass through their doors, you'll never be the same again. I do not claim to be an innocent, as you would say."

It is true that innocence was not what Hobby had to offer me. Nor is innocence what I desire. Innocence is a thing that I can understand. The dark side has the mystery to me, and thus the grace. I fell in love with honor first, but then I came across dishonor, and could not understand it.

Not that Hobby represented it, but we had had our moment of dishonor. It was at an old hotel off the coast of Alabama, where, by a strange string of circumstance, I first met Mr. Underwood. Hobby was there by coincidence as well, and even then we had a past. But there, and how unlike the sterling Northern sea, but along the Gulf of Mexico and Mobile Bay, with hurricane weather, stormy weather, and the palm trees in the heat, tortuous Bellingrath Gardens at nearby Theodore, Alabama, and at the old hotel, among the ancient grounds and gardens, among the green, with velvet lawns and long tables with white tablecloths set up on the lawn for a dance in the black night—moments of hilarity, sweltering in the heat, pitchers of martinis, and the past—conceived a child. It could have been our Al.

And it was for some time thereafter hard to find that rare thing, peace.

There was that time I first met him, in Havana. I could have known. There were the sweet tropic squares and raging Beaux Arts architecture in the night. Only then—a brief week—as among the Senators and the old sinner in New Orleans—does one feel most alive—in the proximity to danger—and to a story that is bigger than you are.

That Governor, the old sinner, was corrupt. There's the other side of the coin. The fascination of the corrupt is not a small thing. It can occupy him who has a love of honor. The eternal dilemma, you might call it. The old sinner's love of the corrupt, at least it was a love that dared to speak its name. And the fascination of the corrupt, these shallow human lusts, and deeper ones, have their dark suave glamour. . . . And this is a conflict that in my opinion is the hardest one in life to reconcile.

A very storm was brewing in the Caribbean. But I knew the tropics—the weather is fickle in the tropics—no doubt it would pass—storms do not last long in the tropics.

It is amazing that I didn't drive Hobby bananas with my worrying, but he himself had what is called peace after a struggle.

But I go to bed and feel my heart crashing in my chest, a sort of convulsion of the frame or flutter of the heart, from sheer nerves and fear. I must have had it years ago on St. Charles Avenue in New Orleans, even in that white house with its sweet gaiety beside the palms, and I recollect it in the Garden District upon moving to New York, and on leaving for Havana. Nerves at night, leaving for Havana, why should that seem fond? But retrospect is always fond.

The charm of Orient is as ever this—that people should concoct forms of innocent amusement and ply their summer pleasures, the guests arriving across the lawn or steaming in on the ferry with blue lights at dusk, fixing drinks for them and spending innocent afternoons on the water boating. Such heedless pleasures were not his, nor are they mine. I do not say that that is right or good. Only that I cannot overcome my memories. It is not for pleasure, but for duty, that I repine and regret. For my disquiet heart, when I my soul despise.

I was walking down the garden path with Al. He said enigmatically, "I guess God took my word."

"What do you mean, Al?"

"I asked God to let you take us to the old house and the park and then you did. So I guess God took my word."

"Oh, Al."

"In God we trust, my dear," he said.

"Now, Al, I'm glad you have religion, son, but where exactly did you learn that?"

"From you. You teach me so many things that when you are here, my house is like a school."

So I guess my Geography was not for naught.

And while sitting on the porch, I see a towheaded boy in a sailor suit with Hobby, and the baby in her carriage, walking down the lane, as quaint as in a very dream. And then I see a group of people, the guests, sitting in wicker chairs on the lawn—a towheaded boy, then I see the friend of my childhood, friend of my youth, since departed. A tender, silly fellow raises a cocktail glass in tones of silly hilarity.

New arrivals were seen on the ferry.

55.   ON THE FERRY to Orient soon were seen
two dark-haired beauties—not the champagne-soaked authors, but Claude Collier and his wife. On the ferry Claude
Collier leant on the rail, and he did not look well. They were
glamorous, however, he and his wife. He in his white summer
suit and white bucks, with the jaunty way his hair came onto
his collar in the back, and his old kind eyes, in which were
seen, despite their humor, an unalterable sorrow. He had a
quiet but extravagant generosity; and he was droll and quaint
as the Colliers for some reason tended to be. His generosity,
however, took a toll on him.

Despite his apparent efforts to entertain everyone in his
party—not on a very sophisticated level, I might say, as for
example he could not ascend a flight of stairs without pretend-
ing to fall down it, causing amusement among the children—
he was a desperate character, and not unlike Hobby, being
slightly seedy, having a dark Southern glamour.

As for his wife, Louise, when she saw her daughter, Anne,
waiting at the dock, she began to weep profusely, not having
seen the child in two months, and the child looked so small
and defenseless and weak—she was overcome with many
emotions and took her children to her heart, in tears.

When the ferry came in from New London, there was a lone
swan in the bay, sign of Orient, Port of Egypt, and at the
dock, as the mother wept, her daughter took her hand.

Anne Collier was very happy at last though she did not
break down, like her mother, and even found her mother's
tears somewhat perplexing. It was a source of perplexity to
her that her mother should weep upon seeing her. She did not
know the depth of her mother's love. Or the trials that her
mother had been through. The little girl had been through her

own trials, but she was a gallant creature, whose purpose was to see her mother happy. So she took her hand while walking from the dock. And when once she let go of her mother's hand and turned around and saw her parents standing side by side, they looked so glamorous to her that she, too, shed a tear.

Claude Collier's wife was what is called long-suffering, and for her husband she felt some element of what is ordinarily felt for a child, Socrates' *filia*, the strong desire to see someone happy. Claude Collier, on the other hand, was the type of person who would bring the taxi driver home to dinner, extending Socrates' *filia* to the entire world. He remained in his old environment, New Orleans, and I sincerely wonder what his behavior would be in regard to the rejected and despised in New York of whom there are so many, whether they would all flock to him in huge droves, which he would accept. But he remained in his old environment, and so I see him in my mind's eye on the Avenue in the black night in New Orleans. That green boulevard at night, underneath the arch of venerable oaks. He walks out of his bachelors' club by the side of an ancient old girl with a crown awry on her head. The bachelors' club, a white mansion with gardens lit up at night, is filled with people but he and the ancient old girl, Mrs. Stewart in fact, depart and walk down the Avenue. There he is entertaining her, and she holding on to his arm, and they are as though out of time, with fifty years' gulf between them as nothing, in the glittering night. Where I come from we honor the old.

Otherwise I see him with his children, as it was his influence on Al, for example, that made the boy to be such a gallant little fellow.

56.   "Mom, can I move to the Arctic?" said
George Collier.

"We'll see about it, dear."

Formerly it was George Collier's purpose to live in a debris
tent (whatever that is) in Wyoming and worship American
Indian gods.

"Dad, is it okay with you?"

"Is what okay with me, my heart?"

"Is it okay if I move to the Arctic?"

"Now why would you want to do that, heart?"

"George, don't move to the Arctic," said Al.

"Why, Al?"

"Because we would miss you too much. But if you were
sad, we would rescue you."

"I forbid you to move to the Arctic, Son," said Claude
Collier. "But when you are eighteen, if you still want to move
to the Arctic, okay. If it's your heart's desire to move to the
Arctic, okay. If your heart leads to you to the Arctic, Son, I'm
all for it. If that's where your heart leads you, I'm—"

"That's not a toy, Dad," said Al. His father was flipping the
frying pan around on the stove, in his customary penchant to
catastrophe. Suddenly it fell on his foot.

"Poor Dad! Poor thing! Did it hurt you?" said Al, in tones
of utmost solicitude. Al's always sitting there observing things
with a calm demeanor, the calm demeanor of the Colliers.

"Let's all keep calm," said his father. "Let's all keep very,
very calm." This family had a theme.

Al grew very pensive, with a troubled air. "He's thinking
about tomorrow night when we go out to the dance," said his
father.

"Yes, I'm thinking about when you leave me, Dad."

"How'd you know that's what he was thinking of?"

"I know my boy," said his father.

"Don't go out dancing, Dad," said Al.

"Why, Al?"

"Because sometimes when Dad leaves, I cry." He looked manfully off into the distance, noting a fact, a melancholy one. "I want to be with my Dad," said Al. "I'm very proud of Dad."

"I'll never leave you, Son," said his father. "I love you very much. Now come over here and sit on my lap in the rocking chair and we'll have some Therapeutic Time Together."

"I'm falling apart, Dad," said Al.

"Well, let's paste you back together, Son."

He was wearing his old plaid bathrobe, an item he had possessed for too many years, I would say. Al sat in his lap in the rocking chair.

"My precious, I'm so glad you're here," Claude said to me. To Hobby he said hello and they shook hands.

"You're looking well," Hobby said.

"Wish I could say the same for you, sweetheart," said Claude with his dark Southern wit with which it was customary for the men to insult each other but in actuality expresses affection. Hobby smoked a cigar and Claude drank club soda sitting for some hours in deck chairs on the lawn. I see them in their seersucker suits years ago walking through the old park, or empty bars, in the tropic spring, with their gruff devotion ten years ago walking through a garden in the late afternoon to shake hands in the old afternoon after work.

It was early October, shortly before the World Series. It was almost exactly five years to the day since I was with Hobby at the old hotel in Alabama. He remarked it. He asked me rather formally to come with him then to his house.

He closed the doors of his study purposefully and sat back

down by me. The usual loud jazz music issued from the record
player. He required loud Mississippi ballads such as "Inseparable" and "Reconsider me" and "One Night of Sin" to be
playing when making a decision that required concentration,
packing, or organizing his itinerary. I found this to be poignant. But then again, I find virtually everything to be
poignant.

The AP Wire was coming through on the computer as there
was an international crisis happening in an Eastern European
country. "Do you think you'll have to go to Teroizia?" I inter-
rupted, naming the place from which the crisis emanated.

"No, I'll work on it from New York. Woolen-clad nationalists . . . riots in the streets—civil war . . ." he mused.
Woolen-clad nationalists? But no one ever said that Mr. Underwood's paper was highbrow. The stories from the bureau
chiefs and writers from all over the world were coming in
over the computer to Hobby with their endless tortured analyses of the international crises for their stories. He was belea-
guered, rumpled, wry. I'm not sure he cared about the
Teroizians. Or it was only the same to him as taking Harry
Locke to the hospital. Maybe this does not differ from anyone
else, but maybe it was that he seemed so often to be in that
position, of responsibility for others, and you could say of him
that he never failed them.

That is why, when I looked at him, I never felt that heavy
mantle of responsibility settle on my shoulders—responsibility
for a man's weakness. Of two hearts one is always the
stronger. But in a man like Hobby, who can take care of
himself, and who is not prone to express Feelings and Emotions—then how should come about our moment of reconciliation, so long after our moment of dishonor—I am not sure,
except that love abides. Thus it is when thou art gone, love
itself shall slumber on.

He sat back down by me, preparing, I could see, for a speech. He said some things. I was nervous. He was masterful. He said, "Sweetheart, I'm late. Five years too late. But when I see you like this and I've watched you, I wish you were sitting right next to me like this, and I could grab you, and hold on to you, and tell you not to worry."

But we had made a heartless decision, really, as well as a pointless one, no matter what you say of it, our moment of dishonor, in circumstances such as ours.

A sudden sorrow in his blue eyes, for the past. It was a hard thing to forgive. And then to think of Grace and Constant and the abundance of their family.

But I heard an accent from the past. He said, "I'm dying for you." Dying for me? An accent long unheard—and I felt that at that old hotel, some years ago in the Alabama night, I had left something behind, and since then, as the poet said, I had searched for it hopelessly, as ghosts are said to do.

Misanthropy is a heartless pursuit, some might say. But misanthropy is the tonic of solitude.

"I treasure you. You are dear to me and I set store by you."

He turned up the volume of the soul songs playing, "Inseparable" and "Reconsider Me." We danced.

Al toddled in. "You looked beautiful," he said, enraptured by our glamour. "Hobby danced so hard that he cried."

I bent down to him. "He cried because he was happy, Al."

"I wanted to marry you," said Al wistfully.

"I'll always be your Storey."

The children were leaving the North. They were returning to New Orleans with their parents. Al and I discussed our town. "The palm trees kill me, Al."

Those boys kill me—Hobby and Claude, in their khaki pants and white shirts in the tropic zone.

"I don't like good-byes, Al."

"I don't like good-byes either, Storey. We're the same. We don't like change, and we don't like good-byes. Also palm trees kill us."

"Oh, Al!"

As I looked at the green lawns of Orient, it almost seemed a paradise, the green of paradise, and with the strains of music.

I was sitting with my two favorites, Al and Hobby. To me it was the sweetest hour. My little Al would call for me and Hobby would say, "Come back here! He gets to see you all the time."

He smiled. His smile was like someone who kept a grand old Rolls-Royce in his garage and every once in a while broke it out and took it for a ride, and then you'd see the fine sight, an old Rolls-Royce coming down the street, as in the London twilight.

He pulled the little boy onto his lap. Before Al left we took him to a baseball game. A gospel choir sang inside the stadium —a dignified old black man led the choir, a Godly thing—and little children threw out the first pitches.

Hobby had a green sweater and his eyes became that color, his dazzling eyes. Such a handsome man. I tell you that he wasn't hard to look at. And I have to say that when I grasped his hand—in forgiveness—it reminded me of the strong and manly hand of Constant. That's it, constant and old, constant as the most steadfast rule, for life has taught them that, and to exhibit their devotion, unworried and unafraid. So I advise you to take up a Hobby. And then you may have a sporting chance.

It was a sultry evening—a light rain fell—humid—hot. New York played Chicago.

$\mathcal{V}$OICES OF THE $\mathcal{S}$OUTH

Hamilton Basso
The View from Pompey's Head
Richard Bausch
Real Presence
Take Me Back
Doris Betts
The Astronomer and Other Stories
The Gentle Insurrection
Sheila Bosworth
Almost Innocent
Slow Poison
David Bottoms
Easter Weekend
Erskine Caldwell
Poor Fool
Fred Chappell
The Gaudy Place
The Inkling
It Is Time, Lord
Kelly Cherry
Augusta Played
Vicki Covington
Bird of Paradise
Ellen Douglas
A Family's Affairs
A Lifetime Burning
The Rock Cried Out
Percival Everett
Suder
Peter Feibleman
The Daughters of Necessity
A Place Without Twilight
George Garrett
Do, Lord, Remember Me
An Evening Performance
Marianne Gingher
Bobby Rex's Greatest Hit
Shirley Ann Grau
The House on Coliseum Street
The Keepers of the House
Barry Hannah
The Tennis Handsome

Donald Hays
The Dixie Association
William Humphrey
Home from the Hill
The Ordways
Mac Hyman
No Time For Sergeants
Madison Jones
A Cry of Absence
Nancy Lemann
Lives of the Saints
Sportman's Paradise
Willie Morris
The Last of the Southern Girls
Louis D. Rubin, Jr.
The Golden Weather
Evelyn Scott
The Wave
Lee Smith
The Last Day the Dogbushes Bloomed
Elizabeth Spencer
The Salt Line
The Voice at the Back Door
Max Steele
Debby
Walter Sullivan
The Long, Long Love
Allen Tate
The Fathers
Peter Taylor
The Widows of Thornton
Robert Penn Warren
Band of Angels
Brother to Dragons
World Enough and Time
Walter White
Flight
Joan Williams
The Morning and the Evening
The Wintering
Thomas Wolfe
The Web and the Rock